TONY

Alvarez Security Series

By

Maryann Jordan

Tony (Alvarez Security Series)
Copyright © 2015 Maryann Jordan
Print Edition

Cover Design by: Becky McGraw
Editor: Shannon Brandee Eversoll

ISBN: 978-0-9864004-5-2

Acknowledgements

First and foremost, I have to thank my husband, Michael. Always believing in me and wanting me to pursue my dreams, this book would not be possible without his support. To my daughters, MaryBeth and Nicole, I taught you to follow your dreams and now it is time for me to take my own advice. You two are my inspiration.

My best friend, Tammie, who for twenty years has been with me through thick and thin. You've filled the role of confidant, supporter, and sister.

My dear friend, Myckel Anne, who keeps me on track, keeps me grounded, and most of all – keeps my secrets. Thank you for not only being my proofreader, but my friend. Our friendship has grown and changed and you mean more to me than you can imagine.

Shannon Brandee Eversoll has been my editor for the past five books and what she brings to my writing has been amazing. She and Myckel Anne Phillips as my proofreader gave their time and talents to making Gabe as well written as it can be.

Thanks go to my beta readers who devote their time to make sure my books will have readers who love them!

My street team, Jordan Jewels, you are amazing! You volunteer your time to promote my books and I cannot thank you enough! I hope you will stay with me, because I have lots more stories inside, just waiting to be written!

My Personal Assistant, Barbara Martoncik, is the woman that keeps me going when I feel overwhelmed and I am so grateful for not only her assistance, but her friendship.

Most importantly, thank you readers. You allow me into your home for a few hours as you disappear into my characters and you support me as I follow my indie author dreams.

If you read my books and enjoy them, please leave a review. It does not have to be long or detailed...just that you enjoyed the book. Reviews are essential to indie authors!

Dedication

As a high school counselor, I have worked with thousands of teenagers over my long career. The pressures and problems that teens face today can seem insurmountable to them. I have had the wonderful experience of working with some amazing therapeutic foster parents, social workers, and Court Appointed Special Advocates—all working to make the lives of children better. This book is dedicated to all those who work with young people, helping to chart their course toward success.

CHAPTER 1

THE FLIGHT WAS long...it never seemed short and this time was even longer. He could not complain though. The U.S. Army had allowed him to go home to see his wife and newborn daughter. For a Special Forces Captain, that was a miracle in and of itself, but his squad was between missions and with the slight downtime, he squeezed in a week stateside.

Pulling out the picture that he carried in his pocket, he ran his fingers over the face of his tiny daughter. Dark hair. Just like both he and his wife. His eyes were brown while his wife's were green. What color would Sofia's be?

The plane was descending as he tucked the picture back into his pocket. Moving through the airstrip, he made his way over to the chopper that would take him to his squad's base. Just in time for a briefing, a planning and another mission.

Tony Alvarez loved the Army. Loved Special Forces. Loved his men. But the trip home reminded him that one day there would be an end to his military career and waiting for him back in Virginia was his wife, Marla, and their daughter. Smiling to himself, he

1

looked forward to that day.

Finally arriving at the base, he was greeted with the handshakes, salutes, and back-patting that goes with a returning comrade. Gabe and Vinny Malloy, twins in his squad, handed him a cigar and then passed them out to the other men.

"Come on, let's see it. We know you've got it right on you," Gabe prodded.

Laughing, he pulled the photograph out of his pocket and his cell phone as well. "Okay, scroll down through these, but this one is getting framed."

"Damn, Captain. She's beautiful, even at three days old," Jobe said. He looked at Tony and laughed. "I got three younger sisters. All gorgeous. You're gonna have your hands full when she gets older. When I get married, I'm telling my wife to only make me boys."

Vinny quipped, "Oh, don't worry. She'll have all of us as honorary uncles. She won't have a chance to date. Ever."

One of the other men looked over at Vinny and said, "You'd better hope she doesn't ever meet anyone like yourself."

"She'd better not try to go out with anyone like me," he said. "I'd have to cut the guy's dick off."

Tony chuckled, adding, "You're just lucky someone's dad hasn't chased you down and cut yours off."

Vinny jumped in, bragging about his dick's ability to withstand anyone's attempt to cut it off. Tony nodded toward the group and headed to his room. It was small, but as the squad leader and officer, he got his own little private space. At least for now.

Lying down, willing his mind to rest before the briefing tomorrow, he turned on his side to stare at the picture now on his nightstand. Marla and he, with Sofia in their arms. They were the perfect couple and now the perfect family. Closing his eyes, he allowed sleep to take over and for tonight his dreams carried him out of the war zone and back to Virginia.

ONE WEEK LATER, Tony found himself lying in the dirt; the memories of his bed with his wife were in the far distance. *This feels like a suicide mission.* The planning had taken longer than usual, because the man they were supposed to rescue was being held in the middle of a compound in a village. *A fuckin' village. Filled with fuckin' men, women, and children.* Gabe had recently seen a child killed in another mission and Tony had watched how it affected him. *And now that I've got a baby? Jesus, what would I do if anything happened to her? Fuck, I'd just stop livin'.*

Crawling through the dirt and dust, his squad came to the hill closest to the compound. The night was cold and clear, the only light coming from the stars above and the fires below. The area looked quiet, but in war time, that could just be a ruse. A few men sat around the central fire, riffles laying to the sides. Jobe, their

Weapons Sergeant, moved to the other side gaining visual. "All clear to the east."

Tony gave the signal and his men began sliding into position. Gabe and Vinny were both Medics, but Vinny was also a Weapons Sergeant and their best marksman and long range shooter. Vinny positioned himself where he had the best visual of the compound, having identified the building his squad members would be entering.

Through night vision goggles, Tony saw Gabe and Vinny look briefly at each other before separating. He had never worked with twins before and was awed by the instinctive way they communicated. But then all of his men worked that way. They ate, slept, played, and trained together for years. He had never worked with a group of men that clicked the way this squad did.

Several of his men slid down the hill carefully then moved through the back of the village like fog. Jobe and Chief Warrant Officer Bryant moved in first, followed by their Engineer Sergeant and Gabe. Tony brought up the rear of the front group moving in. *Please let their contact's info be right.*

Finding the building, they moved toward a window, Jobe peering in first. He gave the signal indicating that it was the right one, then held up four fingers on his left hand indicating that there were four others in the room besides the man they were rescuing. Tony watched as Jobe moved three of his fingers.

Fuck. Three children in the room. He could never get

used to the enemy using children in their wars. Moving up beside Jobe, he peered in as well at the sleeping man they were after and a woman with two small children and a baby. The children were asleep, but the woman was sitting in the corner nursing. The sight of her sent shock waves through him, the memory of Marla nursing Sofia almost sending him to his knees. The plan was to kill anyone who stood between them and their rescue.

Leaning back against the mud-brick wall, he willed his mind back to the mission at hand. *This is not personal. This is my job.* Tony was the quintessential Green Beret. He was the mission. Slowing his heartbeat, clearing his mind, he nodded at the others.

Moving in through the door, Jobe kept his weapon trained on the woman, whose eyes were wide with fright, but she did not make a sound. Bryant moved to the man and quickly woke him, placing his hand over the man's mouth to quiet any noises he might have made when startled. They stood and moved to the door as Tony took over Jobe's position of holding his weapon on the woman as Jobe led the group out of the door.

He began to move to the door as well, following Gabe, and at the last second allowed his eyes to drop from the woman to the sleeping children and the baby still nursing. With a nod, he turned and quickly followed his men out of the door and back to the rest of the squad.

The mission was considered a success and upon arrival back at the base, the men began their debriefing. Afterwards they cleaned up, ate, and celebrated their accomplishment, enjoying their bragging rights. That night in bed, Tony lay awake starting at the photograph next to his bed, hating that he could not be there and yet thankful that she was not being raised in a warzone. *Stay safe little Sofia,* he thought, *until I can get home and take care of you and mommy, always.*

THREE DAYS LATER, Tony was called in to the Major's office. Walking in, the Major immediately walked over and placed his hand on Tony's shoulder, as the base Chaplain walked in as well. His heart began to pound but before he could ask, the Major spoke.

"Tony, we've just received some horrible news. There was a car accident involving your wife as she was driving yesterday. She was coming back from a doctor's appointment with your daughter. Tony, I'm so sorry. Your wife Marla and baby were killed instantly."

The blood roared through his ears and he heard nothing else. The floor rushed up to meet him as his knees buckled. There were no tears. Not then. It was too surreal. Too much for his brain to process. He would later look back and not be able to remember anything else from that day. Not the words from the Chaplain. Or his men rushing to his assistance.

His men.

They packed for themselves and him as well. They boarded the plane with him...all eleven. They drove him to the funeral parlor and sat with him making arrangements. They drove him to his house to help settle matters there. And they stood behind him at the funeral.

For a week they assisted with the insurance forms, mail, neighbors, relatives, and yet knew instinctively when to step back and give him space. And on the day they were to fly back to the warzone, they drove him to the cemetery before they had to make it to the airport.

Tony remembered that day when all the others were a blur. Walking over to the headstones, side by side, he knelt between them. The tears flowed from somewhere deep inside of him that he never knew existed before. Someplace dark and hidden. That place that is buried in all of us that it is only revealed when the loss of someone rips our soul so deeply that it is then exposed. And once opened, like Pandora's box, can never be completely closed again.

As his sobs finally subsided, his men moved silently closer to him, surrounding the area, and with heads bowed prayed for peace. Peace in the world. Peace for the Captain they loved. But more importantly, peace in their souls.

CHAPTER 2

FIVE YEARS LATER

TONY SAT ALONE at Gabe's wedding reception table glowering at the beautiful woman three tables over. Sherrie Mullins. His men, talking and laughing, as they walked by to greet her. And Monty. *Fuckin Monty Lytton.* He did not have anything personal against the FBI agent who had recently assisted Tony's agency on a case. But any man in her vicinity would draw his ire right now.

Tony Alvarez was a man of action who left the Army and started his own security agency and filled it with his brothers-in-arms who had left the Special Forces as well. Men from his squad. Men he trusted. Men whose skills were unparalleled. His agency now handled not only installing state-of-the-art security systems, providing security to any number of dignitaries or functions in the area, but also helped the Richland Police Department on a number of cases where their budget constraints did not allow for the equipment that he had.

He was not a man used to sitting around staring at

a woman who should not even be on his radar. But she was and had been in his sights for almost a year.

He remembered the first time he saw her picture. She had been trying to help her drug-addicted, prostitute sister. Charisse had become involved with one of the biggest gang leaders in the area and Sherrie had put herself in danger to try to help. He remembered seeing the picture of the woman he was tasked to rescue when the gang leader kidnapped her and was attempting to take her out of the country. She was a beauty, but he could see trouble from a mile away. He thought she was probably just like her sister, after all she had been a waitress in a cheap strip joint. *Hell, I couldn't have been more wrong.* Reading her dossier, he discovered she was strong, smart, loyal, and...good. When she realized she could no longer help Charisse unless her sister wanted to get help, she cut her loose.

Tony had kept up with the blonde beauty. She quit her job as a cocktail waitress when she finished her paralegal degree and had once again put herself in danger by trying to do a little digging for Gabe's new wife Jennifer, looking for evidence of the illegal activities of a state Senator. He thought again, remembering how she called him for help when Monty dragged her out of the State Capitol building. It turned out he was undercover FBI, but Tony could still remember the emotions he felt when she called. First, there was fear. Then the adrenaline of a mission to be accomplished. And then...the feeling of a woman depending on *him*.

Shaking his head, he tried to force those feelings out of his mind as he looked back over at Monty leaning in close to her at their table. *Fucker's probably catching a scent of her hair. Or trying to look down her dress. Why the hell is she wearing that anyway?* The green dress was low in the front, showing off entirely too much of her breasts. And from the looks of them, they were gorgeous. Then there were her legs as she crossed and uncrossed them. The whole package was shown to perfection in that dress, causing Tony to glower even more.

SHERRIE LOOKED OVER at the angry visage of Tony. *What is wrong with him? I wore this dress hoping he would finally notice me and all I get are glares. I could have worn a potato sack for all he would care.*

Sherrie tried to give a polite smile to Monty as he leaned closer to chat. Her gaze raked over him. Tall, good-looking, intelligent. The kind of man that most women would be hoping to take home, not only for the night but for forever. Just not her. For Sherrie, the only man in the room was the one man who seemed to hate her.

As Monty turned to talk to the couple next to him, she looked at Tony under lowered lashes. *Yep—still glowering.* Her mind flowed back to when she first saw him.

Hands tied behind her back, lying on a pallet on the floor of an airport hangar at the mercy of the gang leader that had used, abused, and abandoned her sister. Just when she thought her life was over, he came charging in. She remembered ducking when she first heard gunshot and a large man wearing all black came at her with a knife.

He had cradled her and pulled the gag from her swollen lips, assisting her with drinking from his canteen. Using the knife, he gave calm assurances as he cut her bindings and rubbed her hands and feet. She remembered shivering as she gazed into his caramel eyes, not knowing if she were cold, in shock, or simply mesmerized at his face peering down at her.

She had felt him lift her in his arms as easily as a child and all she could think of was that someone had come for her. Rescued her. Once loaded into the ambulance, she tried to thank him, but her voice only croaked a whisper. She had no idea if he heard her or cared. And she realized belatedly, she did not even know his name. Later at the hospital she had tried to slip out unnoticed having heard how injured her friend, Suzanne, was and feeling guilty about her sister's part in the scheme. But Tony had approached, standing in her way. She had looked up, knowing he was too good for her. Too clean. Too…everything. And had slipped around him and out into the night.

Suzanne walked over to Sherrie and slid down in the seat next to her. "Well, doesn't this look familiar?" she quipped with a smile.

"What?" Sherrie asked.

"At my wedding I also remember you sitting at one table trying not to stare at Tony, and he at another table openly staring at you."

"Oh, he's got no interest in me."

"Honey, if you think that then you're either dumb or refuse to see what's right in front of you. And you are not dumb!"

Sherrie huffed, glancing at the beautiful mother of twins, glad for their friendship surviving their ordeal a year ago. With Suzanne's help, she came to realize that she had to let go of the guilt. She was not at fault for the poor choices of her sister.

Wanting to change the topic, she asked, "How's the new clinic?" Suzanne was a vet tech for a friend of theirs, Annie, who had also just had a baby.

"It's fabulous. With both Annie and me having babies, we have a very generous schedule, which works for us. So I get time off with the twins and still get out to work a couple of days a week to have some adult time." Glancing down at her breasts, she said ruefully, "And speaking of babies, I need to go find a place to pump before these huge boobs explode."

Laughing, Sherrie noticed Suzanne's husband heading their way. "Looks like BJ is right on time."

"Oh yeah, he keeps up with my schedule about as well as I do," she said. "But Sherrie, about what we were talking about earlier. Tony and you?"

Sherrie interrupted, "Suzanne, there is no Tony and

me."

Her friend leaned over and gave her a hug, whispering in her ear, "Give him a chance, honey. I really think you two are perfect together." With that, she allowed her husband to give her an assist from her seat and as he winked at Sherrie, he tucked Suzanne under his arm as they left the room.

Sherrie looked wistfully at the receding couple. *That's what I want. But not with just anyone,* she had to admit, glancing at Tony one more time. With her and Tony having the same friend group they had been together on numerous occasions, but all ended the same—him staring from afar and her leaving alone.

The last time he had come to her rescue, she had called him. *He was the only one I wanted to see. Wanted to trust.* But even then, other than the rescue, nothing happened.

The bride walked over and sat in the chair vacated by Suzanne, interrupting Sherrie's musings. "Enjoying yourself?" Jennifer asked, a conspiratorial grin on her face.

"Of course," Sherrie replied giving her a hug. "You're an absolutely beautiful bride."

"Well, you're a stunner yourself in that dress. Anyone I know you're trying to impress?"

"Nope, no one. At least no one who cares."

Jennifer leaned in close, "Oh, honey. He cares. He just doesn't want to, that's all. But Gabe's working on it."

Sherrie's gaze shot back over to Tony, seeing the groom talking to his boss. Her lips in a tight line, she retorted, "But that's the problem. If I was really worth it, no one should have to be convinced."

Giving Jennifer a look of resignation, she turned and asked Monty if he would like to dance. Eyes alight, he stood and offered his hand. Walking out to the dance floor, she purposefully kept her gaze away from Tony and tried to concentrate on the handsome man who had his arms around her.

Tony's glare had turned murderous, but Gabe stilled him with a hand on his arm. "Captain, you've got no one to blame but yourself." Even though the men had been out of the Army for several years, his former squad members still found themselves referring to their boss as their superior officer.

Tony tried counting to ten but found that his Special Forces training had abandoned him when it came to her. She filled his dreams. She filled his thoughts. And as much as he tried to push them away, they came back. Over and over.

"Captain?" Gabe's voice finally cut through. Gabe had been joined by Vinny and Jobe. Tony looked over at his most trusted men. And friends. Gabe continued, "You've had your eye on her for almost a year. She's a great woman. Smart. Tough. Not to mention, gorgeous."

"Think I don't know all of that?" Tony growled.

"You don't act like it. Instead you act like you're

trying to keep her at arm's length all of the time."

Tony looked over at the couple on the dance floor and then turned his anguished gaze back to the others. "What…what do I have to offer a woman like that? I loved once. You were there. Nearly broke me. Can't do that again, and she deserves better than a man who hasn't got much left to give," he admitted.

The silence at the table was deafening. They had accepted the fact that Tony never spoke of his wife and daughter after they left the cemetery that day, five years earlier. Never. For him to bring it up now, told them the depths of his feelings. And anguish.

With that, Tony stood from the table pushing hard against his seat. The scraping noise had Sherrie look over in surprise. For a moment, both held each other's gaze. Warm caramel ones met the summer-sky blue ones. Longing and despair in both.

Tony turned suddenly and walked out of the door, leaving his friends hurting for him. And Sherrie hurting for herself.

CHAPTER 3

THE NEXT MONDAY found the Alvarez core employees in the large conference room for their weekly meeting. While Alvarez Security had a number of people employed, it was this group of trusted friends that were the heart and soul of the agency.

"Gabe get off okay?" Tony asked, referring to the honeymoon.

"Yeah," Vinny answered. "He'll just be gone a week, but they're heading to the sunny Keys."

"That sounds lovely," Lily said softly. "This winter has been harsh. I'm so not a fan."

Looking down at his agenda, Tony began the briefing. "We're pulling out of the Hollywood starlet securities after the fiasco a few months back, but we have some requests from agents with some artists or musicians signed that would occasionally want our services. I'll take those on a one at a time basis with no long term contract unless we have been with them and want their business."

"You get any female rockers that need an escort, I'm your man," Vinny joked. The team laughed as Tony just shook his head.

"Next up, home and business security. Jobe, what do you have on that?"

"The new equipment that we've ordered has come in and when Gabe gets back, we'll look it over and start installing it on newer customers. Didn't know if you want us to offer upgrades to existing clients?"

The group discussed the pros and cons of the equipment contracts for several minutes. Making their decisions, they moved to the next topic.

"Had a request to help find two sisters who have been missing a month," Tony mentioned, opening the file in front of him. This got the immediate attention of the group. "Their grandparents have employed us to look in this area. They are from the D.C. area and by all appearances, they ran away together. According to the grandmother, their step-father may have been abusive. It was reported to the D.C. police, but they're strapped for manpower and the trail is a bit cold. The grandparents hired a PI in the D.C. area and he thinks they took a bus to Richland. So they have contracted us to see what we can dig up."

"You giving this to one person?" Jobe asked. "Cause if so, I'll take it." The group knew of Jobe's overwhelming sense of responsibility when it came to his own sisters and Tony knew this would be a personal mission for him.

"I was thinking of you and Terrance working on it, and with BJ getting his PI license, he can work on it with you. I told the grandparents that we would see what we could find from the bus station security but that they shouldn't get their hopes up too high since the girls left a month ago." With that, he slid the folder over to Jobe who began to thumb through it.

Moving to the next item on his agenda, Tony continued. "As you know, the Richland Police have worked with us in the past and even paid Lily and BJ for their time for some of their computer skills. The Chief knows our reputation and with our friendship with Matt and Shane, it's been easy."

Lily smiled. Her husband, Matt Dixon, and his partner, Shane Douglass, were detectives that had close ties to Alvarez Security and worked with them even when not sanctioned by the Chief.

"Well now, it seems as though we have the attention of the Mayor and Governor as well. So that will probably lead to us having more and more contracts with city as well."

"You okay, Captain?" BJ asked. "You're giving us good news, but seem...I don't know...kind of bored."

"Nah, it's all good. Business is up and you all should be expecting raises by next month." This news was met with cheers all around. His gaze wandered around the room to his core employees. Lily, happily married to Matt and expecting their child. BJ married his long time sweetheart months ago and is now the proud father of twins. Gabe, who was on his honeymoon, was also on his mind. Jobe was still single, but Tony knew as soon as the right woman came along, he'd snatch her up. Vinny on the other hand, was a hound-dog at heart. He was too into tits, ass, and one-night stands to ever fall in love. *Then there's me. I am getting morose.*

Jerking himself out of his musings, he dismissed the meeting and headed back to his office. A moment later, Lily knocked on the doorframe.

Smiling, he stood, motioning for her to enter. Beautiful, blonde hair that just skimmed her shoulders. Neat slacks, professional blouse, and her trademark, colorful tennis shoes. As a below-the-knee amputee, she always wore tennis shoes.

"How are you feeling?" he asked, ushering her to a seat.

"I'm fine. Actually, more than fine."

She sat, awkwardly quiet for a moment. Finally looking at him, she said, "Sir—"

"Lily, we're too good of friends for you to call me 'sir'."

Smiling, she nodded. "I just wondered…well, that is to say…I thought that…" Sighing, she said ruefully, "I'm not making much progress here, am I?"

Tony chuckled and agreed.

"Tony, when I first met Matt, I thought that I had nothing to give him, other than a life with an amputee and that didn't seem fair. I found out later that because of the large scar on his face, he felt the same. That all he had to offer was life with a man with a damaged face. But we were wrong."

Not knowing where she was going with the conversation, Tony just sat quietly, allowing her thoughts to come out in her own time.

Looking down at her hands for a moment, she unconsciously splayed them across her slight pregnancy bulge. Gazing back up into his eyes, she continued. "We've all had pain, Tony. Things that marked us. Changed us. Hurt us. Made us feel like the sun was never going to shine on us again."

Leaning forward, she placed her tiny hand on his much larger one. "I can't begin to imagine your grief and pain. And it'll never go away. I know. I've grieved the death of my sister for ten years. But if you don't allow yourself to feel again, hope again, dream again…you'll never find happiness again."

Seeing him about to protest, she interrupted. "And you can find happiness again. We all did and want that for you as well."

The lump that formed in his throat threatened to choke him, so silence was the only solution. He blinked and nodded, feeling her words slide through him. Not reaching the darkest places. But warming him, nonetheless.

She stood, and walked out of his office saying nothing else. He sat, looking at the papers on his desk but not seeing them. The hall was quiet and he knew he was alone. Pulling out his wallet, he slid the old, faded photograph out. Running his finger over the face of Marla and Sofia once again, he wondered if Lily was right. Was there such a thing as happiness again for him?

SHERRIE WALKED INTO the lawyer's office where she was a paralegal, greeting the receptionist as she moved to her small office. Looking at the pile of files on her desk, she heaved a huge sigh. She used to go to the State Capitol often for business, even if it was just delivering files to a client. But ever since the Senator had been caught in a huge scandal involving payoffs and mob bosses, Attorney Ashton Marks had scaled back as he was winding down his career. He kept his business to just family law, dealing mostly with wills and trusts. Necessary, but to Sherrie, it was a little boring.

She was tired of spending her days stuck in the tiny office, completing legal forms for the clients. She could not help but smile at the memories of helping Jennifer with a little reconnaissance a few months earlier. She had felt alive and needed. Her gaze moved from the pile of folders to a small picture frame on her desk. She and Charisse, her sister. Raised in foster homes, she had gone the route of being a good student and Charisse had decided that prostituting herself for drugs was the way to break out of the system. *Where are you now, sis?*

"Ms. Mullins?" a deep voice called from the door.

Jumping, she exclaimed, "Oh, I'm sorry. I didn't

hear anyone there."

A tall, handsome man wearing a nice, if inexpensive suit, walked in with his hand out. "I'm Simon Tolbert, Mr. Marks' new partner."

Jumping to her feet, she shook his hand, saying, "That's right. I totally forgot it was your first day here."

Seeing the look of disappointment cross his face, she explained, "I was involved in a friend's wedding last week and am afraid my mind was completely pre-occupied."

He smiled and nodded his understanding. "Well, I'll be settling into my office today and I'm sure I'll see you later." He turned and headed back out of her door.

She did not have to wait long for the next time she saw Mr. Tolbert, when Mr. Marks called an office meeting. The receptionist stayed for just a few minutes of introductions and after she left, Sherrie and the two attorneys continued their meeting.

"My specialty is family law, Ms. Mullins; and Mr. Marks tells me you are a CASA worker. I will be making some visits to children in foster care and would like a female to go with me when I am interviewing a child. I find that it makes them more comfortable. With your special training, you will be an invaluable asset. Other than that, I would expect that my needs for your services will be similar as to Mr. Marks'."

Smiling as she walked back to her office, she thought of working on some cases with children as well as her CASA assignment. *This just might be the spark I needed.*

SHERRIE HAD HER first time visiting a foster care home with the attorney that week. As they drove the short distance to the pleasant house, he asked her to call him 'Simon'. "I know Mr. Marks believes in formality, but I prefer a friendlier atmosphere at work."

Nodding, she added, "And you may certainly call me 'Sherrie'."

Arriving at the home, she followed his lead and sat with the child at the kitchen table as Simon asked them some questions. She could not help but look around at the pleasant surroundings. It reminded her of one of her earlier foster homes. When she and Charisse had been younger, the homes were nice. But as her sister's behavior became more erratic, they had been shipped from one house to another. And a few of them, not very desirable.

The interview went quickly and Simon called the DSS worker assigned to the case. After conferring with her for a few minutes, he turned back to Sherrie. "Want to grab some lunch while we're out?"

"Sure, anywhere's fine," she answered.

"Do you know of any good places near the office? I'm still new to this side of town."

"There's a great deli a few blocks from us. Good menu and good prices."

"Sounds like just the place for me," he laughed.

They soon were seated at a table near the back and welcomed the warm cup of cider from the owner. "Ahh," Sherrie said. "This hits the spot on a cold day."

As they were eating, she asked, "Tell me about the cases you'll be working on."

"Special interest?" he asked.

"I was raised in the foster care system. Me and my sister."

At this, Simon's surprised look had her wondering if she should have shared the information. "I hope that wasn't too personal," she said nervously. The crowd in the restaurant was noisy and she found herself leaning in close to be able to hear him.

"No, not at all," he assured her. "I just wasn't expecting that. Please accept my apology for my stupid reaction."

"It wasn't stupid. I just caught you off guard, that's all. But when I was in the system, I never questioned it. But now, well I'm curious."

They continued their conversation for several more minutes while eating. She enjoyed learning about some of the cases he would be working on. It sounded much more interesting than delivering files for Mr. Marks.

Lunch was now over and she rose to put her coat on as Simon made his way to the front to pay. Wrapping her scarf around her neck, she dropped her gloves from her pocket. Glancing around to see where they fell, a strong arm snaked out and snagged them.

Still bending over she looked up to see who was holding them out to her. *Tony.* Just the sight of him had her heart pounding. Taking the proffered gloves, she noticed he held her elbow as she came to a stand.

"Thank you," she said, wishing his eyes were not so warm. So deep. As though…*stop. He doesn't see me that way.*

"You're welcome," he said, his voice raspy in a way that made her want to hear it when she first awoke in the morning after a night of…*Jesus, stop. Just stop,* she silently admonished herself.

Glancing to the side, she saw Vinny and Jobe grinning from a nearby table. Nodding to them too, she realized that Tony's eyes were now cold and hard as he was peering over her shoulder. Twisting her head to see what he was scowling at, she saw Simon standing almost right behind her.

"You ready to head back, Sherrie?" he asked.

"Yes." She turned back to say goodbye, but Vinny and Jobe were already out of their seats and standing next to Tony creating a wall of masculinity.

Feeling self-conscious, she said, "This is the new attorney Mr. Marks hired." *I don't owe him an explanation,* she thought angrily, but could not seem to keep her mouth from running as she made introductions. "Well, goodbye," she mumbled, and with one last look at Tony she turned and walked away.

Tony watched her walk away, having seen the hurt in those sky-blue eyes. *And you put it there, you prick.*

Turning angrily back to toss some bills on the table he caught the look of censure from his friends.

Vinny and Jobe wisely kept quiet as they walked out into the brisk winter air. The three of them continued their silence as they drove to the job site. Tony did not usually do the security equipment installations but felt the need to work with his hands in the cold air as they worked on a new home in an expensive neighborhood—one where millions were spent on not only the homes, but the pools, tennis courts, and state-of-the-art security systems.

If his men were surprised with his presence on the job, they did not say anything. They all knew what it was like to fight the demons in their heads with physical work. And if this was how Tony wanted to fight, then they would allow their Captain anything.

CHAPTER 4

A WEEK LATER, Gabe walked into work tan, rested, and with a smile on his face. The others greeted him enthusiastically and asked about Jennifer.

"It was great to just soak up some sun and eat great food. And to see Jennifer relax. Other than calling my parents every day to check on her brother, she really had a chance to rest."

Vinny looked over at his twin with mock hurt. "You know I'd have kept Ross and we two would have had a great time."

"Are you kidding? We would've come back and you'd have bought him every video game in existence and probably a dog as well," Gabe laughed.

"You two going to stay at your place?" Lily asked.

Gabe gave her a hug, answering, "Well, we decided that we would start looking for a house. One with a yard, and then we'll get a dog."

Vinny's eyes lit up, happy for his brother. The settled-life was not for him, but he loved Jennifer and knew she was good for Gabe.

"Anything new going on around here in the past week?" Gabe asked.

"Nothing much. We had a briefing last week and mostly Tony's been going out with us on security installations. Got some new contracts for systems and Jobe's been going over the new equipment that came in."

Jobe piped up, "Glad you're back. The new systems are amazing but I'll be glad to have you checking them out."

Tony walked over, patting Gabe on the shoulder. "Good to have you back. Been catching up?"

Gabe nodded and asked if there was anything he wanted him to do.

"Just work with Jobe this week, if you would and, let me know if we want to order any more of the new systems."

Gabe nodded and then headed down the hall with Jobe and Vinny to the equipment storehouse. Turning around, he called out, "Hey Tony, would you like to have lunch today?"

"Sure," came the expected response, before Gabe continued down the hall.

Vinny and Jobe looked at each other and then at Gabe. "We're not invited?"

"Nope, not today."

"Hell, I'm your brother," Vinny pointed out.

"Yes, but lunch is with Jennifer and I happen to have it on good authority that she's inviting Sherrie."

Vinny and Jobe chuckled. "You playing cupid, bro?" Vinny quipped.

"And you two don't think it's about time Captain gave it a shot again?"

The two sobered as they pondered his words. "Yeah," Jobe agreed. "I fuckin' do."

Vinny nodded and his trademark shit-eatin' grin spread across his face. "All right, but when it's over, you gotta talk."

The men laughed and made their way into the room to start their day.

JENNIFER AND SHERRIE slid into the booth at the little Italian restaurant in the downtown area. Sherrie noticed her friend looked tan, rested, and…content.

"So married life agrees with you or is that the honeymoon glow I'm detecting?" Sherrie teased.

"Florida was so needed," Jennifer said. "I wanted fun and sun in the middle of winter and was not about to fly out of the country and be so far away from Ross."

"Did he stay with Gabe's parents?"

"Yes, and when we got back yesterday I made Gabe drive us there to pick him up immediately. But he was so entranced with their place near the water that I think he'd just have soon us leave him," Jennifer said.

Before the waitress could take their orders, Sherrie heard Gabe's voice booming. "Well, if it's not my gorgeous bride." She saw him slide into the booth, giving Jennifer a quick kiss. Glad to see him, she still felt a pang having wanted some girl time alone with her.

Jennifer smiled at her husband and then looked over Sherrie's shoulder. "Hi, Tony. Nice to see you again."

Before Sherrie could twist her head around, Tony slid into the booth next to her, effectively caging her in. And not looking particularly happy about it. *Great, I get stuck with the one man on the planet that can't stand being with me.*

Tony glared at Gabe, knowing that he had been set up. *I wonder if Sherrie was in on it.* One glance to the side had him convinced that she was not. And looked about as happy to be stuck in this situation as he did.

The scent of her shampoo wafted his way and his senses heightened. He noticed the way she tried to keep her leg from touching his. The way she nervously pushed her hair behind one ear. The way she sucked her lips in and then nibbled on the bottom one. The way she stole glances his way when she thought he was not looking.

He noticed everything. And his body was reacting. *If there was a woman I could be with, it would be her. But I'm not fit to be with anyone.*

The conversation was led mostly by Gabe and Jennifer as they tried to draw the other couple out. Tony finally relaxed, but noticed that it took longer for Sherrie to begin talking. At one humorous story from

Gabe, she laughed and Tony could not get the sound of her out of his head. Melodious. Sparkling. Stretching his tall frame out, he placed his hand on the back of her seat.

He saw her gaze land on his and she began biting her lip once again. *What I wouldn't give to be on those lips right now.* Giving himself a mental shake, he knew what Gabe and Jennifer were doing. Forcing him to be in such close proximity would break down his barriers. *Why couldn't they understand that the idea of giving in to his growing feelings for her scared the shit out of him?*

Sherrie wished she could stop the pounding of her traitorous heart with Tony so near. The longing she had felt for almost a year was reaching a fevered pitch just because his arm was on the back of the booth. *This is so unfair,* she thought. *Jennifer is going to get an earful when we're alone again.* The one man she would gladly take was the one man who seemed totally disinterested.

Just then her phone vibrated with an incoming text. Glancing down, she saw it was from her sister. *Charisse? We haven't spoken in a year. Not since I told her that I couldn't keep cleaning up her messes and until she was sober, not to call.*

Sick. Need you. Riverfront Hotel.

What the hell are you up to now, Charisse? Looking up at Jennifer's questioning expression, she said, "I'm sorry, I have to leave." Turning to Tony, she implored,

"If you could please let me out."

Tony did not move. Instead he held her gaze and questioned, "What's wrong?"

Blinking at him, she grew angry. "I have a personal visit I need to make. Someone needs me. Now please let me out."

"Not until you tell me what put that look in your eyes."

"Oh no, Tony Alvarez. You do not get to play this game."

"Not a game, Sherrie. I haven't seen a look on your face like that since you were dealing with your sister."

She reared back in surprise, sucking in a shaky breath. "Tony, let me out. I have to see someone." Looking over at Jennifer and Gabe, she said, "I'm so glad you're back safe and sound. Please, let's do this again at another time." Turning to Tony, she just lifted her eyebrow at him waiting for him to move.

He stared for a moment, watching her battle between anger and tears. *She's so strong, trying to hold her shit together, acting like she doesn't need anyone. I'll give you that play; hell, it's not really not my place to push her to talk to me anyway.*

Sliding out of the booth, he let her pass and watched her as she began to walk out of the restaurant. He sat for a moment, realizing he missed her presence next to his. *Damn, and that's my fault.*

Looking down at Gabe and Jennifer, he gave a curt nod and followed Sherrie out of the door.

Jennifer, snuggling in closer to her new husband, asked, "Gabe, do you—"

He cut her off with a kiss. "Don't sweat it, babe. Tony's going to follow her to make sure she's safe." He chuckled. "As for your matchmaking, all it will take for him to make a move is to think she's in danger."

Jennifer smiled and settled into the crook of Gabe's arm as they continued to finish their lunch.

SHERRIE HURRIED OUTSIDE and hailed a cab, giving him the dubious address of the Riverfront Hotel. While it was not the seediest hotel in the run down area, it still rented rooms by the hour. *Charisse, if this is a ruse for money, then this is the last straw.* Perhaps it had been the visit to the foster home that had her nostalgic for the days when she and her sister had been best friends. Running her hands through her hair, she leaned her head back with her eyes closed, trying to steel herself for the reunion.

The cabbie let her off at the front door and asked if she wanted him to wait. Not having any idea how long this would take, or what shape her sister might be in if she were sick, she thanked him but sent him on his way. Turning, she looked up at the building and then quickly scanned to the left and right. A few people meandered around, but no one looked threatening. Her mind went back to the last time she saw her sister.

Charisse had made her bed with the devil and when he wanted Sherrie, her sister called her into a trap. If it had not been for Tony's rescue...

"Why are you here?" came a deep voice from behind. Sherrie jumped, her heart pounding as she twisted around quickly, ready to flee.

Tony? What the hell?

Before she could ask that question aloud, he repeated, "Why are you here?"

"I got a text."

He cocked an eyebrow. "A text?"

"I...someone is...I'm...uh..."

"You wanna just try the simple truth?"

"Not really."

At that he chuckled, stepping closer. Too close. Have to lean your head way back to hold his gaze kind of close. Licking her lips, she suddenly realized that she was glad he was there. She felt safer. As though with him near, she could forge ahead and face anything her sister could need.

"Charisse?" came the question from his lips.

Licking hers, she just nodded.

"Christ, Sherrie. When was the last time you saw her? Huh? When she trapped you, had you drugged and kidnapped? By someone who was ready to haul you out of the country?"

Sherrie snapped out of her Tony trance and glared. "I haven't seen her in a year, okay? She just sent me a text saying she was sick." Dragging her hand through her hair again, she said in a quiet voice. "I'm the only family she's got, Tony."

Sherrie sounded so defeated at that moment, Tony wanted to take her in his arms and pull her close. Chase away the clouds, letting the sun that was Sherrie shine again. He forced himself to hold his itchy fingers back and not take her right then and throw her in his truck and drive away.

Instead he nodded. "Then let's go. We'll see her together. You can decide if you can help and I'll keep you safe."

At this, she just stared. *He would do this for me?* Slowly nodding, she agreed and turned toward the entrance.

"But Sherrie," he stopped her. "If I see anything that I don't like, or if she does anything I don't like...I'm getting you outta here."

Sucking in a huge breath and letting it out slowly as his words washed over her she nodded again. *He cares. Underneath all that bravado, he cares.*

The two entered and with one glare from Tony to the desk clerk, they found out Charisse's room. Taking the elevator to the third floor, they walked down the hall. Tony's senses were alert. His op training had him scanning the area but felt no threat. He could not shake the feeling that something was not right, but he had no warning of danger.

Arriving at Charisse's door, Sherrie knocked several times. When no answer or sound came from within, she turned her gaze to Tony. Before she had a chance to ask, he quickly picked the easy lock. The door swung open, but Tony went in first. He was so tall and broad, Sherrie could not see around him.

"Damn," he called out and before he could stop her, Sherrie skirted around him, running toward the bed. Charisse lay on the bed, drug paraphernalia around. Eyes wide open.

Tony tagged Sherrie around the waist and lifted her easily off the ground. He had seen enough death to know what it looked like. Felt like. Smelled like. And he knew Charisse was dead.

Bicycling her legs, she tried to get down. "Tony, let go. Let me help her."

He wrapped both arms around her, effectively caging her in his embrace. "No, Sherrie. You can't help her," he said softly.

She stopped moving long enough to see that her sister's chest was not moving. No breaths. No movement at all.

"Noooo," she wailed, going limp in his arms.

He was the only thing keeping her upright and he knew he needed to call the police. Turning around and shifting to hold her with one arm, he pulled out his phone, dialing Matt. Giving a quick run-down and location, he shoved his phone back into his pocket, returning both arms to her.

"Tony…you have to let me go to her. I have to see her," Sherrie sobbed. She twisted in his tight hold to see Charisse again.

"Don't want you to touch anything until Matt and Shane get here."

"I won't touch anything, please. Please let me, please, please," she begged.

Knowing he should not, he felt helpless against her pleading. He loosened his hold slightly and she shot out of his arms, kneeling by the bed.

She reached out a shaking finger to just a whisper away from her sister's cheek. Holding her breath, she touched it gently, hoping to feel the warmth. The life. But only ice cold met her touch. Her breath rushed out in a single whoosh, causing Charisse's hair to move in the breeze. Her hair. They had the same blonde hair. Often disinterested, temporary foster parents would not take the time to tell them apart. *Too much like twins,* one had complained when Sherrie corrected them for the hundredth time.

Choking out a sob, she threw her head back, unleashing a wail in the room.

"Shit," Tony ground out as he pulled her up from the floor and against his chest. *Shoulda never let her down there*, he chastised himself. Holding her shaking body tightly to his, he could not help but notice how neatly she fit into him. His arms wrapped securely around her middle with one hand cradling her head that was tucked perfectly underneath his chin with her cheek against his heart.

He had kept her at arm's length for so long, convincing himself that he did not want her. Or need her. Or anyone. But holding her right here, right now, had his mind wondering if maybe there could be something between them. If perhaps he could try again. *No. Don't go there. Not again.* His arms could not seem to listen to his mind as he continued to hold her as sobs racked her body.

She had no sense of the passage of time. She felt her hands bunch his shirt that was pressed closely to her face. Tears soaked the material, but she could not make them stop. Her legs felt gelatinous and at one point she felt his arms shift as if to hold her up. Voices began to murmur in the distance but meant nothing to her.

Matt and Shane appeared, taking in the scene efficiently. Calling it in to get the homicide detectives to the hotel, they quietly asked Tony questions. Tony answered them succinctly and if they wondered about his arms supporting Sherrie, they did not let on. He was grateful. *Don't need them reading more into this than it is.*

Sherrie's sobs had quieted and he could feel her testing her weight as she placed her feet more firmly on the floor. She pushed ever so slightly on his arms, but his brain could not seem to tell them to let go of her.

Looking down, her face was tear-streaked, shock still in her eyes.

"Sherrie?" Matt asked softly. "When was the last time you saw your sister?"

Opening her mouth to answer, her tongue seemed to have swollen, halting the words from coming out. Licking her lips, she swallowed loudly. "It...I..." Giving herself a little shake, she tried again. "A year ago. I haven't seen or heard from her since..."

Matt nodded, well remembering how Charisse led Sherrie into a trap, trying to score a favor with a drug king-pin.

"She...she sent me a text saying she needed me," Sherrie continued, holding out her phone for him to see.

By then the other detectives had arrived and the scene became an active investigation. Matt, Shane, and Tony gave their information to the detective in charge.

"Tony?" she called in a small voice. He looked down immediately, seeing trust mixed in with grief.

"Yeah?" he answered, more gruffly than he should have.

"What...what happens now? With her?"

Sighing, he answered gently, "They'll take the body. They may have to do an autopsy to determine cause of death. They'll let you know when you can have a funeral home come and pick her up."

"Oh." Her brain simply could not process anymore.

Recognizing that he needed to get her out of there, he walked her slowly to the outside of the room and down the hall a little ways. "I'm going to make sure that they don't need you for anything else. Stay here, okay?"

He walked back to the room, talking with Matt and Shane for a few minutes. "Damn, guys. Charisse was a piece of work and now this? Just couldn't stay off the drugs."

"Sherrie gonna be okay?" Shane asked.

"Yeah. I'll take her home in a little bit."

"You were holding her pretty tight when we got in. She finally breaking through that tough exterior of yours?"

"Nah. Just making sure she didn't pass out all over the crime scene, that's all." *Damn, I'm a prick. Can't even admit that it felt fuckin' great to finally have her in my arms, even if it was from this fucked up situation.*

The men chatted a few more minutes and then Tony walked back into the hall. Looking around, seeing it empty, he sprinted to the stairs and out through lobby. A taxi was just pulling away, Sherrie's blonde hair visible from the back.

Standing on the cold sidewalk, hands on his hips, he hung his head. *She must have heard.* Fighting the urge to get in his truck and race after her, he stood his ground stoically. *This is why I'm no good for anyone. I just don't know how to open myself up to those emotions anymore.*

Turning he walked to his truck, pulled himself into the driver's seat and moved into traffic.

CHAPTER 5

A WEEK LATER SHERRIE sat numbly in the seat at the front of the cemetery staring at the casket. She kept things simple, knowing her sister had no friends that would have attended her funeral. In fact her sister had no friends at all, unless you counted pimps, her drug supplier, and perhaps a few strippers and hookers.

She looked at the gleaming casket, glad that the cheapest version did not look like just a box. Charisse certainly had no money, no savings, and no life insurance to help cover the costs. In fact, if Sherrie's friends had not given some donations, she would have been paying off this bare-bones funeral for years.

Her eyes were hidden behind sunglasses even though the day was cloudy. Charisse may have been a mess as a person...but she was still her sister. The stress of the last week was bearing down on Sherrie, causing a never-ending headache. Reaching up to rub her forehead, she wished...*what the hell do I wish for? That Charisse had not been such a fuck-up? That I hadn't been pulling her ass out of the fire since we were teenagers? That I had been better...or more understanding...or something?*

Her friend, Jennifer, reached over and grasped her

hand, giving a gentle squeeze, startling her out of her musings. Annie, Lily, and Suzanne sat on the other side with their husbands sitting in the row behind. The minister had finished his prayer and was walking over to offer his condolences before leaving.

She stood, accepting the hugs from her friends and assured them that she was fine and just needed a little privacy. She watched them as they made their way to their cars, smiling when they glanced back.

She walked slowly toward her car, but spying a bench under a tree she made her way there. Sitting down, she wrapped her arms around her middle, trying to protect herself. From the chill. Both inside and out.

Alone. All alone. It had been her and Charisse for as long as she could remember. No uncles or aunts. No cousins. And now Sherrie was filled with the realization that she was the last in her family. She sighed loudly, the weight pressing on her chest forcing the air from her lungs.

"Do you need someone to see you home?" a deep voice came from behind that she recognized. *Of course I recognize it…it's filled my dreams ever since I first met him. And I am nothing to him. He sees me and just sees an extension of my sister. I'll never be good enough for him.* She closed her eyes for a moment, wondering if his voice was only her imagination.

"Sherrie?" the voice prompted.

She did not turn around as she answered, "No, thank you. I'm fine, Tony."

He walked around to the front of the bench and stopped directly in front of her. "I wanted to say that I'm sorry. About your sister. About…"

Leaning her head way back so that she could see his face, she replied, "It's fine. I'll be fine."

"I'd like to see you home," he said, squatting so that she did not have to lean back so far.

She looked at his face. She had memorized every facet. From his short, dark hair to his square jaw with just a hint of stubble. And those eyes. The color of warm caramel. She wanted to lean into his chest and feel his arms around her. She wanted to know what it would be like to have him take her home, sit with her and hold her.

She stood from the bench, a forced a smile on her face. "Thank you, but I'm fine," she said for the hundredth time that week. *Maybe if I keep saying it, it will eventually be the truth.*

She moved around him quickly and walked to her car, hearing him walk behind her. She opened the door and turned to see that she could not shut it with him standing in the way.

"Tony, you're good to go. I don't need babysitting. I'm just going to go home and rest for a while."

He stood for a moment, indecision written plainly on his face before just nodding and closing her door. She drove slowly out of the cemetery and told herself that she would not look in the rear-view mirror. But she did…and seeing Tony standing there alone instead of holding her almost broke her heart.

A WEEK LATER, Sherrie found herself back in her car with nothing in her rear-view mirror but highway. Mr. Marks had called her in and told her that he was forcing her to take a break.

"Listen to an old man, my dear. I've buried loved ones before and you need to take some time for yourself. I talked to my wife and we agreed that we'd like you to get away. We've got a little cabin that's less than two hours from here that's in the mountains. It's kind of rustic, but we keep it stocked and with a few of your own groceries, you'll have everything that you need."

After much protesting on her part and insisting on his, she acquiesced. Her girlfriends had all come by the day after the funeral to check on her but right now seeing them only brought to mind what she did not have. Family. They were all married, some with children. *I love them but right now, I just need to get away.*

After packing for a weekend trip, she loaded her car with luggage and some food. Glancing at the gray sky that matched her mood, she put the directions in her GPS and started out. After a while, she gave Jennifer a quick call to let her know where she was going.

"Sherrie, are you crazy? Haven't you heard the

weather reports?" Jennifer asked with concern.

"I haven't really had the TV on this week," Sherrie had to admit.

"Honey, there's a snow storm coming. In fact, it's heading our way right now and you're heading for the Blue Ridge Mountains where it's going to hit before Richland."

Sherrie sighed, a moment of indecision flitting through her mind. "Jennifer, I'm going on. I just need to get out of town and I'll be fine. Once I get there, I'll just sleep and read. That's all I need right now."

"Oh, honey. Please be careful. I'm worried about you."

"Don't be. It's not like I'll be out in the weather. I'll be snug in a cabin and can just weather the storm." Giving a snort, she added, "Kind of like I've been doing my whole life."

"Sherrie, just make sure to take care of yourself, let me hear from you, and stay warm. And when you get back, we'll talk."

She smiled. Jennifer was a social worker who worried about everybody and being her friend was comforting as well as fun. "Fine, as soon as I get back, we'll get together."

With goodbyes and promises to be careful, they hung up. Sherrie leaned forward looking at the darkening sky. Glancing back to the GPS, she should only have thirty more minutes to drive. Flipping on the radio to distract her, she found a country station and listened to songs of lost loves and found loves. Her mind, as always, went back to Tony as she tried to accept that he fell into the 'I'll never have love' category.

As soon as Jennifer hung up the phone with Sherrie, she called Gabe.

"Hey gorgeous," he answered.

"Honey, I'm sorry to bother you at work, but it's about Sherrie."

"What about Sherrie? Is she all right?" he asked, glancing up at his co-workers, his gaze focusing on Tony whose attention was riveted on him. "Hang on, babe. I'm putting you on speaker."

"I don't know that I should be worried, but she's been so quiet this past week. I know that's normal, but I couldn't get her to talk about her feelings, or her grief, or her sister at all. Now her boss has offered her his cabin in the mountains as a retreat to get away from it all for a bit."

Gabe, a confused look on his face, said, "Babe, I think that sounds good. It may be just what she needs."

"Honey, she's going there now. Right now. She hadn't listened to the news or weather and I told her a huge snow storm was coming but she went anyway. What if her electricity goes out? Or she's stuck there for a week?"

Tony's voice cut in. "Where's the cabin?"

"I don't know. She said it belonged to her boss, Mr. Marks. Should I try to call him?"

Tony's eyes cut over to Lily, his computer guru, and understanding his look she immediately began to search.

"Hang on, baby. Lily's checking," Gabe said. "How did she sound?"

Jennifer sighed. "It's been two weeks since Charisse died and I know that Sherrie is grieving. I wished she would talk to me, but I get the feeling that she feels like none of us would understand. Or that she feels like she's a bother to us. Nothing could be further from the truth, but she has been on her own for so long I don't think she knows how to open up. I checked with Suzanne and she said the same."

At the mention of his wife's name, BJ nodded. "Yeah, Suzy says that Sherrie has just pulled back into herself."

"Got it," Lily announced, having located the cabin's address.

Tony was already standing as Lily jotted it down. "Jennifer, don't worry. I'm heading out now," he replied. He left the conference room to grab some items from his office, while Gabe finished the conversation with his wife.

As Tony walked back in, he saw the eyes of his brothers-in-arms staring at him. A man of action, he was not used to needing to explain. "I...I—"

Gabe stood, followed by Vinny and Jobe. "No need to explain, sir. She needs your help. Whatever you need from us, you have."

Tony nodded curtly then turned to walk out of the door. He stopped, his back still to his group. Hesitating. Turning back around slowly he looked at his men, his employees...his friends. "This...she's...more than a mission," he finally admitted. Both to them and to himself.

The group smiled in unison. "Yes, sir," Gabe said. "You need us, you just let us know."

TONY RAN TO his apartment to grab some cold-weather gear. He kept his SUV loaded in the wintertime with the necessary items, but he quickly grabbed some warm clothes and made sure his apartment was secure before heading out. Punching in the address in his GPS, he pulled onto the highway heading out of town.

What the hell was she thinking, driving to the mountains with a snow storm coming? He thought of her usual dress...pencil skirts and heels. *She probably doesn't own a pair of snow boots.* The idea of her getting stuck in snow before arriving at the cabin had him in knots.

Listening to country music on the radio, he wondered when she became more than a mission. Was it when he rescued her the first time and saw not only gratitude but a sadness hidden deep inside those blue eyes. Or was it when she called him by mistake when she was trying to help Jennifer and it just so happened that his number was the first one on her call list?

Maybe there was not a certain moment, but a combination of lots of little moments over the past year. The way she jumped in to help others, regardless of the safety to herself. The way she had tried for years to pull her sister's ass out of the fire. Even the way she looked at him when she thought he was not looking. He knew that look. Longing. Wanting. Hoping.

It was the same look he gave her, but for a year was determined to not give in to those desires. *What about Marla? What about taking chances and loss?* Rubbing the back of his neck in frustration, he suddenly realized the snow was beginning to fall. He had tried twice to call Sherrie's number but it had gone straight to voice mail. Glancing at the GPS, it looked like he could be there in about forty minutes…as long as the storm cooperated.

WITH THE SNOW making the road hard to see, Sherrie had to admit that perhaps Jennifer was right. She could no longer see the lines of the small two lane that was leading her higher. *Thank God for GPS,* she thought as she pulled off the road onto a gravel lane that winded around through the trees. *Oh, Jesus. I hope it's here soon.*

Finally coming into a clearing that was already filling with snow, she pulled up to the front of a little cabin. The storm had snow falling so hard and fast that she could not get a good look at the cabin's exterior but decided that she did not care how rustic it was. *Warm, dry, and no critters…that'll be perfect.*

She got out of the car and quickly pulled her suitcase and the bags of groceries out of the trunk. It was cumbersome, but she did not want to make another trip back to the car. Awkwardly making her way to the front steps, she finally reached the porch. Once under the porch roof, she looked back, surprised to see that her windshields were already covered with snow. Finding the key, she unlocked the front door and it swung open. She stepped in, trying to maneuver her suitcase in front of her. Tripping, she landed on her knees on top of her luggage, her long blonde hair falling in her face.

Huffing, she pushed herself up trying to move the suitcase while dropping the groceries onto the floor. Kicking the door shut with her foot, she pushed her hair out of her eyes and looked around.

Oh, my. This is perfect, she thought, heaving a sigh of relief. When Mr. Marks had offered her the vacation cabin, she never questioned him what it would be like. Jennifer had her wondering what she was getting herself into, but this seemed like a dream.

Small and rustic, it still oozed charm. To the left was a long living room with exposed beams in the vaulted ceiling. The room went the full length of the cabin, with sliding doors leading out to the back. A stone fireplace with built-in bookcases took up much of the left wall. An overstuffed sofa sat in front of the fireplace with two worn leather chairs flanking it. Stepping over her suitcase, she moved into the room. The large window at the front porch let in little light with the storm, but she could imagine that in better weather, the morning sun would stream in. The dark wood floors held braided rugs. She flipped a switch on the wall and the lamps sitting on the end tables lit.

Turning, she saw an old wooden dining table and chairs on the opposite side of the front door and a kitchen further back. Walking into the kitchen, she saw that it was old, but gleaming. She imagined the Marks family when their children were little, running through the house and enjoying vacations here. *Vacations. With family.* Having never experienced a vacation, she felt a pang of envy, but pushed it down, determined to have her first vacation even in the middle of a snow storm.

Rounding back out of the kitchen, she moved further and found two doors. The first one opened into a bathroom, not small but not opulent. A single sink, toilet and bathtub, and linen closet were there. She reached over, pleased to see water rushing as she turned the knob. Quickly using the facilities, she eyed the tub longingly. *First thing on my vacation list—a long hot soak.*

Moving to the only other door, she found the bedroom. Quaint, with a queen sized bed, night stands, and dresser, she flopped down on the bed for a moment, reveling in the comfort. *Mine. All mine. At least for the weekend.*

Getting back up, she quickly put her grocery items into the kitchen and dragged her suitcase into the bedroom. *One bedroom? I guess the Marks' children must have slept in the living room.* Imagining a cabin in the mountains as a child, she thought that spending the nights on the pull-out sofa or sleeping bags must have been an adventure.

Turning on the water to fill the bathtub, she poured just a little bath oil in before walking back to the living room to look out at her car in the driveway. It was buried in snow but as safe as she knew how to make it. Going back to the bathroom, she stripped and settled into the tub, letting the warmth and aroma of the scented oil soothe her. Slipping in her earplugs, she listened to the melodic sounds of music, taking her to a peaceful place that she had not known in weeks.

As always, images of Tony filled her mind, but she pushed them away. *I'll never be good enough for him. Whatever he needs or whatever he's looking for…it's not me.*

TONY'S GPS HAD HIM turning on a non-existent road between two trees. He'd given up seeing the road, relying on instinct and training, moving slowly. Finally it looked as though he were there. Moving between the trees in what could have only been the path, his headlights finally illuminated a cabin in a clearing. Lights were on from the inside and he saw a snow covered car in the front. Parking next to it, he hauled his duffle bag from the back, as well as his supplies. Walking over to the snow covered vehicle, he gave it a quick swipe with his hand and saw that it was Sherrie's car. *Thank God. So why hasn't she been answering her phone?* Not knowing if he wanted to spank her or kiss her, he made his way up to the front door.

He knocked, but immediately thought that she might be frightened. "Sherrie," he called. No answer. He knocked again. No answer.

He tried the doorknob and found that with just a hard jiggle, it came unlocked. *She's out here with virtually no security, not even a front door that locks properly.* Stepping inside, he set his things down and glanced around, his gaze seeing and categorizing everything. As he shut the door behind him, he saw that there was a deadbolt that she had not secured. *A spanking is definitely first on my list*, he thought angrily.

"Sherrie, it's Tony," he called out. No answer. Seeing light from a partially open doorway that was just behind the kitchen he stalked over and looked in.

Sherrie was lying in the bathtub, eyes closed with earplugs from her Ipod in her ears. Her long, blonde hair was piled on top of her head in a messy knot, tendrils escaping along the side of her face. His gaze raked down her body, rosy nipples peeking from the water.

Knowing he should turn and walk away, his feet seemed rooted to the floor. His dick swelled painfully in his jeans, straining the zipper. Even that simple act of tamping down his desire seemed foreign to him. A master at controlling his body as well as his emotions, he was not used to getting a hard-on just from looking at a naked woman. He allowed himself to get off when he needed anonymous sex, but could not remember the last time he had trouble controlling his dick.

Starting to back out of the doorway, he saw her eyes open and before he could say anything she moved faster than anyone he had ever seen.

Screaming, she jumped up, the earbuds popping out as her feet slipped in the tub, sending her backward, her head going under the water.

Tony rushed forward, trying to grasp the slippery women while dodging her flailing arms. One of her hands slammed into his nose as he pulled her out of the tub before slipping on the wet floor, somehow managing to keep her from hitting her head as he landed on his back. Her wet, naked body was plastered against his as she continued to wiggle to get free.

"Stop," he ordered, knowing there was no way he could keep his erection from pushing into her stomach. Standing, he pulled her up with him, setting her on the bathroom rug while grabbing the towel from the toilet lid.

"Sherrie, it's me," he shouted over her screams as she tried to see through her dripping hair and cover herself at the same time.

Realizing who had just plucked her naked form out of the bathtub and was now standing in front of her holding a towel up to give her some sense of modesty, she glared up into his face.

If looks could kill, I'd be incinerated, he realized.

CHAPTER 6

S HERRIE STOOD IN the bathroom, staring into the mirror. She had not planned on washing her hair but after the dunking in the bath-oil water she had no choice, and her wet, combed hair hung down her back. *Oh Jesus, he pulled me naked from the tub. How the hell do I face him now?* Looking at her reflection, she saw her pajamas. A soft flannel set that covered her head to toe. *Not exactly sexy. No, that doesn't matter. I wasn't here for entertaining.* Gripping the counter with white knuckles, her mind whirled. *What the hell is he doing here? How did he find me? And why?* Pursing her lips tightly, she thought, *Another rescue. That's what he's doing. I'm nothing but a rescue mission to him—again!* Eyes snapping, she pushed off the counter and prepared to face him.

Tony had put away the provisions he had brought after making a cursory tour of the small cabin when Sherrie appeared out of the bathroom. Covered in flannel with only her tiny toes peeking out completed her comfortable ensemble, but it did little to blank out the image of her curvy, naked body. Wet hair, now combed and pulled away from her face allowed him to see that she was angry.

Putting his hands up, he said, "Before you get your panties in a wad, you've got some explaining to do."

"Me?" she sputtered. "Me?" she repeated, unable to think of anything else to say.

"Yes, you. You leave Richland without telling your friends of your plans. You haven't watched the news lately so you completely missed that the snow storm of the winter was coming our way. Your phone has been off for the past several hours, keeping anyone from checking on you. I get here to make sure you're all right and all it takes is a jiggle of the doorknob to get in since you forgot to turn the fuckin' deadbolt. What if it had been someone else besides me?"

"You self-righteous prick," she answered back. "I don't owe anyone an explanation of where I go or what I do. I may not have known I was heading toward a storm but I made it just fine. I have warm clothes and food, so I hardly think that I am totally unprepared. And what rapist or murderer would possibly know about this place or be able to find it in the middle of a storm? And on top of that, what the hell are you doing here?" she yelled, eyes snapping with her hands on her hips.

Stepping forward, he yelled back, "Don't turn this on me. You put yourself in danger."

"How am I in danger? I'm here safe and sound, was enjoying a fabulous bath and then you come barging in, invading my privacy!"

"You're lucky it was me and only me invading your privacy." *Infuriating woman. Jesus, she's the only person who makes me lose all control.* Standing toe to toe they glared into each other's eyes, anger morphing into something more primal.

Pulling her to him quickly, he covered her mouth with his own. Deep, wet and hard. An unrestrained kiss that spoke volumes as their arms entwined. Lifting her up, she wrapped her legs around his waist as her arms clutched his shoulders. Moving their heads from one side to the other, their tongues dueled in a frenzy for dominance.

Thrusting his tongue deeply into the warmth of her mouth, he tasted the heady combination of mint and her. Distinctly her. Two more steps forward had her back against the wall. Her breasts pressed into his chest, as one arm held her ass and the other was wrapped around her back. She sucked his tongue into her mouth and could not tell if the animalistic moan came from her or him...or both.

He pushed her more firmly against the wall, supporting her so that he had both hands free. She immediately began to grind herself on his torso, desperate for the friction to ease the ache that was deep inside.

He grabbed the bottom of her shirt and whipped it up over her head, their kiss only breaking long enough for the material to pass their lips. After lifting her hands, allowing her top to fly off, she grabbed his head holding it tight as she delved her tongue back into his mouth.

She had not put her bra back on after her bath and his hands quickly found the heavy globes that fit perfectly in them. He moved his thumbs over her nipples, alternating between pinching and gently rubbing.

Throwing her head back against the wall, she allowed his lips to leave a wet trail of kisses from her throat down her neck to the tops of her breasts. She thrust them forward as an unconscious offering and one that he was more than willing to take. Sucking a nipple deep into his mouth, he licked, nipped, bit, and suckled until she was writhing wildly. Moving over to give the other nipple the same attention, his hand slipped down her pajama bottoms and found her panties soaked. Pulling the bottoms and panties over her hips, he jerked them off her legs then picked her back up.

Lips locked once more, he hefted her up in his arms long enough to unbutton and unzip his jeans, freeing his swollen cock. Having lost all control he held her over the tip, finding her slick folds ready for him. His mind, filled with the pounding need that roared through him, was barely conscious of her small hands holding him closely. Needing to be inside of her was more important than his next breath.

"Please," she begged, her mind equally filled with desire and longing that drowned out all other voices in her head. She only felt. Experienced. Every fiber of her being tingled with the need of him deep inside. *I've waited forever for someone like you. No, not like you. Just you.*

With one swift plunge, he seated her firmly and completely on his dick, barely hearing her head bang on the wall behind her. *Damn, she's tight. Too tight. Something's wrong—*

Before he could process that thought, she was moving on his cock, trying to ease the ache. With one hand on the wall beside her head to maintain his balance, he thrust up and down, fucking her as he had wanted to for the past year.

Her fingernails scored his back as she felt the tingles that had tempted her as she rubbed herself on his jeans now intensified as her entire sex clutched at him. Strung tight as a bow, she was aware of every movement of his thick cock stretching her tighter. Tighter and tighter until she was sure she would snap.

He could not remember the last time he had felt like this. Barely aware of anything other than the roaring in his ears, he moved one hand down to her clit, thumbing it in rhythm to his thrusts. Finally, with his name screaming from her lips, she felt her sex clench and electric jolts moved from her core, spreading outward in all directions.

As her incredibly tight inner walls milked his cock, he found himself pouring his seed deep into her. Continuing to stroke the inside of her until every last drop was emptied, he rested all of his weight on the arm against the wall, holding him up.

Sweating and panting together, her head was resting next to his arm, eyes tightly closed as the sensations flowed over her. *I've wanted him for so long.* Opening her eyes to see his face, she saw that he was looking down as he pulled out of her. Waiting for him to say something profound or romantic, she wanted him to look into her eyes.

"God, that was a mistake," came the agonized words.

His words slapped her with cold as if she were standing in the storm outside. Pushing against him, she slid out of his arms as she looked to see her virgin blood on his cock. *A mistake?* If she thought the idea of being alone in the world was the worst pain, she realized she had just slipped even deeper into agony.

Tears welled in her eyes as she ran into the bedroom, slamming and locking the door. Lying on the bed, she felt the sobs overtake her as the realization that the most perfect moment in her life up to now was only a mistake to the one man that she ever cared about.

STUNNED, TONY STOOD in the hallway trying to process what had just happened. *Shit, that wasn't what I meant.*

Stepping to the bedroom door, he pounded as he

called out, "Sherrie. You took that the wrong way. I didn't mean that it was a mistake. Not what we did. Well…it was, but not how you think. I just meant that it was wrong. No, not wrong. Just done the wrong way. But that's my fault." No sound came from the room, other than the sound of heartbreak.

Resting his head on the door, he said, "Sherrie, nothing's coming out right. Please don't cry. Let me explain, but let me do it face to face."

Nothing.

Moving to the bathroom, he washed the blood and semen off and then pulled his pants back up. Washing his hands in the sink, he looked into the mirror. *You're a royal fuck-up. When the hell did that happen? You just took a virgin up against the wall. Without a condom.*

Stepping back into the room, he saw her pajamas and panties on the floor. Bending to pick them up, he was filled with shame. Another emotion he had not felt in a long time. *Jesus, I've broken the record on the number of new emotions in one day for me. All because of her.* One petite, blonde with a curvy body and a personality that pulled him in. Or rather pulled himself out of his constant morose mood.

Deciding she needed time to cry and possibly plan his demise, he walked back to the window looking out over the front yard. The snow was still swirling, his SUV now as covered as hers. His gaze expertly took in the room once again, this time landing on the stone fireplace and the pile of wood stacked nearby. Starting a fire, he felt the warmth in the blaze as he rubbed his chest, wishing the tightness to go away.

LYING ACROSS THE BED, tears spent, Sherrie stared up at the ceiling. Shame filled her belly as she wiped her wet cheeks. *How could I have read the signals so wrong?* Ruefully, she acknowledged her inexperience. From the time she was fifteen years old, she had witnessed Charisse's sexual escapades. Her sister used sex as a way to escape. And to score drugs. And as power. *Hell, she used sex for everything except love.* Sherrie decided early on that her body would only be given to someone special. All those nights spent waiting on drunk customers while trying to keep an eye on her sister when she was stripping, made her an expert at seeing men at their worst. It only made her more determined to find her hero. The first time she had looked into those caramel eyes when he rescued her she knew she had found a good man. A good friend. Someone she could fall in love with.

And now, with her virgin's blood spilled, her hero had called her a mistake.

Sitting up in the bed so that she could breathe with her stuffed nose, she swung her legs over the side grabbing a tissue. Blowing her nose and wiping her eyes, she glanced out of the window. The night was black, no moonlight coming through the window.

Wondering if it was still snowing and if she could manage to drive back to town, she quickly dismissed that idea. The last time she had peered out, the snow was already in drifts around her car.

Sighing deeply, she thought about spending the next couple of days locked in this room so that she would not have to face him. *I could only wander out to go to the bathroom or to eat. Eat?* The tantalizing smell of food was drifting into her room.

Anger filled her as much as hunger. *This is my cabin for the time and he's the intruder.* Determined to stop hiding she moved to the door. Lifting her head, she threw open the door and marched out. *It's not the first time I've been hurt...and won't be the last. I've been pretending for most of my twenty-six years...and this is no different.* As she walked out of her room, she knew she was lying to herself.

NOW KNOWING IF SHE was going to come out that evening, Tony decided to fix some dinner just in case. He walked into the kitchen and pulled out some chicken breasts, putting them into the oven. After a while he covered them in marinara sauce and put them back in the oven. As he put some noodles in the boiling water, he heard the bedroom door opening.

Turning, his heart pounding, he looked as she walked into the living room toward the fire. Now wearing sweat pants, thick socks, and a sweatshirt, she looked…armored. *Against me, no doubt.*

She walked over to the fireplace, lifting her hands to the warmth. She could feel when he approached from behind, but feared turning around. Seeing the look of regret, disinterest, or worse, pity on his face terrified her no matter how strong she tried to be.

"Sherrie," his voice called out softly. "Please look at me."

Swallowing her pride, she turned to face him and to her surprise saw anguish. He stepped closer, not crowding, but just close enough that she could not take her eyes off of him.

"Tony, it's okay. Really. It was silly of me to think that it would mean anyth—"

"Stop," he ordered placing his fingers on her lips. Her lips were swollen from their kissing and as he moved his fingers over them, he felt them quiver. But then he looked into her red, puffy eyes and knew he had to make this right.

He slid his hand from her lips slowly down her arm to her hand. Taking her hand he walked toward the sofa, gently pulling her down next to him, twisting so that he could look into her face.

She went silently along with him, both curious and dreading. *This is where he tells me that he doesn't do commitment. Or I'm not his type. Or he was grossed out. Or—*

"Whatever fucked-up shit's going on in your head,

please stop and listen. I need you to listen," he pleaded.

Startled out of her musings, she just nodded.

He opened his mouth and shut it several times. Finally dropping his head, he stared at their hands, still clasped, for a moment. *Man up. Time to man up.*

"Sherrie, I'm not good at this."

"At what?" she asked in confusion.

"Explaining my feelings. I try to say things and they come out all fucked up." He looked at her, grateful that she stayed silent, giving him time to gather his words. "With my men, it's fine. I'm comfortable in command. I plan, I strategize, I execute the mission. But emotions...it's hard."

Sighing, he looked into her blue eyes that seemed to see deep inside of him regardless of the barriers that he tried to erect. "I never meant that what we did was a mistake. Never. It was..." he searched for the right word and could only come up with, "special."

Her eyes seemed to light at that word so he hoped he chose the right one. Again, she stayed still, allowing him time to think. He rubbed his coarse fingertips over her tiny hand, finding strength in the feel of her skin.

"I didn't come here to seduce you. Or take you up against the wall."

She watched as his face twisted in a mix of anger and disgust. "Why did you come exactly, Tony?"

"Jennifer called Gabe to say that you were traveling alone toward a snow storm. And I just jumped up to come find you. I needed to make sure you were safe. I needed to make sure…nothing bad was happening."

"You feel the need to rescue me all the time?" she asked, needing to understand his motives.

"Yes. No. Not really." Running his hand over his face, he started over. "When I first saw you almost a year ago, I thought you were beautiful. But I assumed I'd never see you again. Then, when we had the same friends, I got to know you. You're smart. Loyal. And dauntless when you're trying to right a wrong."

He looked down at their hands again, noticing that this time she was rubbing circles on his hands.

"I thought you didn't like me," she said shyly.

Giving her hand a gentle squeeze, he shook his head. "No, my problem was that I didn't *want* to like you."

He saw the look of confusion cross her beautiful face, and he struggled for the right words again. "There are things in my past…things that…well, made me not want to feel again. So whenever I saw you, I tried to force myself to not think about you. Stay away from you. I figured I was too fucked up for you, anyway.

"When you leaned into me when we found Charisse, as bad as that was for you…it felt right to me. You being in my arms. Leaning on me. Trusting in me. That felt right. I made a dumbass comment to Matt and Shane that I know you overheard and when I realized you had gone, I knew I hurt you. When you pushed me away after the funeral, I figured that I needed to stay away.

"But when Jennifer called, I didn't over-think for once. I knew this was the place I wanted to be. I wanted to make sure you were safe. I wanted to be here in case you needed something. Or needed me. But what happened there?" he nodded toward the wall behind her. "That should have never happened. Not like that."

Silence filled the room except for the crackling of the logs burning in the fireplace. Licking her lips, she pondered his words. *Such a contradiction, I hardly know what to think. He acted like he didn't like me, but he does. So what now? Just friends? Or more?*

He watched her pink tongue moisten her lips and it was all he could do to not lean over and capture them, but he refused to lose control once again. He lifted his gaze to her eyes and once again saw uncertainty.

"I'm still fuckin' this up, aren't I?"

"I want to understand, Tony. Please help me understand why it was a mistake. Is it because you just want to be friends? Because you don't *want* to want me?"

"Sherrie, you were a virgin. You should have had your first time in a bed with candlelight and someone taking their time to make sure you were ready and then have them go slow and easy."

He focused on her eyes, cupping her face with his free hand, feeling the soft skin against his rough. "I wanted you. I've wanted you for a long time. I'm used to controlling everything about myself but one look at you, standing in your pajamas arguing with me had me lose control. I just went on emotion and took you against the wall."

She lifted her hand as well and caressed his cheek, trusting the caramel eyes that had captured her a year ago.

"In a bed or up against a wall...I've wanted you," she said.

"Can I ask you something really personal?"

"Tony, I think we're way into something personal already," she grinned.

"How is it that you are...were still a virgin? I mean someone like you?"

At that, the humor left her face and he wondered what he had said wrong.

"Someone like me?" she asked, pulling back from him. "What do you mean, Tony? A poor girl from the foster system? Or a cocktail waitress in a strip joint? Or just because my sister was a—"

"No," he interjected. "No, none of that. I just meant... you know. Someone as beautiful as you. I can't imagine that you haven't had men dying to meet you."

"Oh," she said softly, her eyes going misty. "I guess, I was just holding out for a hero. And then I found him."

"Baby, I'm no hero," he admitted, a flash of regret passing through his eyes.

"You are to me," she whispered.

Leaning in, he kissed her softly, promising himself to maintain control. Just then the water began to boil over and they both leapt up as he jogged into the kitchen. Turning down the stove eye, he placed the pasta in to cook. Looking over his shoulder at her standing at the kitchen entrance, he said, "I didn't know when you might come out but I fixed some dinner."

"It smells good," she admitted, watching him pull the chicken out of the oven. Deciding that their serious talk was over for now and she could rest easy knowing they were friends, she found the plates and set the table. Several minutes later, they sat to dinner in companionable silence and he opened one of the bottles of wine she brought.

Eying the other bottles, he lifted his eyebrow at her in question. She could not help but giggle as she said, "I thought I might drown my sorrows in wine while I was here alone."

"Well, I'm glad you're not alone to drink all of this," he quipped.

"Me too," she added seriously.

Finishing their meal, she offered to clean up since he cooked. Tony stepped outside on the porch to see how the storm was progressing. While out, he made a quick call to Gabe to report that they had both made it and would be in touch when they could, knowing that Gabe would let the others know. His men were like that—all of one mind. Finding more wood piled on the corner of the porch, he brought several loads inside.

Kneeling as he placed more wood into the fire, he could feel her presence behind him. He saw her standing near the sofa, fingers nervously twisting the bottom of her sweatshirt. *Hell, I've talked more to her in the past hour than I have to anyone in a year...and there's still so much more to say.* Turning back to the fire as the new wood began to catch with flames, he replaced the antique fire screen.

Standing, he faced her, knowing that she was still unsure of what his feelings were.

"What's it like outside?" she asked quietly, as though trying to find something to say.

He chuckled. "Cold. Windy. And blowing in one helluva of a snow storm."

Sucking her lips in, she glanced toward the dark window. "I was foolish to come here, wasn't I?"

"I wouldn't say foolish, but maybe unprepared. Honestly, honey? I kinda blame Mr. Marks for not checking the weather before offering you his cabin. He shoulda known that your mind wasn't on looking at the news."

"I think he was just worried about me. I did receive a text message from him and I let him know I got here safe."

Nodding toward the sofa, he asked, "You want to sit by the fire for a little bit?"

Her face lit up with a smile and she moved to where she had been sitting before supper. He watched her smile and felt the piercing in his chest once again. Right over his heart. She moved gracefully, everything about her elegant. He did not know how long he stood there just staring at her until she broke his trance.

"Tony? Are you going to sit too?"

Settling his large frame next to hers on the over-stuffed cushions, he could not help but smile himself. It felt strange on his face. A smile. *Jesus, when was the last time I really smiled?* Her hand was resting on the sofa between them. Not too close to seem grasping, but available if he wanted to take her hand again. Small. Delicate. Beckoning.

He reached out and slid his fingers around hers. Just that connection felt right, as though he were beginning to see her as a life-line. Something to hold on to that was real. "Did you...understand what I was trying to say earlier? Before dinner. About us?"

Looking down at their clasped hands, she admitted, "I understand that you were avoiding me because you care for me but don't feel like you should. And that you wished we hadn't had sex up against the wal—"

"Not as your first time," he interrupted. "Sherrie, I never lose control. If I lost control in the Special Forces, men could die. With my agency if I lose control, a mission can go wrong and others can get hurt."

"So…," she hesitated. "You're not sorry we had sex, but sorry you lost control?"

"Yeah."

"But Tony, sometimes life is about losing control. Giving into feelings. Going with your gut reaction. Not everything in life is going to be like a planned mission."

Shaking his head, a sadness crossed his expression as he said, "I don't like the feeling of not controlling things around me." He looked up and continued, "We haven't even touched on the part of me not using a condom. I swear I'm clean. I've got the papers to pro—"

"I trust you," she said quickly, hating the turn of the conversation.

"Well, if you get pregnant you've got to tell me—"

"Stop, just stop," she said, her anger beginning to rise. "I will not be your mission again. Poor little virgin gets pregnant and you have to rescue her one more fucking time!"

The silence stretched between them. She saw the shadows of the firelight flicker across his chiseled face. His demons still existed deep inside and until he could let go of them, she would never really have him to herself. *I don't mind you having a past, but if I can't have all of you…*

Several minutes passed, both lost in their thoughts. "What are you thinking?" he asked softly, both wanting and dreading her answer.

Licking her lips, she kept her gaze steady as she answered, "I've wanted you for a very long time. There's so much about each other that we know and yet I'm sitting here thinking that we're still such strangers." With a final squeeze of his fingers, she stood, looking down on him. "I gave myself to you gladly. Was it spontaneous? Yes. Was it amazing? Absolutely. The difference is that you have regrets because of whatever-the-hell keeps you from really living life. I get that something's in your past that keeps you wanting complete control. We all have our demons, Tony. And for someone who is all about maintaining control, you have lost it with them."

At that, his gaze shot up toward hers in question.

"Yeah, Tony. You say you're in control, but whatever has hold of you...whatever holds you back? That's what really controls your life."

With that, she walked toward the bedroom alone. At the doorway, she paused but did not turn around. *If I look at his face, I won't be able to be strong.* Sighing deeply, she added, "I want you Tony. But I want all of you. I deserve all of you. Not just the little part that you're willing to give to me." *I want more than friendship.*

She walked into the bedroom and closed the door. Sliding out of her sweat pants and sweatshirt, she pulled on her pajamas again and crawled under the covers, glad that the heat was still working in the cabin.

She wondered if she would be able to sleep, but exhaustion took over and she drifted off. For the moment, peace was only found in slumber.

CHAPTER 7

SLEEP DID NOT come so easily for Tony. He sat for a long time, looking into the flickering flames dancing in the firelight. Strange, but fire was comforting to him. It always took him back to the campfires he and his men would sit around. On cold nights in Afghanistan, it was sometimes the only warmth they had. Tony's mind opened and he allowed himself to wander back in time.

It was easier then...to talk, share, feel. At least before. Before life came to a screeching halt and the coldness seeped in to stay. After that, the campfire conversations centered around their missions. Looking back, he knew that was when the missions became his life. His control. Nothing else mattered but getting in, getting the job done, and getting all his men out safely.

Reaching into his back pocket finding his wallet, he pulled out the faded, worn picture. His fingers traced the faces once again. *It's getting harder to remember your face, Marla. But I remember how you made me feel. Happy. Like I was the center of your fuckin' world.* He thought about how old Sofia would be by now. *Running around? Playing? What would be your favorite food?* As much as his heart ached, he could not picture what she would look like if she were still alive. In his mind, she would always be the tiny, wrapped up infant he held the day she was born.

What would you want, Marla? You gotta tell me, 'cause I'm lost here. I'm afraid to move forward...to open myself up to that kind of pain again.

"Life without pain, isn't really living." *Where have I heard that? That was what she told me when she was in labor with Sofia.* The memory washed over him as he thought back to the long, arduous labor. He hated seeing her in pain and had told her that he would take it all away if he could. *She just looked up at me between contractions and said, "Life without pain, isn't really living."*

At the time, he simply thought she meant that without the labor there would be no baby. But maybe, just maybe she meant more. Was telling him more. Was even giving him permission to live again, even if it opened him up to pain.

I want to try again, Marla. I want to try with Sherrie. He did not feel out of control. Panicked. Unsure. Instead, for the first time in a very long time, he knew what he wanted to do. *Tomorrow,* he vowed, *I'll start something new with her. Show her what I can be. What we can be. And treat her the way she deserves to be treated.*

Sighing, he stretched his long frame on the sofa, pleasantly surprised that it accommodated his height. With his head on the arm, he lay with the photograph on his chest while staring at the fire. His eyes finally closed, falling into a troubled sleep.

In the middle of the night Sherrie quietly got out of bed to go to the bathroom. Not seeing Tony at first, she tiptoed toward the fire, seeing him asleep on the couch. Unwilling to disturb him, she turned to move away when a photograph on his chest caught her eye. She took one step closer, peering down to see a faded picture of a younger, smiling Tony with a beautiful dark haired woman holding a newborn baby.

Heart pounding, she felt sick as her mind raced. His hand, curled around the baby had a wedding ring. *He was married. Married.* Her thoughts swirled as she ran through the possibilities. *He'd never leave his wife and baby which can only mean...oh my God. They must be...* Not letting her mind accept the possibility that a young mother and baby could have died and what that would have done to a man like Tony, she numbly tiptoed back to her room.

A heavy weight pressed on her chest as she lay back down in the bed. *A beautiful wife. A new baby. A smiling Tony.* She rolled to her side, as a silent tear slid down her face landing on the pillow.

I'm a poor girl from a foster background with a dead, fucked-up druggie sister who had threatened his friends. I'm not good enough. I'll never be good enough. It looks like he had perfect. I am nowhere near perfect.

Wiping her face, she realized that it was time to cut Tony loose. Time to let go of the idea of them together.

Time to move on.

TONY WOKE SUDDENLY, his military senses on alert. Not used to sleeping so soundly, it took a moment to figure out what he was hearing. Jumping up off the sofa, he caught sight of the photograph that had landed on the floor. Grabbing it, he slid it back into his wallet. Torn between feeling lighter than he had in a long time and knowing that something was not right, he glanced to see the bedroom door was open and then sprinted to the front door to see the noise coming from the outside.

Throwing open the door he halted, stunned at the scene in front of him. The snow was still swirling creating a winter wonderland, completely covering their cars. Sherrie's suitcase was sitting on the front porch and she was...*what the hell is she doing?*

She was wrapped up in her coat, scarf, hat, and had tromped over to her car where she was attempting to rake almost a foot of snow off with her little scraper. If he was not so pissed, he would have been amused.

"What the hell are you doing out here?" he yelled.

She turned and looked at the angry man on the porch. Legs apart, hands on his hips, sleep tousled hair. *Damn, this had seemed like a good idea when I got up.*

"What does it look like I'm doing?" she yelled back. "I thought I would try to clear my car off so that I could go back home."

"Woman, so what if you clear off the car? The driveway and roads are still impassable. You're not fuckin' going anywhere."

"Well, I'll be ready when they are clear," she yelled back.

"Then what's your suitcase doing sitting on the porch?"

"Um..." she said, no quick response coming to mind.

"Get your ass back in the cabin right now," he ordered, his irritation ratcheting up to anger.

"You can't order me around," she yelled, now feeling foolish. The snow was landing on her face, freezing little crystals that made her cheeks hurt. Glancing over at her car, the small amount of snow that she had scraped off had been replaced by a fresh layer.

Sighing heavily, she turned toward the cabin trying to step in snow that had drifted in small mountains that came to her knees. Two steps in, she lost her footing falling face first into a pile.

Grabbing his boots and sliding his feet into them, he headed down the steps toward her. By the time he reached her floundering form, she was pushing herself up. She looked up, extending her hand toward him.

Ignoring it, he scooped her up and toss her over his shoulder, giving her ass a slap in the process. Tromping through the snow, he carefully mounted the steps, snagged her luggage with his free hand and set it inside the door before kicking it shut with his boot. Walking over to the fire, he set her down and put his hands on her shoulders.

Bending down to her eye level, he said, "We're talking about this stunt later. But right now, we're getting you undressed and warm, then I'll go whip up some breakfast."

Pulling her gloves off, her cold fingers fumbled with the buttons on her coat. He moved her hands away and unbuttoned it, pulled it off and gently pushed her down onto the leather seat closest to the fire. Kneeling, he pulled her boots off and rubbed her feet to try to get some warmth back into them.

Standing, he looked down sternly and said, "Stay," as he turned to walk into the kitchen.

"I'm not a dog to be ordered around," she groused.

"Don't push me, Sherrie. You pull another stunt like that and you'll find your ass bared and reddened," he barked from the other room.

She looked askance, not remembering anyone ever threatening her with a spanking before. Not as a child and certainly not as an adult. A retort was on the tip of her tongue, but she wisely decided that she would not tempt fate. And she had to admit that the fire's warmth was penetrating her frozen hands and toes.

A few minutes later the smells of coffee and bacon were drifting from the kitchen. *He's going to think I can't cook since he did supper and breakfast. Nope, doesn't matter what he thinks. I didn't invite him here anyway,* she thought stubbornly.

Standing up, she made her way to the kitchen, watching the scene in front of her. Tony's back was to her, the tight t-shirt stretched across his muscles. *He came out into the snow in just a t-shirt to see what I was doing.*

Feeling small, she said, "I'm sorry, Tony. I didn't mean for you to rescue me again."

His head dropped as he said, "Quit with the fuckin' rescue talk."

Huffing, she whirled around and stomped to the table, tossing some plates onto the surface.

"Pouting now?" he quipped.

Furious, she stalked over to him, poking him in the chest. "Yes, I'm pouting. I came up here to get away. To be alone. To think. To grieve. Now I'm stuck in the snowstorm of the century with a man who really doesn't want to be here, doesn't want to be with me like I want to be with him, and can't let me in." Chest heaving, she turned away, knowing the tears were coming.

She heard his footsteps come up behind her and felt his large hands on her shoulders. "You're wrong. I do want to be here. And I do want to let you in."

Not even bothering to wipe the tears sliding down, they dripped from her cheeks onto her shirt. He rounded her chair, seeing her ravaged expression. Kneeling, he cupped her face wiping the tears with the pads of his thumbs. "Oh, darlin'. We seem to be constantly at odds, don't we?"

She nodded, saying nothing, but held his gaze.

Her tear-filled, luminescent blue eyes held his. Leaning forward until his lips were a breath away, he said, "I do want this. When I said I wanted you last night I meant that I wanted to be with you. I want a relationship. I want everything. I just don't know how anymore. Will you help me? Can we help each other?"

He wants me? Us together? Am I enough to help him? What if I agree and my heart gets broken? Can two people, who seem to be broken help each other become whole again?

He rubbed her cheek with his rough thumb. "What's going on in that mind of yours, Sherrie?"

Sucking in a deep breath, she looked up into his eyes. *I may never be enough to fill his emptiness and my heart may get broken in the process. But yes. I deserve this, however long it lasts. I deserve to be happy. I want to take a chance with this man.*

She nodded one more time, allowing him to slip in, placing his lips onto hers. This time calm. Gentle. A whisper of a kiss. But one that held promise.

She leaned back, searching his face for signs of regret. But there was none. Not this time. Offering a small smile, she said, "We keep having arguments right before meal time."

He grinned back, happy that they were finally on the same page. "You want breakfast, babe?" Standing, he moved back to the kitchen and served the eggs, toast, and bacon onto two plates, placing them on the table.

Hungrier than she realized, she ate heartily noticing that he ate almost three times as much as she did. He caught her eying his plate and laughed. "I'm bigger...gotta keep up my strength."

"For what?" she queried. "We're just going to be stuck here until the storm is over and they can plow the roads."

"I may have to chop wood. Or dig us out. Or wrestle abominable snowmen."

She looked up, a bite of egg still on her fork halted on its way to her mouth. "Did you just make a joke? Tony Alvarez made a joke?"

Tossing a piece of bacon at her, he quipped, "Eat your breakfast, smart-ass."

Grinning, she did exactly that. *I have no idea what's going on, but if it keeps that smile on his face, it needs to stay!*

TRUE TO HIS WORD, he did go out and make sure that they had enough firewood. The heat was still working in the house, but he cleared the snow and ice away from the heat pump to keep it efficient. *With this storm, trees could fall right on the power lines and we'd be without power for a while.* A shed was built next to the house on the kitchen side, and upon investigation he discovered a generator and fuel. Grateful that the

Marks kept the house stocked, he checked to see what other supplies might be around.

He had lost track of time, and when he went inside he did not see Sherrie. The wind had stopped howling and it appeared that the snow was beginning to lessen. Trekking around to the back patio, he saw Sherrie standing there, trying to shovel the snow from the door.

"Woman, get back in the house," he ordered.

"Will you quit calling me 'woman' and quit telling me what to do?" she argued.

Taking the shovel from her hands, he gave her a quick kiss. "Sorry darlin', but I just can't deal with you out here freezing when I can do this so much easier."

What had taken her almost ten minutes to shovel only took him a few minutes to cover twice the area. Crossing her arms over her chest, she glared.

"What?" he asked.

"You're still controlling."

"Yeah, well now I'm enjoying controlling you," he said, gently pushing her back inside as he stomped off his boots. "I did find a generator that we can use if the electricity goes out."

At this, she turned her gaze to him, confusion in her expression. "I...I don't know what a generator is," she admitted.

"It runs on gasoline and you can plug in your most important appliances or heaters while your electricity is out."

"Oh," she said, turning away as she walked slowly toward the fire.

Coming up behind her, he hesitated for a moment then pulled her in for a hug, grateful when she did not pull away. She felt…right. This felt right.

"What're you thinking?"

Twisting in his arms, she leaned way back to look into his eyes. "Tony, if you hadn't come after me, I'd be here all alone and wouldn't know any of this survival stuff."

"Darlin', you've got a fireplace, a roof over your head, and food. You woulda been fine." Looking down at the doubtful expression of her face, he added, "But I woulda come for you." Placing another gentle kiss on her lips, he said again, "I'll always come for you."

She allowed him to pull her body tightly into his, the warmth from him seeping into her. His massive arms held her close as she pressed her head into his chest, his heartbeat a comfort beneath her cheek. She wanted to ask him more. What he meant. What he would do. How he felt. But not now. Now, she just wanted to feel him wrapped around her.

By that afternoon, the snow had stopped and they stepped out onto the front porch to take a look around. The air was cold but the sun came out, turning the view into a blinding white wonderland. Snow clung to each branch and the Cardinals sat proudly in the cedar trees, the green and white a perfect background to their brilliant red.

"I found some birdseed in the cupboard. Do you think they'd like some?" she asked.

"I think they'd love it."

Sherrie ran inside and grabbed the two bags. By the time she came out, Tony had removed the tops of the feeders that hung near the porch. After pouring some in each of the feeders, they sat in the rockers bundled under blankets as the cardinals, blue jays, and others became brave enough to eat from the feeders.

Tony looked over, seeing her eyes riveted on the feeders, watching the birds. Her eyes were sparkling, cheeks rosy, and her lips were curved in a gentle smile. Rubbing his chest once again, he knew that she was worth it. Worth the pain, because she was worth the living.

"You cold, darlin'?" he asked.

Turning her head, she saw his eyes staring at her, a soft expression in them. Smiling, she nodded. "A little. But it's so pretty, isn't it. Like a fairyland." She turned back to the shimmering landscape in front of them. "It seems clean and fresh. Not tainted by anything ugly yet." Turning her head back to him, she added, "You know how snow is so perfect when it first comes down and then by the time the snow plows come through the snow gets all dirty? I always hate that."

He saw the little frown that marred her face and wanted to keep that frown from appearing. "Then maybe we'll just stay out here and let the snow melt naturally and we won't go back into the city until all the dirty snow is gone."

A giggle erupted as she said, "I'd like that."

He looked back over the diamond-like brilliance of the yard and said, "Me too."

They sat in companionable silence for a little while longer before he rose and stretched out his hand to her. "Come on in, babe. The sun is moving behind the trees and it's getting colder."

She reached out her delicate hand and placed it in his as he pulled her gently from her rocker. His hand felt warm. Strong. Capable. Like him.

THAT EVENING SHE insisted on fixing dinner, digging around in their food to see what she could manage. Dicing the leftover chicken, she quickly stir fried it with some egg, vegetables, and rice that she had boiled. Luckily the Marks' had soy sauce in their pantry. She had brought some frozen eggrolls that she loved to munch on, so with her chicken fried rice she served up a hot meal.

Scooping a huge serving onto his plate, he grinned appreciatively at her. "Smells good, looks good and," after taking a bite, says, "tastes good, darlin'."

Beaming with his praise, she sat down to eat as well. This time, their meal was not eaten in silence. The conversation flowed as two people getting to know each other. As they finished cleaning up after dinner, he grabbed two wine glasses and another bottle. Jerking his head toward the fire, he led the way over. This time he sat on the sofa and she piled up on the floor near the heat.

"So tell me about working for Mr. Marks. How did you decide to become a paralegal?"

Taking a sip, she watched the flames quietly until he thought she might not answer.

"I guess the easy answer is that I was interested in law and knew I'd never be able to go to law school, so it was something attainable."

"Why no law school?" he asked. The question was simple, but he wanted to know more. Wanted her to open up to him. Wanted to understand this woman that had had him tied up in knots for a year.

She sat in silence again for a moment. *How much do I tell him? But then, how can I ask him to let me in if I'm not willing to do it myself?* Heaving a huge sigh, she began.

"My parents were teenage lovers who had to get married when mom got pregnant with Charisse. She was a preacher's daughter and they really had no choice. Mom was cool, but dad…he just never got used to having his wings clipped at such a young age. I don't remember much about him. He wasn't bad…he just wasn't there. He drank a lot, hung out with his friends. Hell, from what I heard when I got older he probably slept with any woman he could find, refusing to be tied down."

She turned her gaze back to him, saying, "But mom loved him. Crazy, isn't it? To love a man that treats you so badly." Shaking her head, she admitted, "I just never understood that."

The fire snapped and she gave a little startle before continuing. "When I was eight and Charisse was ten, dad died. An accident at work we were told, but I always wondered if he hadn't been drinking when it happened. Mama just couldn't live without him." Rubbing her finger around the rim of her wine glass, she seemed lost in thought.

"We needed her, but she wasn't there for us. She withered away. I now understand that she was depressed, but then it just seemed like mama didn't care. For the next two years, Charisse and I cooked, cleaned, got ourselves ready for school. One day, I got home from school and Charisse was sitting outside with the police around. She wouldn't let me go in. Said mama was gone.

"It took years for me to understand that mama committed suicide. She took a bunch of pills and just went to sleep. No note. No goodbye. No 'I'm sorry girls'. Nothing."

Shit, he thought, looking at her composed face. *She holds her shit together all the time. Always composed. Always in charge. How the fuckin' hell does she do it?*

"Charisse and I ended up in the system. We had one really good social worker who worked to keep us together and for a while it wasn't hard. Two cute little girls...we were easy to place. Then Charisse began to act up. I think she was just so desperate for attention." Giving a rude snort, she looked up, "Did you know that studies show that girls who lack a strong father figure in their lives often become promiscuous in their teen years?"

Tony silently vowed at that moment that if he was ever graced with another daughter, he would shower her with love.

"Anyway, the Charisse that you knew used to be a sweet little girl who just turned into a teen that found out that boys might not date her because she was a poor foster kid, but they'd pay her to blow them. And then later, she started hanging with a crowd that gave her plenty of attention. She'd stay high and started selling her body for drugs.

"I tried. I tried so hard to keep her clean and out of trouble but...well, by the time Charisse was eighteen our foster family booted her out and even though I wasn't like her I think they just wanted me gone too."

Leaning back against the leather chair, with her legs stretched out before her, she felt the warmth from the fire toasting her toes. Sighing as the wine warmed her as well, she looked up at him staring at her. "You asked about law school and I've been giving you a rendition of my life story. Pathetic, isn't it?"

"Not at all. I'm sitting here, listening and admiring you more by the minute. Keep going. I want to know everything."

Admiring me? She sat silently for a moment, letting her thoughts flow back through time. "Eventually Charisse got into more and more trouble. She got a job at Club Edge and began stripping. Then she caught the eye of a gang leader. I tried so hard to run interference for her. I was out of high school by this time and the state will assist for college costs if you were in foster care. My last family agreed to have me stay with them on the condition that Charisse never came there again."

"That must have been hard," he said.

"They had little children, so I got it. I was never going to be able to afford a full university and law school after that, so I decided that if I could get my paralegal degree then I could start making money. I'd been working as a cocktail waitress…well you know the rest of that story. I had to finally make a choice between keeping Charisse out of trouble or having my own life. I guess she saw it as the ultimate betrayal and sold me to the gang leader. And that's when you rescued me the first time."

Tony smiled at her, nodding. "Yeah, that was my lucky day."

Lifting an eyebrow in question, she decided not to pursue that statement as they sat in silence once more, each lost in their own thoughts.

"It's not your fault, you know?" he spoke softly, watching the light play off of her beautiful features.

"Intellectually, I know that. I gave her an ultimatum a year ago. If she was going to continue to have a relationship with me she had to get clean and I'd help her any way I could. If not…" she let the statement hang out there.

"You did more for her than anyone else did and that includes your parents."

"Yeah, that's for sure. But when someone is an addict, it's so hard to know when to pull them along and when to step back." She gave a little shrug. "I wish…oh, hell. Wishing won't help now. But I do miss the Charisse of old. The one who would hold my hand during a thunderstorm. Or would read to me when mama wouldn't. Or who taught me to ride a bike. That's the sister I miss."

"Then that's the sister you should remember."

Her eyes sought his at this statement.

His hand cupped her cheek, willing his touch to soothe. "Remember the sister that did all the right things. The sister that fills your memories with smiles. And let go of the part that hurts your heart."

"What about you, Tony? Do you let go of the part that hurts your heart?" she asked softly.

Silence was the only answer.

CHAPTER 8

STANDING, SHERRIE PICKED up her wine glass and walked to the kitchen. Rinsing the glass out, she put the cork back in the bottle and placed it in the refrigerator. It had felt so good to talk about Charisse. To let go of the guilt and allow grief to progress normally. *Tony did that for me. But he can't do it for himself.*

She saw the look on his face when she asked if he let go of the past and knew what the answer was. He had been closed off for so many years she wondered if he even knew how to start living again. Heaving a huge sigh, she left the kitchen and stood for a moment watching him stare into the flames. She could see why he was good on missions...she could not even see movement from his breathing. But she knew he was breathing. And thinking. And hurting.

"Goodnight, Tony," she said softly, almost afraid to speak and disturb his thoughts. "I hope you sleep well." With that she turned and walked to the bathroom. Finishing in there, she moved into the bedroom. Slipping into her pajamas, she stood at the dresser brushing her long hair, exhaustion beginning to overtake her.

"I was married," came the deep voice from the doorway.

Her gaze saw him in the mirror as her hand halted the progress of the brush. She stood frozen, eyes locked on the reflection. Indecision was written on his face and she was afraid to speak. Afraid to break the spell he had woven around himself.

"I was overseas. Special Forces. I got to come back between missions when she went into labor. Made it just for the last few hours before our baby was born."

Silence.

She slowly lay the brush down and turned to face him, no longer wanting to see him only through the mirror.

"We had a baby girl. Named her Sofia. After my grandmother." Another flash of pain crossed his face. "So fuckin' perfect. So tiny. Never been around babies, so I had no idea how she'd fit in my hand."

He shuffled his feet momentarily as though the memory caused physical discomfort. She wanted to offer that they sit down, but was afraid to interrupt the moment.

"Spent a week at home. A week with my wife and baby." He rubbed his hand over his face and continued, "Went back and celebrated with the men."

His eyes sought hers, gauging how much she wanted to hear. She had no idea what expression was on her face but she wanted everything. She wanted him to give her everything. All of his pain. All of his memories.

"Had a mission and when I came back, I was called into the office with the news. Car accident. No one's fault. Just a fuckin' car accident. And they were both gone."

"Oh, Tony," she whispered, her heart aching for him. She wanted to go to him. Touch him. Hold him. But she held back, not knowing what he needed.

"All my men came back stateside with me. Made arrangements. Had the funeral. Helped with every-thing. Then...we went back to Afghanistan. My life here was over and my country still needed me."

"Your men followed you when you left the Army, didn't they?" she asked.

"Yeah. Most of us were discharged within six months of each other and some of them followed me back and joined my company."

She walked over slowly until she was standing right in front of him. Reaching down, she took his hand, holding it tenderly. Raising her head, she saw a single tear slide down his cheek and she lifted her other hand to gently wipe it away.

"So this is me, telling you, that no...I haven't let go of the past that constantly hurts my heart."

She gave his hand a gentle squeeze, letting him know that she was still there...*even if he can never be mine.*

This time, he squeezed back and her eyes sought his again. "But I want to," came the simple words from his heart.

He saw the questioning expression wrinkle her brow and with his free hand, reached up to smooth the lines.

"What I'm saying, Sherrie, is that I want to remember the good times and learn to let go of the hurt. For so long I didn't want that. They were gone, my little girl would never grow up," he choked out. Clearing his throat, he continued, "So I wanted to be miserable too. I wrapped my grief around me like a blanket. As long as it was with me, surrounding me, they'd be with me. But the reality is that they aren't with me." Sighing deeply, he continued, "But now...I don't. I don't want to be miserable."

"Maybe," she said softly, "We can help each other." She added hesitantly, "Even just as friends, if that's what you need."

A tiny smile appeared on his face as he pulled her a little closer. "Sherrie, you're the only woman I've ever been interested in since...Marla. I've tried so hard to not be attracted to you. To not want you. Hell, to not like you. But I'm tired of fighting the feelings I have."

By now, he had slowly pulled her closer so that his arms wrapped around her body. He rested his head on the top of hers, noting how perfectly she fit. Heartbeat to heartbeat, they just stood in a doorway of a cabin in the middle of snow covered woods...grieving and letting go, together. He letting go of his fear of loving again and she letting go of her insecurities.

She knew it would take time, *but if he's willing, then so am I.* Sherrie had no idea how long they stood there, but she felt him gently push her away.

"Darlin', I'm sorry. You're standing here in bare feet and your pjs. You need to get in bed and get warm."

She eyed the big, comfortable bed, thinking of lying in it with him. Comfort. Warmth. Caring. Leaning back, she asked, "Will you come to bed with me?"

He smiled, answering, "As much as I would love crawling into bed with you, I want to do this right. And jumping into bed with you just because we gave in yesterday, isn't what I want to do."

"What do you want to do?"

"Well, what I want is to take you to bed, make love to you and worship your body all night."

She blinked her large, blue eyes slowly not having a response to that.

He chuckled, glad that she was innocent enough to not have a practiced comment to fling back. "But I don't want sex to be what we do to forget when we've just had the conversations like we've had."

Nodding, she agreed. As he turned and started to walk away, she quickly said, "So just come and sleep. Hold me as we let it go." Looking at the mattress, she added, "And the mattress is much more comfortable than the sofa."

She let go of him and walked over to the bed, turning down the covers. He looked at her ass as she bent over the bed. For the first time he really noticed what she was wearing. Over the last year that he had dreamed of her, he pictured her in sexy nighties, barely there wisps of silk. But this? The material looked soft, warm, and comfortable. And utterly sexy. *How the hell can she be covered and look sexy as hell?* He did not have an answer but knew that he could be happy seeing her in those pajamas every night for the rest of his life. *Happy?* Smiling, he felt lighter than he had in years. *Yeah, happy.*

"I'll be right back," he promised and headed back out into the great room. Checking the doors, he banked the fire before he walked back into the bedroom. She was already under the covers, her blonde hair spread across the pillow and her beautiful face beaming at him. Quickly shucking his clothes, he slid under the covers with her.

Pulling her tightly into his embrace, feeling her warm breath against his skin, it only took a few minutes for him to slip into a peaceful sleep. *I'm ready to live again, even if there'is pain,* was his last thought.

THE NEXT MORNING TONY woke up to a warm body snuggled next to his. Answering the call of the wild, his cock was already twitching and eager to play. *Down boy, none of that now.* Determined to continue spending time with Sherrie that did not involve ravishing her again, he willed his dick to obey.

The warm body rolled over, spearing him with her brilliant, blue eyes. "Good morning," she said shyly, snuggling deeper into him. "This is nice. I've never woken up with someone before."

His heart pounding, he could not help the macho realization that he was her first. Her first in everything. Cupping her cheek, he kissed her with all the tenderness he felt inside.

Smiling, she pushed the covers off and felt the chill of the room. "Ohhh," she exclaimed as her bare feet hit the floor. She hustled to grab her jeans and sweatshirt before running into the bathroom.

A few minutes later she emerged, dressed warmly, announcing that she was fixing breakfast.

He lay in bed a few extra moments, not able to remember when he was this relaxed. Or lighthearted. Smiling, he jumped up as well and after taking care of his morning business he made his way into the living room to get the fire going again.

"How's the firewood holding out?" she called from the kitchen.

He wandered in to help saying, "We should be good for a while."

"Tony?" she said, turning from the stove. "How long do you think we'll be stuck here?"

He rubbed the back of his neck, saying, "Don't know, darlin'. I figure they'll get the road plowed today or tomorrow. The problem is this long-ass driveway. I'll try getting hold of someone from VDOT and see if we can get a plow to get us out of here."

Nodding, she set plates on the table and they dug into the hearty, warm food. After cleaning up, he asked, "You wanna go outside and see what's around?"

Her smile lit her face as she glanced out of the windows to the glistening clearing and woods around. "I'd love to," she agreed.

Soon, they were layered in clothing, wrapped up like Eskimos, and tromping through the snow. Just like the day before, the sun shone brightly in a perfectly blue sky and they needed their sunglasses to ward off the snow blindness. There was more than a foot of snow on the ground, with drifts up to Sherrie's knees in some places. Tony held tightly to her hand as they walked across the clearing toward the woods near the back of the cabin. During the storm they had not been able to see the small lake that was there. Ice covered the water for a ways from the shore, creating the perfect Norman Rockwell scene.

Walking to the snow covered dock, she pulled out her phone and declared, "Selfie time," handing it to him. With his long arms, he made several pictures of the two of them, tucked tightly together with the winter landscape in the background. Before handing the phone back to her, he quickly sent the pictures to his phone.

He wanted to keep them from the edge of the water

for safety's sake, so they made their way back around the cabin and down the driveway. Tony walked a little way ahead to see if he could tell where the path lie. Suddenly he was smacked in the back with a snowball.

Whirling around, he saw Sherrie trying to look innocent. "Where did that come from, I wonder?" she shouted.

Without saying a word, he stalked toward her. "Oh, I think I know exactly where it came from, darlin'. And you're gonna pay."

Screaming, she tried to run but he caught up to her in just a couple of steps, tackling her around the waist. They rolled over several times in the snow. He moved so that she was on top, but held her tightly in place. Tendrils of blonde hair fell from her cap, framing her porcelain skin with pink tinged cheeks. Her smiling lips were rosy red and as she looked down at him, her luminescent blue eyes once again saw deep inside of him.

"I thought we needed a little roll in the snow," she giggled.

"Oh, yeah? Well, I guess you got what you wanted, didn't you?"

She softly said, "I did get what I wanted, Tony. What I wanted was you. All of you."

He lifted his head to capture her cold lips in a searing kiss. The kiss quickly heated her lips and other parts of him as well. Wondering how the snow was not melting all around them, he rolled her to the side so that he could hoist himself up, pulling her along with him.

Her kiss-warmed lips opened slightly in surprise. "Where are we going in such a hurry?"

He swooped her up in his arms, kissing her soundly once again. "Wanna get you inside and get you warm, baby."

Baby? He called me baby. She could not help the grin on her face, realizing that she had never been anyone's 'baby'. Holding tightly to his neck, she pulled him in closer.

Walking through the front door, he kicked it closed behind him, then carried her over to the fireplace. Setting her down gently, he noticed her wet pants. "Start stripping and I'll get you something warm to put on."

She watched as he took off his jacket, pulling a gun out from the pocket, checking it and then laying it on the table by the sofa.

He saw her questioning look and smiled. "I carry a weapon, darlin'. Never know what critters may have been out there. Four-legged or two."

"Will you show me how to shoot sometime?" she asked, looking down at it.

"Absolutely. We'll practice later. Right now, you need to finish getting out of those wet clothes."

Her fingers and toes ached as she pulled off her boots and wet socks. She managed to get out of her jacket by the time he returned with her sweatpants, but her fingers fumbled with the button on her jeans.

Brushing them aside, he quickly had her jeans unzipped and slid them down her legs.

"How do you do that? You were outside too, so how is it that your fingers work and mine don't?" she asked, trying to pull her sweatpants up.

He was attempting to not look at her near nakedness as he stripped out of his outer garments as well. "Training," was his reply.

Cocking her hip, she looked up at him. "Training? How on earth can you train to not have cold fingers?"

He laughed as he pulled dry socks onto her feet and moved her closer to the fire. "I was Special Forces in the Army."

"Oh."

He looked at her and smiled. "You don't know what that means, do you?"

"Well, kind of. I've seen it in movies. It means you earned the Green Beret, right?" She pushed him down on the rug in front of the fire and said, "Let me get some hot chocolate for us and I want to hear about it."

Returning a few minutes later with steaming mugs, she sat down next to him. "Okay, Mr. Green Beret, tell me how you learned to not have cold fingers."

Laughing, he said, "Not much to tell you other than we trained for-fuckin-ever, in the water, in the cold, in the heat. You learn to withstand the elements, work through them, keep going."

"Did you always want to go into the Special Forces?" she asked, noting the pride in his voice as he spoke.

"My father was Army. My grandfather was Army. I did college and then officer training school, by that time I knew I wanted to be part of the elite."

"What about the others? Gabe and Vinny and Jobe?"

"We all were assigned to the same unit. They were under me. We worked in squads of twelve. Tighter than brothers. You gotta know their thoughts as well as their moves and they sure as hell had to know mine."

"Do you miss it?"

Tony thought for a moment, the firelight playing across the angles in his face. He shook his head slowly. "Nah. I don't miss it. If I didn't have them working with me, then yeah, I'd miss the camaraderie. The closeness. That bond that just happens when you share the good as well as the worst. But it was time for me to get out and as it happens, they felt the same."

"What about the security business? When did that become your dream?"

"I started thinking about it a year before I got out. I didn't have anything except for the Army. Not after…" Rubbing his hand over his face, he said, "Just felt the need to use my skills. To protect. To…" Looking at her, he said, "You know those commercials about serving in the military to make Americans safe? Well, I knew that you don't have to go overseas to fight in a war to want to make people safe. I could do it here in my own backyard."

They sat quietly for a few minutes, letting the crackle of the fireplace fill the silence. He leaned back and watched her as she closed her eyes inhaling the scent of the hot chocolate. *Haven't talked so goddamn much in years as I have in the past two days.* Smiling, he realized that it felt fuckin' good.

AS SHERRIE CLEANED up from dinner, she heard Tony on the phone. "Tomorrow? Any chance you can get to the Marks' cabin? It's a driveway right off of County Road 147, Lakeview Road. Yeah, if you can get someone to plow a path from the cabin to the road, we'd appreciate it."

She watched as he moved into the kitchen. She could watch him move forever. Lithe. Like a panther. Big and strong, but silent and always moved with a purpose. *Tomorrow?* Why, suddenly, did tomorrow not sound good? Why did she find herself wanting more days stuck out here with him? *Because I love him. I've loved him for a very long time. And now, maybe, it will finally go somewhere.*

"So the snow plow's coming tomorrow?" she asked, trying to keep the longing out of her voice.

He walked up behind her, wrapping his arms around and pulling her into his chest. Leaning down, he nuzzled her neck. "You don't want to leave? You're not sick of my company?"

She turned in his embrace, saying, "You want honesty?"

"Always, baby."

"I came up here to get away. Get away from everyone and everything. Including you." She leaned way back to see into his eyes. "I know what my sister became and no one in my life knew what she was like before. I felt so sick at heart after we found her. And then just numb. And then angry. And then just incredibly sad."

He brushed her hair back from her face, listening to the words but hearing with his soul as well. *Been there. Oh, yeah. I've been there.* Nodding his understanding, he encouraged her to continue.

"The past couple of days with you have been a whirlwind. You want honest, Tony? I've cared for you for a really long time. In fact, ever since I first saw you. But I figured I was never going to be good enough for you."

At this, his eyebrows rose in surprise. "What the hell? You not good enough for me?"

Shrugging, she said, "I always thought you just saw me as an extension of my sister. You know…guilty by association."

"Baby, I never thought that. I got a dossier on you when I was sent in to rescue you. I knew you were nothing like Charisse. In fact, I had nothing but the highest respect for you."

"Then why? Why did you always avoid me?"

"I promised myself after Marla and Sofia died that I'd never get that involved with someone else again. The pain of losing them was too much. I had feelings for you immediately, but tried for almost a year to bury them."

"But Tony, life without pain isn't really living. It's just existing."

He stiffened in her arms and she shot a look of concern at him. He leaned his head back, eyes closed tightly, trying to block out...*what?* She gave him a little squeeze and he dropped his head, his warm gaze spearing her.

"Are...are you okay?" she asked.

Smiling, he just nodded. "Yeah. Perfect. Now that I'm with you."

They walked, arms around each other, over to the sofa sitting down once again. Sherrie giggled, saying, "I'm going to miss this room and fireplace. We've spent a lot of time right here."

"Maybe the Marks' will let us come visit sometime," he suggested.

Her eyes lit up at the thought. "Would you want to?"

"Hell yeah. Baby, anywhere with you is where I want to be, but you're right. This place has memories."

He leaned over and pulled her onto his lap, his lips sealing hers. Slowly exploring until he captured her moan and the kiss became wilder. Cupping her face with both of his hands, he angled her head for better access. Tongues tangling, he tasted the sweet wine and essence of her. His hands slid down to her shoulders, along the sides of her breasts to her small waist, finally resting on her ass. Kneading the soft globes, his straining cock was pressed against her core.

The little moans that she continued to make were driving him wild, but he was determined that this time would be different. Special. Loving. *Loving?* Hesitating for only a second as that word flashed through his mind, he resumed his kiss with more ardor. *Yeah, love.*

Pushing the coffee table away with his foot, he scooped her up, then lay her gently on the thick blanket in front of the fireplace. Looking down at her face, he saw trust. *I want to earn that trust, baby. And keep it.*

Slowly he explored her body, moving his fingers lightly over her curves discovering every peak and valley. His lips followed his fingers as the firelight danced across her curves. Her skin, like silk, beckoned him to continue his discoveries.

Moans escaped from deep in her chest as her eyes shut tightly, afraid if they opened it would all disappear.

"It's not a dream, baby. Open your eyes. I want to see you watch me love you. I need to see you," he ordered gently.

Pulling off her pants and panties with one swift movement he then stood, quickly removing his clothes.

She opened her eyes, seeing his warm ones gazing at

her as he lowered himself between her legs. Clasping her hands in his short hair, she sucked in a huge breath as he lapped her wet folds. Determined to keep her eyes on him, she watched as he licked and sucked his way to her clit. No longer able to resist the urge, she threw her head back against the soft rug and shattered into a million pieces as her orgasm rolled through her.

He watched her face in the throes of ecstasy, as he continued his way up her body. Tugging her shirt up over her head, he added it to the pile of clothes on the floor. The firelight danced across her skin as he watched the flickering reflection in her blue eyes. Quickly rolling on a condom, he seated himself at her entrance, looking down as her eyes opened up to him. The smile on her face was all the permission he needed as he slowly pushed his way in to the hilt.

She felt each stretch as her body accommodated his girth, being touched in places that were unaccustomed to invasion. Her hand grabbed his shoulders as she accepted his ride. He bore his weight on his hands looking down at her, his smile just as intense.

Over and over, he moved inside of her, bringing her to the edge once more. Lowering himself, he continued to piston as he tugged a nipple into his mouth, sucking voraciously.

That was all it took to send her over the peak, screaming out his name as he roared hers at the same time. Falling down and rolling, he pulled her across his body, arms holding tightly. Their ragged breathing slowly calmed as their heartbeats began a more regular cadence.

Smoothing her hair back from her face, he kissed her forehead, wishing the moment would never end. Wishing the last remnant of guilt over being happy would disappear. But also knowing that for him and Sherrie…it was only the beginning.

CHAPTER 9

THE NEXT MORNING dawned as bright as the previous day with the sun beaming through the slit in the curtains. Sherrie opened her eyes and stretched, the soreness between her legs reminding her of the night before and a smile crossed her face.

"Hey, beautiful," Tony said, pulling her in closely. Missing nothing, he asked, "How are you today? Are you too sore? Did we do too—"

She pressed her fingers to his lips, halting his words of concern. "I'm fine." Smiling again, she repeated, "Really fine."

They heard the sound of a diesel truck nearby and he said, "Must be the snow plow. Let me go and thank them for coming out here." He kissed her quickly, sliding out of bed and into his clothes. She watched him leave the room and snuggled deeper into the covers for a few minutes. *What now? What happens when we return to the real world?* Sighing deeply, she realized that she had no idea what he would feel once they were back around their friends.

Tossing the covers back she quickly dressed and headed for the kitchen. Glancing out of the window, she saw a large truck with a snow plow attached to the front and the driver talking to Tony. They chatted for a few minutes before she saw him pull out some money, handing it to the driver. The plow driver tried to wave the money away, but Tony insisted. Shaking hands, he made his way back to the cabin as the driver plowed around their vehicles before driving back down the driveway.

She hurried outside before he had a chance to come in, wanting to prolong their time at the cabin. He looked up as she stomped through the snow. "You promised to show me how to shoot."

Smiling, he took her hand, leading her to the side of the house. Pulling his pistol from its holster, he acquainted her with his Glock 19. "This is a good one for you to use, baby. No kickback, easy to hold, semi-automatic."

She nodded nervously as he placed it in her hand. Standing behind her, he showed her how to take her stance, aim, and pull the trigger. With his warm body behind hers it was hard to concentrate, but she wanted to show him that she could do this.

They practiced several minutes, firing at trees until she was able to hit them with a degree of accuracy. Twisting around, she looked up at him smiling as she said, "I'll be in good shape to defend myself if I'm ever attacked by a tree."

"Smartass," he said, smacking her on her ass. Then looking serious, he said, "I'll get you a weapon when we get back and take you to our firing range. I do want you to be able to defend yourself."

"I just aim for the trunk, right?" she said, still smiling.

Laughing, he added, "You're not too wrong. Actually the creed is to aim for center mass." Seeing her questioning expression, he said, "That means aim for a person's chest."

He took the pistol from her and they headed back toward the house. He sent her on ahead while he checked the vehicles again. She decided to fix lunch before they had to think about leaving.

Tony came in, stomping his boots off at the door. Looking up, he saw Sherrie standing in the kitchen staring at him and he could not stop the smile on his face. *God, what would I give to see that every morning?* Stalking over, he immediately took her face in his hands and pulled her in for a long, wet kiss. She opened immediately allowing his tongue to slip inside, drinking in her essence.

She wrapped her arms around him, wanting to feel his hard body pressed into hers. The kiss went on until she was not sure where she ended and he started. Finally pulling back to catch her breath, she moved her cheek to his chest, feeling his heartbeat.

Letting him go slowly, she smiled but he noticed it did not reach her eyes.

Turning, she moved to fix the coffee but was held back by his hand on her arm. He moved her back into him, lifting her chin with his fingers. She looked up questioningly.

"You gonna tell me why that smile doesn't seem like it's real?"

"I guess I'm just thinking about what we need to do. We need to clean the cabin and get everything packed up. Then load up all our stuff before we leave. And then—"

"Darlin'?" he interrupted, looking directly into her eyes. "I don't want to know what all we've got to do. I want to know what's going on in that beautiful head of yours."

Pursing her lips, she retorted, "So you think you can read me now?"

He threw his head laughing. "Yeah, baby. I think after watching you for almost a year and spending every second of the past three days with you, I know you. So give it up, Sherrie."

Sighing, she said, "I just…well, this has been really nice, although kind of surreal. So I was just wondering…um…what happens when we go back." Feeling the blush rising up from her chest to her face, she tried to look away, but his hand on her cheek halted that plan.

"Oh, no, darlin'. I want to see your eyes when I tell you exactly how it will be. What we did last night was no casual fuck for me and I thought you knew that. But seeing the doubt on your face right now, means I didn't do a good job getting that across and that's on me. So,

I'll set you straight right now. As far as I'm concerned, we're now a couple. This weekend has shown me that I can be happy again. And I want to be happy again. And that happiness can only be with you."

Watching her face as his words washed over her, he saw the smile that he had sought, move from her beautiful mouth to her sparkling eyes. "And I'm gonna make a promise to you, baby. I may be rusty about letting anyone know what I'm thinking, but I never want to see that worry and doubt in your eyes again, so I'll work to make sure you know just how much you mean to me."

Pulling him in tight again, she once more pressed her cheek against his chest, hearing his strong heartbeat.

Several hours later, after securing the cabin and a last, longing look backward, they pulled out of the driveway.

PULLING INTO THE DRIVEWAY of her little, Victorian house, Sherrie noticed that Tony was still right behind her. She had wondered if he would head straight to his place. *I don't know where he lives.* She got out of her car, looking at the plowed driveway, including a shoveled sidewalk leading to her front door. She turned around, exclaiming, "Someone plowed me out!"

As he climbed down from his SUV, he had a grin on his face.

Stunned, she said "Do you know who did this?"

By that time, he had made it to her and held her tightly as they walked to the door. "Yep," he answered.

"Well are you going to impart this knowledge on me?"

He took the keys from her hand and opened her front door. "I asked the guys to make sure everything here was secure for when you came back."

"Secure?" she said, watching him hit the keypad of a new...*security box?* "Tony? When did that get put in?"

I had Jobe and Vinny come over here yesterday to get you set up with security and they said they made sure your driveway and sidewalks were shoveled. I've got to make sure you're safe."

She could tell this was really important to Tony, and she knew why. In an effort to lighten the mood, she stood with her hip cocked, tapping her foot, and glared. "That's very high-handed of you."

He looked down at her snapping eyes and said, "Yep."

"All you have to say is 'yep'? And how did you know where I lived? And how the hell did they get into my house?" She began to push back on his chest.

"Not letting you get yourself in a snit, baby," he announced, scooping her up and walking into her living room. Setting down on her sofa, he maneuvered her so that she was straddling his lap. Staring into the face that first captured him a year ago, he noticed the thin line of her mouth. *Oh shit.*

"I found out where you lived after rescuing you last year. I just…wanted to know. I told myself at first it was because I wanted to make sure you were safe. But then…I just wanted to see you sometimes. Didn't take long to see that you have few outside lights and no security."

Ignoring that he had been noticing her for a year and stalking her, she pounced on his last statement. "But I do. I have a deadbolt on my front and my back door," she announced.

"If it was so good, then how come my boys were able to get in here so easily?" he quipped.

"Be…be…because, they know how to break into stuff," she stammered.

"Yeah. And…" he continued.

"And what?"

"Darlin, if they can get into your house easily, to put in a security system, then someone who did not have good deeds on their mind could have gotten in just as easily."

At this, Sherrie looked down. "I knew when I had that lousy apartment, in that crappy neighborhood, dealing with Charisse's druggie, prostitution life spilling over into mine that I needed to be cautious. But when I moved here," she said with a soft expression as she looked around, "I felt safe. Clean. Like a real person and not just some poor kid from the wrong side of the tracks."

Tony's eyes roamed around the quaint room.

When he had first seen that she had moved, he assumed she would move to an upscale condo; so when he drove by the little house he was surprised. An older, Victorian home with the look of a gingerbread house. It was blue with white shutters and a matching white front door. The wrap-around porch was painted white as well.

Now that he was more intimately acquainted with her, he knew that it was perfect. The pencil skirt, coiffed hair, and heels that she wore for work were part of the image she wanted to project. But when she came home…a little house, set back from the road with a picket fence around it was…just her.

"You've got a nice place here, darlin'," he said, sliding one hand up to the back of her neck. Gently pulling her down, his lips met hers. A soft kiss. One that speaks volumes without shouting.

She melted under his embrace, then gave a little mewl when they separated. Licking her lips, tasting him, she smiled. "It's an old house and it has taken some work to get it fixed, but I love it. I have sunk all my money into it." Blushing, she added, "That's why I had to go as cheap as possible on the funeral…I just didn't have the money saved up for a rainy day."

Looking around, she smiled again. "I know this sounds silly, but when I was little, I saw a doll house that looked almost just like this. One of our foster families had it for their daughter. Charisse and I could look but not play with it. So I would just sit for hours, not touching it, but imagining what it would be like to actually live in a house like that."

Tony's heart lurched for the little blonde girl, sitting and staring at a playhouse and not being able to play with it. Reaching up, he smoothed her hair back from her face, tucking it behind her ear. Rubbing her cheek with his thumb, he vowed to take care of her always.

"You want to see the rest of the place?" she asked, standing and pulling on his hand. Grinning, he allowed himself to be pulled up and followed her across the foyer into the dining room. An antique oak table graced the room with a large oak china cabinet and side bar next to the wall.

A hall cut through the middle of the house leading to the kitchen behind the living room. Spacious and updated, he could see her right at home here. *Making breakfast. For both of them.* Before his musing could take him further, she pulled on his hand again.

"Back here is the laundry room that leads to the back yard." They peeked out together, viewing the snowy vision of her yard with mature trees. Leaning down, she noticed that her back patio had been shoveled as well. "Your employees are certainly efficient, aren't they?"

He laughed as he pulled her into his arms. "Yes, they are. But they're even better friends."

Looking up, she said softly, "So they did all this for you?"

"Darlin', you still don't understand, do you? When Jennifer called Gabe to say that you were heading into a storm, any one of them would have driven to make sure you were all right. But what they really wanted was for me to pull my head outta my ass and be the one to go to you."

"I could have handled myself you know. I've been on the streets and I've been on my own."

Tucking another strand of hair behind her ear again, he leaned down to kiss her forehead. "Yeah, but you don't have to now. So I called Jobe yesterday and asked if he would clear out your drive and just case out your house for a security system, he jumped on the chance to help. Not just for me...but for you as well. There's not a one of them that wouldn't do anything to help you."

Smiling, she led him into the room across the hall which turned out to be a study with built in bookcases lining one wall. The bay window had a cushioned seat, perfect for reading. He walked over to look at her books and saw romances mixed in with her paralegal text books. Turning to look over his shoulder, he lifted an eyebrow.

Catching his questioning gaze, she just shrugged and said, "Well, a girl's gotta have something to read besides legal books."

"Thank God."

Laughing, she walked out, waving for him to fol-low. Up the wooden staircase, they came to a small landing. A quick glance showed two smaller bedrooms with a bathroom in between and then she led him into the master bedroom. Over the study, it also had a bay window with a cushioned window seat. A queen bed with a floral comforter graced one wall, with a dresser and chest of drawers on another. The master bath featured a shower and separate tub along with a double sink.

"This is really modern for an older house," he noted.

"The former owners had done a lot of renovating before having to sell. They had done the bathrooms and kitchen. Then my neighbor and I have been working on the inside."

Instantly on alert, he asked, "Neighbor?"

Sherrie wandered out of the bathroom, saying, "Yeah, he lives next door."

"And just who the hell is 'he' that lives next door?" Tony growled.

Turning around, she asked incredulously, "Are you jealous?" Giggling, she continued, "He's a darling man with a lot of house renovation experience who volunteered to help me with any of my projects."

Stepping close, Tony said, "Well, from now on, he can take his project helping somewhere else."

Swatting his arm, she said, "He also happens to be about seventy years old."

Grumbling, Tony said, "Don't think that old man doesn't check out your ass every time you bend over in front of him."

"Well, I said he was seventy, not dead."

Turning to run out of the room, she screeched when he scooped her up and tossed her on the bed.

"He'd have to be dead to not check you out. But seriously," he said looking down into her eyes as he leaned over her body, "You need help around the house, you've got me now."

Grinning, she pulled him down for a kiss but his cell phone ringing interrupted the moment. Glancing at it, he looked back at her as he answered. "Yeah, Jennifer, what do you need?"

"Good morning to you too, grumpy," she laughed. "I just wanted to make sure you and Sherrie got home safely. I tried calling her phone but she's not answering."

"We're good," he said, giving his patent short answers.

"Good as in safe or good as in *good*?"

"Good as in that's as good an answer as I'm going to give," he replied.

Sherrie, laying under him listening to the conversation, grabbed the phone from his hand. "Jennifer? We're safe. And not just good, but great. So great that he's on top of me on my bed and your call interrupted what would have been a phenomenal kiss." Hearing Jennifer squeal to Gabe in the background, she said, "So goodbye and I'll talk to you tomorrow when I'm back at work."

Disconnecting the phone, she tossed it to the side while never losing he gaze. "So where were we?"

A hungry look flashed through his eyes just before he recaptured her mouth. Her lips were warm and pliant beneath his. Hint of coffee and mint filled his senses as he licked the inside of her mouth, exploring as though afraid he would forget her taste all the while knowing that it was committed to memory.

Her doorbell rang interrupting them once again.

"Fuck," he said, "Ignore it."

It rang again, followed by a knock. "I can't ignore it, Tony."

The moment broken, he groaned as he rolled off of her. Lying on his back with his massive hard-on pressing into his jeans, he listened to her jogging down the stairs.

"Bernard. What brings you over on this cold morning?"

Finding himself wanting to know who the hell Bernard was, he headed down the stairs adjusting himself.

"Wanted to check on you, darling. Saw some men over here yesterday and I came over to see what was going on. They seemed all official but I've been keeping an eye out for you."

"You are so sweet. I was stuck in the storm but home safe—"

"Bernard, is it?" An outreached hand came from behind her toward her neighbor, who was looking up at

Tony whose body was pressing into the back of hers.

"Yes, and who might you be?" Bernard asked, curiosity written on his face, shaking the extended hand.

"Tony Alvarez, Sherrie's boyfriend. And those were my men who were installing her new security system."

She watched in amazement as Bernard's eyes lit while pumping Tony's hand up and down.

"A boyfriend. 'Bout time she finally decided to stop being single. Been after this girl to get her a man for months."

"Well, she's got one now," Tony said, smoothly wrapping his arm around her shoulders once Bernard finally let go of his hand.

"Never was a fan of a girl living by herself. Me and Ethel tied the knot as soon as we got out of high school, God rest her soul. Now this one here," he said pointing to her, "hasn't had a man here since she moved in."

"Good to know I'm the fir—" Tony grunted as her elbow made contact with his ribs.

"I'm right here, gentlemen. There's no need to talk about me as though I'm not," she grumbled.

Bernard laughed and turned to leave. "You got yourself a good 'en," he called out. "Girl, you call me for your next project, you hear?"

She could not help but smile, watching as her neighbor made his way back to his house before being pulled back into Tony's embrace.

"Hate like hell to leave you, darlin', but I need to

get to the office to check on things."

"I know. I'll be back at work tomorrow, so I thought I'd get some things done around here."

Bending down to kiss her, the taste of coffee and mint was just as potent as before. Dragging his lips from hers reluctantly, he pulled her head into his chest and held her tightly. "Gotta tell you, these past few days have meant the world to me."

"Me too," she whispered.

Leaning back, their gazes locked as words went unspoken. Words of grief relieved. Words of healing hearts. Words of futures promised. Unnecessary words only because they both knew them in their hearts.

Kissing the top of her head goodbye, he headed out the door calling for her to set the alarm after him.

CHAPTER 10

M ONDAY MORNING FOUND SHERRIE back in the law office, regaling the office staff with her weekend adventures. She stumbled over the parts that included her new relationship with Tony, but the smile on her face gave her away.

Mr. Marks said, "My dear, I have to tell you that my wife was fretting something fierce until you called to reassure us of your safety." Giving her a fatherly hug, he said, "I'm glad you have someone in your life. You deserve that."

Simon walked over, smiling as he congratulated her on her first storm survival. "I was stuck in a snow storm once, but confess to not having a beautiful woman with me. I envy Mr. Alvarez."

"Alright, enough about my adventures or misadventures," she laughed. Looking at Simon, she asked, "What about my CASA cases? Anything new?"

"Actually, I've got a young woman I'd like you to talk to. She was referred by the courts, but won't talk to me, so you've been assigned as her worker. She is a runaway and currently in a foster placement. You can visit her at her foster home this afternoon if you can fit it into your schedule."

"Sure. I've got quite a bit of catching up to do, but I'd love to."

That afternoon found Sherrie sitting at the kitchen table of the foster home, talking to Betina. She was the only one talking because Betina refused to speak. The young woman was fifteen years old and a natural beauty. Long, black hair and tan skin, the Latina teenager looked furtively from side to side as though searching for an escape.

"Betina, I want to explain why I'm here. I'm your Court Appointed Special Advocate but we shorten that to CASA. Has anyone explained to you what that means?"

A quick shake of her head was the only answer given.

"The judge in your case assigned me to work with you, talk with you, and make sure you are safe. I will be interviewing your teachers and parents to get a good idea of how things are with you so that when I make my report to the judge, he will have your interests in mind."

The young teen sat stoically, not responding.

"Betina, I was noticing that this seemed like a pretty nice house. I grew up in foster care and had a few nice ones, but also had some that were not so nice. Do you like it here?"

A short nod was the only answer.

Sherrie continued as though the girl had given her a

dissertation. "Good, I'm glad. Are you in the same school as before?"

A shake of her head gave her nonverbal acknowledgement. "Is that hard, moving to a different school?"

For the briefest of moments, Sherrie saw a flash of regret pass through Betina's eyes before being quickly replaced by practiced indifference.

Jumping on that, she moved the conversation to school. After several minutes, Betina seemed to relax a bit and actually answered a few questions about classes.

After a slight pause, Betina looked out of the kitchen window and simply said, "Art. My favorite class."

"Do you have any drawings?" Sherrie asked, trying to keep Betina from shutting her out again. "I'd love to see anything you've done. I'm afraid I'm not very artistic myself but love to look at other's work."

Looking furtively around again, the teenager pulled out a small notebook from her backpack and pushed it across the table to Sherrie. Thrilled that she had made the slightest inroads with her, she eagerly opened the notebook. The pages were filled with pencil drawings, with clear lines and incredible detail. Most of the drawings were of people's faces, with a few scenes depicted amongst them.

Several were of other teen girls and boys, and a few adults mixed in. Mesmerized at the intricate drawings, she asked if they were her friends.

Another emotion flashed through Betina's eyes and Sherrie could have sworn she saw fear for a moment.

Years of working in seedy bars to make money to go to college had Sherrie an expert in reading expressions, but she had to admit that Betina's ability to cover up quickly made it difficult to ascertain what she was thinking.

"Some," came the simple answer.

"Well, they're amazing. Really beautiful. How do you capture their faces in such detail?"

Betina smiled for the first time and Sherrie wondered if praise was something that the young girl rarely received. Shrugging, Betina just added, "I watch people. I see them."

"You see them?" Sherrie prodded.

"You know. Like really see them. The inside of them," came the halting answers.

"Well, they are phenomenal." Sensing that she had gotten all out of the young woman that she was going to get, she patted her hand as she pushed the notebook back across the table, noting Betina's aversion to the touch on her hand.

Filing that away for future reference, she stood saying, "Goodbye for now and I'll be by to see you again in a day or so," carefully watching the expression on her face.

Betina did not smile but gave the slightest encouraging nod, which Sherrie took as a positive. Back in the office that afternoon, she met with Simon going over the interview with Betina.

"I know there is something going on and I wish she

would open up," she said.

"She lived with her mom and a man they called her stepdad, but he and mom never married. He runs some local businesses in the area. Pays his taxes and doesn't seem to have anything going on with him."

"Sexual abuse, you think?" she asked.

Simon answered, "Thought about it, but the girl has not indicated anything untoward."

"Well, something makes her run away," she said, frustration clear on her face.

"The DSS worker who placed her in the foster home said that the medical exam did not show bruises so physical abuse was ruled out. The mother claims the girl keeps running away to see a boyfriend and was staying out all night, but the fear shown from the girl indicated that something was going on."

"So what happens now?"

"If Betina won't talk, then she'll probably be placed back in her home. Foster care was just temporary anyway and she may have to go spend some time at the Juvenile Detention Center."

At the thought of 'juvie', Sherrie shuttered. Her sister had spent plenty of time at the detention center when picked up for drugs when she was a teenager. The idea of Betina going there was unacceptable to her.

"Well, I'm going to try to find out what's going on so that doesn't happen," she stated emphatically.

Her cell phone rang and at a quick glance her smile returned. "Hey," she answered softly.

"Hey yourself," Tony replied. "How's your day going?"

"Busy, but it's almost over. What about you?"

Tony shook his head, thinking of the way his friends had reacted to him spending the weekend snowed in with her.

Walking in that morning to Alvarez Security, he expected some questions but not a joyous inquisition.

Lily, immediately placing her hand on his arm, peered into his eyes as though trying to see deep inside of him. "Are you alright?" Receiving his nod, she continued. "Is Sherrie all right?"

"Yes, we're both fine."

"No, I mean are you two really okay? Together?" she prodded.

Tony, unused to talking about his personal life to anyone, found his weekend with Sherrie had released him from being quite so uncomfortable. "Yeah, Lily. We're great."

Turning away from her smile, he was accosted by BJ and Gabe.

"So, you finally went after the girl, huh?" BJ asked.

BJ had not served with them in the Army, so he would not have gone through their experiences together. Tony saw Gabe's expression, knowing his friend was both happy for him and understanding how life-changing this was.

Tony's eyes did not flash irritation at BJ's question, but instead found it hard to keep the smile from crossing his face.

"Not that my personal life is anyone's business, but yes. I went after the girl," he said.

Vinny and Jobe walked up, hearing the end of Tony's one-sentence speech, each smiling. BJ had continued on toward the conference room, but the others stood in the hall with Tony.

"Captain, can't tell you how happy I am for you," Jobe *spoke, sincerity filling every word.*

Tony looked at his former squad members, now friends as well as employees. The men who had stayed with him as he picked out the white matching caskets. And secretly held him when he fell apart, careful to keep anyone else from seeing. He now saw the emotions clearly written on their faces. Happiness. And relief.

Smiling, he just nodded. They slapped him on the back as they too headed into the conference room.

Answering Sherrie, Tony said, "Everyone was happy we made it through the storm safely."

"That's it? No one had anything else to say?" she prodded.

"Like what, babe?"

"Oh, like BJ calling his wife, Suzanne, to tell her that we were now a couple and Lily calling her husband, Matt, to tell him as well. And then they told Annie and Jennifer, who by the way already knew before Gabe could call her."

"Jesus, my men are as bad as you women," he exclaimed.

"Humph," she grumped, then heard him chuckling. "Oh, you're just being mean."

"Just joking with you, darlin'. I told everyone this morning that we were together and they were all real happy." He could almost hear her grin through the phone and his heart felt lighter than it had in a long time.

"Well, besides turning into a jokester, did you have a reason to call?" she asked.

"Besides just wanting to hear your voice? Actually, I thought you could come to my place for dinner after work."

"I'd love to," she effused.

Giving her the address, he saw where another call was coming in. "Sorry to rush but it looks like Shane is trying to get ahold of me." With a quick goodbye, he switched calls.

"Shane? What's up?" he asked.

"I hear congratulations are in order," Shane said.

"How quickly did the news hit the Richland Police?" he asked his detective friend.

"About a long as it took my wife to find out from Lily, and BJ's wife."

"Well, thanks, man. Surely you called for some other reason than to bust my chops?" he asked.

"You got time for Matt and I to have a conference with you and some of your men?" Shane asked.

Serious now, Tony said, "Always got time for you all. Come on over and I'll gather everyone."

MATT DIXON AND SHANE DOUGLASS, detectives with the Richland Police department and close friends with Tony and his group, sat around the conference table discussing their latest investigations.

"We're working on a case of money laundering and have centered our investigation on Quentin Salazar. His name keeps cropping up but once again, like so many we try to investigate, they bury their illegal businesses so deep, our resources can't reach them."

Shane added, "He has also been mentioned with some sex clubs along the riverfront, but again nothing concrete. We've got a feeling that his hand is in much more, but we were wondering if Lily and BJ could do some digging for us. And…"

His pause had the others looking up. "We were wondering if perhaps, your team could put a few security cameras around his office. Unofficially, of course," he said with a grin.

Tony said, "Got no problem with that, but nothing we get will be admissible in court."

"We're just looking for others in league with him, anything that gives us an idea where to look and what we're looking for."

Nodding, Tony agreed. "All right."

The meeting continued as the group broke off into two teams. Matt went with Lily and BJ to talk about what they needed from their computer searches. Shane stayed with the others to discuss what cameras would be needed and where they could place them to get the most intel.

"He's got an office in the same block of buildings that one of the clubs is in. He's not been seen going into the club, but we know he's just being a sneaky bastard."

"We'll get BJ to look at the floor plan of that old building and see what connections we can find," Tony added.

"One other thing," Shane interjected. "Talk on the street is that this club will start servicing men who are looking for children, especially teens or pre-teen virgins. We've got no proof yet, but that's what one informer said."

"Shit," Jobe bit out, shaking his head.

"We want these guys and we want them shut down."

Standing, Tony shook Shane's hand. "Whatever you need from us...you got."

HERNANDO VALESQUEZ MOVED from the front of his prosperous grocery store to the back office. Walking in, he was pleased to see Juan waiting for him.

"What do you have for me?" he bit out.

"Betina is still with the foster family. Had some visitors, but nothing suspicious."

"I want that little bitch watched. If she hadn't run off and gotten picked up by the police, we wouldn't be worried."

"She's not talking. Got too much to lose. She knows her mother will suffer if needed."

"My little wife?" Hernando questioned with a laugh. "Easy bait for Betina." Sobering, he ordered, "Keep me informed. I want no surprises."

The tall, dark-haired man nodded and walked out, closing the door behind him.

Hernando sat down in his squeaky chair as he rubbed his temples. *Too much to lose, little Betina, if you can't follow orders.* He knew the organization was much larger than himself, but he loved the power he wielded. Working his way up the chain, he was now a regional manager. *And not of his grocery store,* he thought with a smirk. *No, the store provides the perfect cover. Providing the only Hispanic grocery in the area, I am loved.* While he had never married Betina's mother, she also helped with the cover. Meek, mild, and so pleased that such a successful man wanted to be with her, she was easy to manipulate.

He only had one boss and that was Quentin Salazar. He frowned for a moment, realizing that he had no idea if Quentin was the top of the chain or if were just one more in the chain, but right now he did not care. His duties as regional manager meant that he had to manage the recruiters, who in turn recruited almost all of the teens his organization needed. Free labor. Free sex. Smiling to himself, he thought of the women in his group as well. *Nothing like the fear in their eyes when on their knees sucking me off.* Hernando was careful to never use the minors for sex. Too risky. And he hated little, skinny bodies. He wanted a mature woman, the bigger the tits, the better.

Finding his dick swelling at the thought, he opened his office door and motioned to one of the workers in his store. He ignored the look in her eyes as he focused on her huge breasts discreetly covered. A few minutes later as he fucked her pendulous breasts freed from her shirt, the thought ran through his mind just as he moved to her mouth to unload...*I must be the luckiest man alive.*

As the woman adjusted herself and then went back to his respectable business, his mind turned toward Betina. The smile left his face. *I've come too far for that little bitch to complicate matters.*

CHAPTER 11

TONY HEADED TO his apartment after work to fix dinner in anticipation of Sherrie's arrival. Walking in, he looked around for the first time in a long time. Really looked around. And realized how stark he had been living. Or existing.

Moving to his kitchen, he began to prepare the meal, knowing she would be arriving in a few minutes. By the time he had the potatoes baking, the steaks seasoned, and the vegetables sautéing, his doorbell rang.

Anxious to see her, he jogged over to throw open the door. His breath caught once again as he took her in. Blonde hair was sleeked back in a low ponytail. Neat, grey pinstriped pencil skirt paired with a pale pink blouse. Demure pumps that still gave off a *fuck-me* vibe, although he was willing to admit that may have been because that was the only vibe he could think of.

Her smiling face gazed up at his, a touch of makeup highlighting her sparkling eyes, and her lips were gently glossed with something kissable.

God, I'm so fucked, he thought as he stood, unwaveringly staring at her.

"Um, can I come in?" she asked, a questioning look

on her face.

"Yes. Yes," he grunted as he stepped back to discretely adjust his swelling dick. He saw her eyes dip to his crotch and then lift quickly back to his face, a blush creeping from her chest to her cheeks.

"Oh, hell," he growled, no longer willing to hold back. Pulling her tightly to him, he crushed his mouth over hers. She opened quickly and he wasted no time in plunging his tongue into her depths. Minty. With a hint of something fruity as he licked her lip-gloss off.

Her tongue tangled with his, as she melted into his embrace. He was so much taller, she stood on her toes to reach her arms around his neck, then squealed as she felt herself lifted. Once again, she found herself plastered against the wall as he jerked her tight skirt up to her hips and rested her core on his knees.

Losing themselves in the kiss, they startled when the kitchen buzzer alarmed. Lowering her quickly, he took a ragged breath as he pulled her head back against his massive chest.

Hearing his strong heartbeat, she knew there was no place she would rather be.

Moving away, he snagged her hand and gently pulled her toward the kitchen. "Gotta get the steaks in, baby." Giving her a quick lift, he perched her on a bar stool and leaned over to kiss her forehead. "Sit here and keep me company."

Smiling, she watched him place the steaks into the broiler, then pour a glass of wine placing it in front of her. As he finished the dinner, she glanced around. His apartment was spacious but…devoid. Devoid of any personality. The living area contained a large sectional sofa in a soft grey, with a black coffee table in front. It faced a large-screen TV, but she noticed there were no rugs, throw pillows, or any color in the room at all.

She moved off of the stool and wandered over to an end table where she saw a small, framed picture. Picking it up, she recognized Gabe, Vinny, and Jobe amongst the other soldiers in the snapshot. *No family pictures. No pictures of his wife or baby.* As her gaze continued roaming, she imagined this apartment looking the same as the day he moved in.

"Was this place furnished?" she asked, curious about his answer.

"Yeah, why?" he called from the kitchen.

"It just looks very…"

"Boring?" He glanced up from the stove to see her blush rising across her face again. Laughing, he added, "It's okay babe. It is boring. Just never had any desire to do much with it since it's just a place to eat and sleep."

But it should be a place you live, she thought sadly. *And he hasn't really lived since his family died.*

Lost in her musings, she did not hear him walk up behind her until his arms came across her body pulling her back close to his front. "Whatcha thinkin'?" he asked.

Twisting around so that she could study his face,

she noticed his arms had not loosened their embrace. "It just doesn't seem very homey."

His gaze wandered around the room as he nodded. "Yeah, compared to your place, it's kind of bare." Giving a shrug, he continued, "But honestly, I haven't had a *home* since I've been back. I just couldn't see one without Marla and Sofia…" His eyes glazed over as he looked out of the window. Then he shook his head and smiled at her, though it didn't quite reach his eyes.

"Do you want one?" she whispered, afraid of the answer.

He looked down at the woman in his arms. Strong. Independent. Kicked by life multiple times and yet came out on top. From foster homes to a quaint Victorian home, filled with…her. It suddenly hit him in the gut…*I want that. I want that with her.*

Smiling honestly, he nodded. "Yeah, baby. I do want a home." Seeing the smile light up her face, he kissed the top of her head. The kitchen stove timer went off again and they moved to get dinner on the table.

Conversation slowed as they ate in companionable silence, but as they neared the end of the meal he found his gaze wandering to her continually. He had memorized her face from the moment he saw her picture in his dossier last year, but was amazed at how beautiful she was. A few strands of straight blonde hair had escaped the ponytail and he watched her as she tucked them behind her ears. Every movement screamed *classy* and he wondered once again at how different she was from her sister.

Sherrie noticed his intense gaze and self-consciously brought her napkin to her mouth, wiping at the non-existent crumbs. His gaze never wavered. "Do I have something on my face?" she asked, wiping again.

Startled from his staring, he said simply, "Beauty." At her questioning expression, he added, "You have beauty written all over your face."

Her eyes sparkled as a giggle erupted from deep inside. "That almost sounds like a bad pick-up line, but honestly, I loved it," she admitted.

He joined in laughter, shaking his head. "God, it did sound cheesy, didn't it?" Sobering, he stood and walked to her side of the table reaching for her hand. "But it's the truth, darlin'. You're so goddamn beautiful that I can't believe what a lucky fuck I am."

She placed her small hand in his as he led her from the table down the hall. Moving into his bedroom, she barely noticed that it had the same blankness of the rest of the apartment. But then the only thing that was really on her mind was the large, king-sized bed. As he turned to face her, she felt her nipples tightened at the look on his face.

As though in response to her thoughts, he lifted one hand to a breast, kneading the mound and flicking the nipple through the material. Her hands moved to her blouse, wanting to remove the offending garment, but his hands pushed hers out of the way. Slowly he undid each button as his lips stayed locked onto hers. Kissing, nipping, licking…his mouth savored hers as he slid the blouse off of her shoulders and onto the floor. Keeping his hands behind her, they moved to her waist and unzipped her skirt letting it fall to the floor next to the blouse.

Lifting her in his strong arms, he lay her gently on the bed before leaning over her body with his. Her breasts, spilling over the tops of her bra, were quickly released by the flick of his fingers on her clasp. He pulled a rosy nipple into his mouth, sucking deeply, eliciting a moan from deep within her. She began to writhe on the bed as he slid one hand down into her barely-there panties finding her folds slick and ready.

Releasing her nipple with a pop, he moved back to her swollen lips, his tongue thrusting in rhythm to his fingers embedded in her slick channel.

Her hands found the bottom of his t-shirt and she maneuvered it up toward his head. Desperate to feel his solid chest muscles against her naked breasts, she wrestled with the material.

Chuckling, he broke the kiss, sitting up on his knees as he jerked the shirt over his head. "In a hurry, darlin'?"

"Yes," she panted, her hands already to the button on his jeans. Getting them unzipped over his impressive cock was proving equally difficult so he rolled over to quickly divest himself of them as well. Shucking his boxers, his dick was standing at attention as he turned his gaze back to the gorgeous woman lying in his bed. *His bed.* He realized that he had not had a woman in *his* bed since his wife had died. The few times he sought company to take care of his needs, he had followed the woman from the bar to her place. No ties. No recriminations. Just two people who knew the score.

"Where'd you go?" Sherrie whispered, wondering at the expression on his face.

"Nowhere important, baby," he assured. "Just realizing how lucky I am that you're here."

Determined to make love to her, he moved slowly, licking and sucking from her lips to her neck to her breasts once again. His fingers found their refuge deep inside as she felt herself climbing higher and higher.

The taste of her was intoxicating as the kiss went deeper. She tasted of wine and the sweetness of their dessert. Licking his way down her body he found the sensitive skin of her neck before moving lower. Giving each breast attention, he elicited moans from her as her hips began to press against his body.

"Patience," he chuckled, his mouth moving lower. Using his hands, he spread her legs wide as he completely exposed her pink folds to his eyes. With a growl rumbling deep in his chest, he dove in, licking her wetness before sucking her clit into his mouth.

"Aughh," she moaned again, her hips rising. He moved one of his hands up to her stomach and gently pressed her back down.

Plunging his tongue inside, he continued to lap her juices, loving the taste of her. His hand on her stomach rose higher until it palmed her breast, pinching the nipple lightly.

"I need..." she panted, feeling the coil of tension deep inside her core ready to spring. "I..." was all she managed to say as he gave each nipple a tug as he sucked her clit deeply to his mouth. Her inner walls clenched and her orgasm raced through her sending all of her nerves tingling outwards. Throwing her head back, she screamed his name once again.

He finished licking her glistening folds before kissing his way back up her boneless body until he plunged his tongue back into her mouth.

"Please...I need you inside of me," she begged.

"Baby, this was about you. Just you tonight," he responded, wanting to give her everything she needed.

Her imploring gaze sought his as she captured his strong jaw in her hands. "This is what I need. This is what I want," she explained. "I. Need. You. Inside. Of. Me."

He held her eyes for just a moment, seeing nothing but truth and trust. Growling he grabbed a condom and rolled on top of her, stilling his cock just at her entrance. Holding her legs apart, he looked down at all her beauty. Pale skin gleaming in the moonlight. Blue eyes looking into his. *She's truly mine.* A sexy smile lit her face and he swore his heart stopped as her arms rose up to him.

Plunging to the hilt, his dick reveled in the soft warmth of her body. Leaning over her, his hands on either side of her head, he pounded deeply, trying to reach the innermost part of her soul. Hanging on to his self-discipline by a thread, he was determined for her to come again.

"Close, baby?" he panted.

"Yes, yes." She grabbed his shoulders, holding on for all she was worth. The sparks shot from her womb out through her limbs as her orgasm rocketed. Digging her fingers into his arms, she cried out once again.

He followed her, his neck thrown back as the cords of muscles strained. Continuing to thrust until every last drop was drained, he fell to the side taking her with him. Holding her close, he wrapped his arms around her trembling form, pulling her tight into his chest. Legs tangled. Arms wrapped. Breaths mingled. Heartbeats pounding in unison.

Slowly awareness crept in and he looked back into her face, seeing her smiling at him.

"Are you okay, baby?" he asked.

"Oh yeah. I couldn't be happier," she whispered back.

Pulling her back tightly to him, he threw his leg over hers as his arm wrapped around her waist.

Tucking her sated body next to his, he allowed the sound of her deep breathing to lull him to sleep.

A DREAM OVERTOOK his sleep, as he wandered around the battlefield of his mind.

The dust. The dirt. The blood. He began to run, wanting to escape the desolation of the war-torn country. Something green was on the horizon and his booted feet pounded toward the color. As he came closer, he could see a beautiful, green park and in the distance was a dark haired woman holding a baby. Marla and Sofia. With his last ounce of strength, he continued to run toward them. But the park became a cemetery and he had to wind his way around the tombstones to try to reach them. They disappeared, but as he stumbled to a halt, he looked at the closest tombstone.

Their names were carved in the cold marble. Beloved wife and beloved daughter. There were new words at the bottom and he dropped to the ground to see them. Wiping the grass away, he read There is no life without pain.

"I'm letting you go, Tony," he heard behind him. Turning he saw a smiling Marla, standing with the light shining behind her head, Sofia tucked safely in her arms. He stood, his breathing sharp and ragged. "Now you have to let me go too," she said again.

He reached his hand toward her but she began to slide toward the light. "Marla?" he whispered.

"Be happy, my love. Be happy with Sherrie," came the only response, as she and Sofia disappeared.

For the first time since his family had passed away, he did not waken with sadness. Instead he continued to sleep, peacefully, his soul finally at rest.

Turning over, he clutched Sherrie closer to his chest as dreamless sleep calmed him.

Sherrie lay awake, her heart pounding in her chest, a sharp pain with each breath. She tried to quiet her breathing, but found that nothing stilled the ache.

She had not imagined it. She could not will it away. She could not pretend it had not happened. He had cried out *Marla* right before pulling her in tightly. *He may be holding me, but in his mind he's holding her.* Pain sliced through her, knowing her body was just a replacement for his wife's. *He tried, I know he did. But maybe we were just fooling ourselves to think we could move beyond the past.*

Silent tears slid down her cheeks as she slowly left the bed. Gathering her clothes from the pile on the floor, she dressed silently and moved to the living room. Slipping into her shoes then grabbing her purse, she left his apartment and drove home.

Arriving, she quickly stripped again before pulling on her pajamas. Soft. Comfortable. *Not as comfortable as his arms around me,* she thought ruefully, dashing the tears again.

I may not ever be much, but I deserve all of him. She

continued to lay in bed although sleep eluded her. *But if I can't have him, he's ruined me for any other man. I love him,* she realized. And allowed the tears to fall once more.

CHAPTER 12

TONY WOKE THE next morning, rested and relaxed in his bed for the first time in...ever. Rolling over to see Sherrie's beautiful face, he found the bed empty. Senses alert, he knew the cold side of her bed indicated that she had left hours ago. He jumped up and as he bent to snag his jeans off of the floor he noticed that his clothes were the only ones there.

Stalking into the living room he instantly saw that her purse was missing as well. *Goddamn it. Where the hell did she go?* He grabbed his cell phone but his call went to her voice mail. A niggle of doubt crept in.

Like any mission, he carefully thought back over the evening. He knew he had not read the signals wrong. *She wanted to be here. She wanted to be with me. So what went wrong?*

Walking back into the bedroom, he sat on the edge of the bed as he pulled his socks and shoes back on. Determined to find her, he intended to let her know that the next time she thought about leaving in the middle of the night, she had better wake him first.

Wake him. I was sleeping so deeply, I can't believe I didn't hear her get up. What had me sleeping so soundly?

My dream! Damn, that crazy dream. His body stilled as he remembered. *Marla holding Sofia. The cemetery. She's letting me go and telling me to be with Sherrie.*

Startling, he jerked stiffly. *Sherrie? How did Marla know her name?* It was a dream...but felt like more. He realized that Marla had spoken to him. Somehow, somewhere...she knew.

Standing quickly, he grabbed his wallet, cell phone and keys and headed out of the door. Driving as fast as he dared, he pulled into Sherrie's driveway. He jogged up the front stairs and pounded on the door. Torn between anger at her sneaking out and desire to crush her body against his, he waited impatiently.

"She ain't home," Bernard's voice called out from the fence.

Tony headed over to greet the older man. "Did you see when she left?"

"Yeah," he said, pushing his hat back from his forehead a little, his squinty eyes steady on the younger man. "She left out of here early. Not usual for her on the weekends."

Tony's mind raced for a moment, trying to work the problem.

"You ain't asked the right question yet, sonny," the older man quipped. At that Tony's gaze shot back up to Bernard's.

"And what would the right question be?" Tony growled.

"What did she look like when she left here?"

Tony rubbed his large hand over his face, stilling his frustration. "Okay. What did she look like when she left here?"

Bernard nodded, saying, "She was carrying a few of the winter roses that my wife gave her years ago that she keeps protected on her back porch. And she was wiping her eyes."

Tony's mind raced for only a second before quickly surmising, "She was upset. And heading to the cemetery."

Bernard smiled a slow smile. "Thought you were a smart man when I met you."

"Thanks," Tony shouted over his shoulder as he jogged to his truck, pulling his tall frame into the driver's seat. He arrived at the cemetery as quickly as he could and parked near her car. He looked over, seeing her kneeling at the grave marker of Charisse. Suddenly feeling like an intruder, he sat in the truck for a few minutes, allowing her time to grieve privately.

I love him so much Charisse. If you were here you'd be drooling over him and telling me to go for it. I just want something…something that's all mine. I don't mind that he has a past. I hurt for his loss, but I'm not jealous of his deceased wife. But Charisse, I want all of him. Not to be the shadow of what he had.

Kneeling next to her sister's grave-marker, she pushed the grass away from the nameplate. *I wish I could afford to buy you a tombstone too. As soon as I can, I promise I will.* The cold wind whipped around her tiny frame, as she stood, wrapping her arms around her. Protecting her from the wind. Protecting her from the hurt.

Sighing deeply, she wiped her tears before kissing her finger, leaving a lipstick stain on the end of her forefinger. Leaning down, she touched the grave marker transferring the lipstick kiss. *That's my kiss goodbye until next time, Charisse.* She turned and started to walk away, then stopped suddenly, twisting around one last time. *I love you, sis.*

Tony's heart ached for the woman he loved as he witnessed her open grief. *I've had years to learn to deal with my grief. Deal? Hell, until Sherrie, I was just existing, not dealing.* Wanting to wrap her in his arms, he stepped out of his truck, startling her.

She looked up, eyes wide in surprise. Her blonde hair was tucked under her winter cap but a few tendrils blew about as the wind whipped them. Her cheeks were red, both with the cold and the tracks of her tears.

"Tony? What are you doing here?"

"You left," he accused gently.

Looking anywhere but into his eyes, she mumbled, "I had somewhere to go."

"Here? Is this where you had to go? 'Cause if so, darlin', I'd have driven you." He noticed that her gaze never met his. Stepping forward slowly he lifted his hand to her face, cupping her frozen cheek. Rubbing the cold tear tracks he leaned down, desperate to see into her eyes.

"I...um...just..." she faltered.

"Sherrie? What's going on in that head of yours?" He moved his hand so that her face lifted to his. Anguish gazed back at him. Icy fear slid through him as he wondered what she was thinking. Cocking his head to the side, he asked, "This is more than you just visiting Charisse's grave, isn't it?"

Bringing his other hand up, he pulled her gently toward him until her face was resting on his warm coat and his arms were enveloping her body, cradling it next to his.

Sherrie allowed herself to take in his warmth. Soak it in. Feel it float through her veins. *I have to let him go. And he deserves nothing but the truth.*

Lifting her hands to his chest, she pushed gently moving away from him. Forcing her gaze to his questioning eyes, she said, "I can't do this, Tony. I've cared for you since the first day I met you, but...I can't be someone's...replacement."

His eyebrows darted together as he questioned, "Replacement? What the hell do you mean by that?"

Sighing, she stepped back, noticing that he allowed her to. "I—"

Grabbing her hand, he turned and said, "Come on." Gently pulling her along with him, they stepped amongst the headstones making their way to another section of the cemetery.

She wanted to ask where they were going, but was too afraid to ask. Too afraid the tears would start again. Too afraid.

Tony noticed her stumbling behind him and he wrapped his arm around her shoulders, tucking her safely into his side, noticing her arms stayed around her body and not around him. Arriving at their destination he stopped, facing a double headstone.

Sherrie looked down, wondering why they had stopped. Until she read the words.

Marla Renee Alvarez Beloved wife and mother
Sofia Carlotta Alvarez Beloved daughter and Angel

Oh my God. Tears stung the back of her eyes once again, as she choked back a sob.

"Sherrie?" he asked gently. "Do you understand why I brought you here?"

"I know you loved. And lost."

He brought his hands to her face once again, cupping her frozen cheeks in his warmth forcing her to look at him. "Yes baby, I loved and I lost. It ripped my heart out and I never thought anything could ever make me happy again. And I was good with that."

"I'm so sorry, Tony," she whispered, another tear sliding down her cheek across his fingers.

"Sherrie, until you, I was ready to just exist. Just be glad I had that kind of love for a little while. But now...baby, don't you get it?"

Her gaze narrowed in confusion as she tried to decipher what he meant.

Sighing, he continued. "I don't wanna just exist anymore. You make me want to...feel again."

Turning with her in his embrace toward the tombstone, he looked down at the familiar words. *The strange ache was no longer coursing through his veins. Thinking back to his dream, he realized that Marla had given him permission to live again.*

"Tony?" came the small voice beside him.

He looked down at her large, blue eyes, still filled with pain.

"What are you saying?" she asked.

"You called yourself a replacement a few minutes ago. Babe, I have no idea what made you think that. You're no one's replacement."

"Last night," she stuttered, then cleared her throat. "You wanted her."

Tony reared back, his hands sliding from her cheeks to her shoulders. *What the hell is she talking about?* Forcing himself to be calm, he took a deep breath. "I still have no idea what you are talking about."

Wrapping her arms around her middle again, girding herself she said, "You may have been lying with me but it was her name that you called in the middle of the night." Embarrassed, she stepped back. "I don't blame you, I really don't. You love her. She was your wife, the mother of your child. She was the one you wanted to be with for the rest of your life. It's just...I can't compete with that and…" Steeling herself, she gazed directly into his eyes. "I don't want to compete and always feel lacking."

Turning, she began the walk back toward her car, making her way through the cemetery as tears streamed down her cheeks. Part of her wanted him to run after her. Follow her. Chase her down and tell her she was wrong. *I won't look back.* Passing by Charisse's gravesite, she glanced down. *No more looking back.*

TONY STOOD ABSOLUTELY still watching Sherrie walk away. Heart pounding. Mind reeling. *What just happened? I called out Marla's name?* His mind flew back over the dream he had the previous night. The one where Marla let him go. *Shit! I must have said her name out loud and Sherrie heard.*

Looking up he saw her car pulling away from the cemetery. He wanted to run after her. Chase her down and explain, but he did not move. His eyes shifted back down to the marble headstone, finding the familiar ache of loss had intensified. *I'm such a fuckup, Marla. How do I make this right?* His gaze drifted over to Sofia's name and his mind jumped to how he would feel as a father if someone she loved had hurt her and did not try to make it right. *I'd pound the shit out of the guy that ever hurt my baby.*

Heaving a determined sigh, he stalked over to his

truck. *Time to stop living in the past. Time to make this right.*

SHERRIE WALKED INTO her kitchen reaching for the coffee, needing the fortification. Her phone chimed as a message came in and she saw Betina's name on the screen.

Can you come see me?

Wondering what the young woman wanted, she immediately texted her reply back indicating that she was on her way. As she drove across town, she called Simon to see if he knew what was going on.

"I received a message from her social worker that she was being returned back to her home," he answered.

"Well, I'm heading there now, so I'll see if she needs something."

Betina met her at the door of the foster home before she had a chance to ring the doorbell.

"Hey, sweetie," she greeted. "What's going on?"

Betina ushered her into the den as the foster mother smiled before leaving the room to give them privacy.

Sitting on the comfortable sofa, Sherrie smiled encouragingly hoping that Betina would open up more about what was on her mind.

"I'm going back," she said, her words filled with

pain.

"Yes, I heard about that. How do you feel about moving back in with your mom and stepdad?"

"He's not my stepdad," Betina stated emphatically.

"I'm sorry, you're right. But how do you feel about moving back in with them?" Sherrie prodded again.

Betina's arms crossed her middle as her eyes darted to the side. Sherrie recognized evasive posturing and tried to put the girl at ease.

"I'm sure it will seem strange to go back after being here."

Betina's gaze came back to Sherrie's face and she asked haltingly, "Can...I call you? If I ever...need you?"

"Of course you can. Honey, I'll still be your CASA worker until the courts decide that I'm not needed but even if I wasn't, you can call me anytime."

The relief on the teen's face was visible, sparking suspicion in Sherrie's mind. "Do you have a specific reason for not wanting to be around your ste—um, mom's boyfriend?"

"No," Betina bit out quickly.

Too quickly, thought Sherrie, suspicions continuing.

"Are you sure?"

"We're good. I just don't like him, that's all."

"Betina, has he ever tried—"

"No, never," she said shaking her head. "I just don't like him."

Not wanting to break the tenuous trust that they

had, Sherrie did not question her further. "Well, if you ever need me, you just call or text."

Receiving the first smile of the day, she was relieved that Betina had reached out. With a heartfelt hug, she drove back to her house, her mind filled with thoughts of the young teen.

MARCELLA SAT LOOKING at her boyfriend as he ate dinner. She usually kept quiet because that was the way he wanted it, but she risked his anger anyway.

"You know Betina comes back tomorrow?" she spoke hesitantly.

"Not stupid woman. Of course I know," he grunted between mouthfuls. "She best stay in school and do what she's supposed to do from now on, if she knows what's good for her."

"She's a good girl," Marcella defended. "She always does good in school."

"Umh," he grunted again. Finishing his meal, his chair scraped across the floor as he pushed himself up. Wiping his mouth with the back of his hand, he moved into the small living room flipping on the TV.

Marcella sighed as she cleaned the table. She knew he had never hurt Betina, so why did her daughter want to leave? Hernando was a hard man, but had been good to them. He was the reason they could afford the little house they lived in. Kept them in clothes. After

Betina's father had died when she was only three, Marcella worked long hours to take care of her daughter, but life had been hard. When Hernando had moved to the neighborhood, it was hard not to notice the charismatic man. Surprised to be the one to catch his eye, she was thrilled when he moved in. He'd made it clear that he was not interested in marriage but she would take whatever he was willing to give as long as he helped to take care of Betina. And if he strayed? She had heard the whispers that she was not the only one he took to bed. As long as he helped them out financially, she could put up with a lot. Pursing lips as she finished wiping off the counters she glanced into the den, seeing Hernando watching a game on the TV. She could not wait until Betina was home tomorrow, but had to talk to her daughter. She could not take a chance on Betina's behavior costing them Hernando's protection.

CHAPTER 13

TONY DROVE TO the north side of the city, pulling to the front of a small house next to the river. The house sat up on a hill and as his gaze roamed over the area he smiled, letting the familiarity settle over him.

The door, unlocked at usual, opened easily as he let himself in.

"Dad?" he called, walking into the living room seeing the older man sitting in a recliner in front of the TV.

"Son? I didn't know you were coming for a visit," his father answered, as he moved out of his chair. Standing, he embraced Tony before moving to the kitchen to grab another beer. "Sit yourself down," he said as he walked back into the room.

Tony settled onto the worn sofa, twisting the cap off of the beer as his father sat back in his recliner. The two men drank their beers in silence for a few minutes, both knowing the words would come when the time was right. Tony's gaze moved from the TV to his father, still in good health and looking very much like an older version of himself. Tall, with now graying hair but the same brown eyes. *Alvarez Eyes* his mother always said.

After another moment, his father lifted the remote turning the sound down. "You ready to talk, son?"

Smiling, Tony knew that his dad was fully aware that he had not just dropped by. "You always could read me, couldn't you?" he said.

"It's what parents do," came the easy answer, then a quick look of sorrow crossed his father's face. "I'm sorry, son," he apologized.

The slicing pain that Tony expected from any comment about parents and children did not come. A dull ache was in his heart, but he just sighed, saying, "It's okay, dad. I can't resent others being parents just because that was taken from me."

A silence ensued once more, this one slightly less comfortable. Rubbing his hand over his face, Tony blurted, "I've found someone dad."

His father's sharp eyes cut over to Tony's face. When no other statement came forward, he prompted, "And…?"

"I've already fucked it up."

"This woman like you too?"

Tony leaned forward, placing his forearms on his knees, hanging his head. "Yeah."

"Then I'd say you haven't really fucked anything up too badly that can't be repaired, son."

"I never thought I'd find someone after Marla. I sure as hell wasn't looking," he said shaking his head.

"You're a young man, Tony. You had love once,

but no reason to think you can't have it again. Your mother, God rest her soul, would be singing from the rafters to know you had found a woman again."

Tony thought of his mom who passed away two years earlier after a long battle with cancer. His dad was right…his mom would have wanted him to be happy, but at the time all he could do was grieve. For her…for Sofia…for Marla. Death had stalked him, or so it seemed. Rubbing his hand over his face again, he turned toward his dad once again.

"I met her a year ago on a rescue mission. Name's Sherrie. She's smart, worked hard to make something of her life from a shit beginning. I looked into those scared blue eyes, and felt something, dad, that I hadn't been prepared for."

His father chuckled while nodding. "Yeah, it can hit you like that." Sobering after a moment, he asked, "So what's the problem?"

"I…I spent so much time after Marla and Sofia died thinking that that was it for me. I'd loved. I'd become a father. And I lost it all. One phone call and it was all gone. I wasn't prepared to ever…feel again."

"You been dating this Sherrie for a year?"

"Nah. I've been fighting my attraction to her for a year. We just hooked up recently."

"And…."

"I finally decided that I couldn't fight it anymore. Even though being with her felt great, at first I felt guilty, like I was cheating or something. But I went for it anyway, and I think she knew that. Then I had the craziest dream." Tony looked at his dad wondering what he thought about all of this.

Plunging ahead, he told his father about the dream where Marla told him to be happy with Sherrie. "But I must have said her name in my sleep and Sherrie heard, so she left. She thinks I won't be able to love her."

"Did you explain? Did you tell her what you're feeling?" his dad asked, concern etching his face.

"No. I just let her walk away."

His father huffed as he brought his recliner back to a sitting position. "Son, you let her walk away because *you're* the one who doesn't think he deserves a second chance at love." At this, Tony's gaze jumped to his dad's, but before he could say anything, his dad continued on his roll.

"You felt so goddamn responsible for Marla and Sofia's death, when in truth there was nothing you coulda done to prevent it." Seeing that Tony was about to speak, he threw his hand up. "And don't give me that cockamamie excuse of 'if I wasn't overseas bullshit'. The plain fact of the matter is that they were at the wrong place at the wrong time. Ain't no one to blame anymore than I can blame someone for the cancer that took your mama. And the idea that we can only love once in our lives? Where the hell did you get that?"

Tony knew better than to interrupt his father and if he was truthful with himself, he craved the words his father was giving him.

The older man leaned forward, his warm gaze holding his son's. "You and I loved good women. I got to have mine a helluva lot longer than yours. And I got to see my child become an adult. You got gypped out of both of those things. But son, that don't mean your life is over. You can love again and that don't take one goddamn thing away from what you and Marla had. You're a good man with a lot of love to give, if you'll just allow yourself to give it. It also means that you know a good thing when you find it."

The corners of Tony's mouth turned up slightly at the vehemence of his dad's words. *I know a good thing when I find it. I sure as hell do. And Sherrie is it.*

Nodding slowly, he added, "I needed to hear that, Dad. I knew it deep down inside, but I needed to hear it."

His father leaned his recliner back and settled in facing the game on the muted TV once again. "So, when am I gonna meet her?" he said with a smile.

"Soon I hope, dad. But first I gotta win her back." With that Tony stood and leaned over to embrace his father before letting himself out of the house. Feeling lighter than he had in years, he knew what he needed to do. Driving home he began to plan out his attack. Sherrie just became his new mission.

GABE, VINNY, AND JOBE met Tony at a small Mexican restaurant near their apartment complexes. Tony had sent out a meeting notice and the brothers-in-arms jumped to meet, no questions asked.

The three looked at their former commander and saw the familiar steely look of determination in his eyes.

"Captain, what's up?" Jobe asked.

Tony looked around at his friends, feeling uncomfortable. "Need some advice." He glanced at Vinny and joked, "Although I've got no idea why in the hell I had you come."

Leaning back, Vinny looked at him in surprise.

Jobe, laughing, just said, "Then it's gotta be advice about a woman."

Throwing his hand across his heart, Vinny declared, "Hell, Captain. I'm the man you want if you need advice on women. I got more experience than all of y'all put together."

Gabe rolled his eyes, saying, "Uh huh. And that's just why he doesn't need your advice. You can't keep one around long enough to know what the hell advice to give."

"I'll have you know, women leave my bed plenty satisfied. Haven't heard any complaints yet, bro," Vinny added.

Tony began to doubt his sanity in talking to his closest friends. *Hell, I shoulda kept this to myself.*

Jobe, seeing Tony's reticence, spoke up. "You know we're here for you, right Tony?"

The twins sobered at seeing the look on his face. "Is it Sherrie?" Gabe asked.

"Yeah. We finally hooked up at the cabin and I thought things were progressing. Then I started getting in my head, thinking about Marla and just when I knew it was okay to move on with my life, I said her name in my sleep and Sherrie heard."

"And she got pissed?" Vinny surmised.

"No, not at all," Tony admitted to the others, seeing the surprise on their faces. "She just interpreted it as my trying to replace Marla with her. So she walked away and like a dumb fuck, I let her. I need to get her back but have no idea how to do this."

The three friends silently watched Tony struggle with his emotions. They had watched their leader bury his grief in missions and getting the job done. And they had watched their friend shut out life. Now with the possibility that he was ready to move on with life, they were ready to do anything to help.

Tony rubbed his hand over his face, sighing loudly. "I married my college sweetheart right after graduation and with basic training, Officer Candidate School, and then Special Forces training, we weren't together all that much. We were young, in love, and willing to put up with the long distance marriage just to be married. And when she got pregnant, hell I thought I'd won the lottery."

His eyes stared off into the distance and his friends would not have interrupted him for anything. Tony talking about his feelings…they would protect them with their lives.

"The truth is that I don't know much about dating. Or women. Or how to fix things when they get fucked up. But Sherrie is worth me knowing what the hell I'm doing." His gazed leveled at them as he vowed, "She's worth it and by God, I'm going to get a second chance at living."

"Thank God," Gabe stated emphatically.

Vinny just leaned back, a shit-eating grin on his face. He did not see himself ever settling on one woman, but if that was what his Captain wanted then he would see it done.

"Flowers," Vinny declared. "That'll turn her into mush. Women love that shit."

Gabe popped his twin on the back of his head. "Yeah, this coming from the man who can't keep it in his pants for one woman."

"Hey," Vinny groused. "I've never met a woman who could stay pissed when they got flowers. Big ones. Real expensive and showy."

Tony looked dubious, saying, "I don't see Sherrie being impressed with a bouquet of flowers that some flower shop sent."

Gabe piped up, "Nah man. Do what I did to win Jennifer over. Jobe suggested I find out what was missing in her life and do that. Turned out it was just something for fun, so I took her out for a carriage ride."

Tony doubted that a carriage ride would make

Sherrie not doubt his feelings for her. He glanced over at Jobe, usually the voice of reason.

"Once again, you all stagger me in your ignorance of women," Jobe said, shaking his head. "My family had very little money growing up and I never doubted the love between my mother and father. Still don't, for that matter." Looking at Vinny, he declared, "Flowers can be a nice gesture but they sure as shit don't mean anything without the words behind them."

Looking at Gabe, he admitted, "You did good by giving Jennifer something just for fun, but that's not Sherrie. She'd doubting Tony and probably even herself."

Vinny, throwing back his beer, said, "Okay genius, what's your solution? If you're so wise, let's hear it."

Jobe looked Tony in the eyes and asked, "Do you love her?"

Vinny snorted as Gabe jerked his head around to peer closely at Tony also.

"Yes," Tony clipped, not wasting any time in answering.

"Have you told her yet?" Jobe continued.

Shaking his head, Tony admitted, "No. I honestly wasn't sure until today but there's no doubt in my mind that I do."

"Then it's simple," Jobe declared. "Tell her. Honesty is what Sherrie craves. She's been used and lied to before. All she needs is simple honesty."

Gabe agreed, saying, "I think Jobe's right."

Vinny lifted his eyebrows in question but wisely kept quiet. He knew that just because he had no desire to settle down with one woman, if his friend was in love then he was happy for him.

Tony, deep in thought, slowly nodded. "She hasn't had a lot of honesty. First, being bounced around foster families, then trying to keep Charisse out of trouble. The gang her sister was involved in lied to Sherrie to keep her from turning them in to the authorities. She's learned to guard herself to try from getting hurt."

"Then that's it, man," Jobe prodded. "She's not looking for you to buy her anything. She doesn't need jewelry, flowers, expensive dinners. She just needs you…and to know that you are giving yourself to her. You love her, Captain? You gotta tell her."

Throwing down the last of his beer, Tony shoved his chair back. Tossing some bills on the table, he said, "Thanks guys. Buy another round on me. I've got somewhere I need to be." With that he walked out of the restaurant, feeling the smiles of his men following him out of the door.

SHERRIE SAT PROPPED in bed, her Kindle resting on her knees as she tried to read. *It's no use trying to fall in love with the characters in my novel when all I can see in my mind is Tony.* She sighed, tossing her Kindle to her nightstand.

Turning out the light, she slid down under the covers, pulling them up to her chin hoping to keep warm. Closing her eyes, she hoped she could sleep without dreaming of a tall, gorgeous man with caramel eyes.

Loud knocking sounded and she jerked up. Glancing at the clock, she saw it was after midnight. The knocking sounded again and she jumped out of bed, grabbing a blanket as she made her way to the door. Peeking through the peep-hole, her heart beat loudly as she recognized the man of her thoughts.

Unlocking the door, she opened it then immediately shivered as the cold wind rushed in. Jumping back, she ordered, "Hurry, get in." She wrapped the blanket around her shivering body.

Tony stepped in quickly, his hand on her stomach pushing her backward as he kicked the door closed with his boot. Looking down he took in her sleep tousled hair, flowered pajamas wrapped in a soft, green blanket, and as his gaze lowered he saw pink fuzzy socks peeking out from the bottom. *Fuckin' adorable. And mine.*

Her surprised expression morphed into concern. "Tony, what's wrong? Why are you here so late?"

"We need to talk," he said simply, taking her hand and leading her over to the sofa. Sitting, he pulled her down onto his lap. Her hands came up and pressed against his chest, but he protested, "Oh no, baby girl. I want you right here."

"Humph," she groused. "Maybe I don't want to be

this close while we're talking."

"Baby, I'd give you just about anything you wanted, but right now we're playing this my way. I got stuff to clear up and I want you close, not pulling away."

Pursing her lips, she stilled her hands, letting them drop into her lap, not willing to have them be tempted to hold tightly on to him. Lifting her eyes, she peered deeply into his face wondering what needed to be said in the middle of the night. *Please, no more heartache, Tony. I can't take it.*

Tony, no longer unsure of his feelings, jumped in quickly. "I've fucked things up between us and I'm here to unfuck them."

She blinked slowly, not sure she understood what he was saying. *Unfuck them?* She had no idea what he was talking about but a sliver of hope peeked in her heart.

"You were partially right at the cemetery. I did love Marla and when she and Sofia died, I died with them. I planned on staying single the rest of my life 'cause I figured I had loved once and something like that just can't come along more than once in a lifetime. But I was wrong. I've been fighting my feelings for you since I first saw you and when we finally got together up in the mountains, I was willing to go all the way with you. Then it all got fucked up when you heard me say her name in my sleep. But baby, it wasn't what you thought."

He ducked his head so that he peered directly into

her eyes, checking to make sure she was understanding. What he saw was confusion and…doubt. *How do I get her to understand?*

"Tony—"

"No, babe. You gotta let me finish."

She nodded, sucking her lips in, looking at his anguished expression.

Satisfied, he continued. "I had a dream that night and yes, Marla was in it. But baby, you have to believe me. She was letting me go, knowing that I was ready. As much as I had feelings for you, there was still the past holding me back. But that night, Sherrie babe, she told me to be happy with you."

She sucked in a gasp, tears stinging the back of her eyes, as she watched the emotions play across his face. She lifted a hand, cupping his strong jaw, the rough stubble underneath her fingertips. His black hair looking as though he had been running his hands through it continuously. And those caramel eyes. Warm. Full of emotion.

Finally, she's getting it. Giving a tenuous smile, he said, "Baby, you're no replacement. I've loved and lost. But if I'm lucky enough to find love again, then I'm grabbing it for all it's worth and hanging on."

"You…you've found love again?" she asked, her voice shaky.

A smile slowly curved his lips as he leaned in for a kiss. The soft touching of lips. The gentle promise of a future. "Yeah, Sherrie. I love you." Touching her lips again, he leaned back saying, "Please tell me I'm not too late. Please say I still have a chance with you."

Her answer was to grasp both of his cheeks pulling him in for a kiss. This one full of understanding. Forgiveness. Then morphing into passion.

After a moment of letting her lead, he took over the kiss, angling her head for better access. Plunging his tongue deep inside her warm mouth, he tasted her mint toothpaste as he plundered every crevice. Feeling something wet on his hands, he leaned back seeing tears sliding from her blue eyes over his fingers.

Wiping her cheeks with the rough pads of his thumbs, he whispered, "Baby, don't cry. Please don't cry."

Standing suddenly with her in his arms, she squealed as he headed back toward the stairs. Taking them two at a time, his precious load held tightly to his chest, he made his way into her bedroom, setting her down by letting her body slide slowly along his front. Pulling the blanket from her shoulders he let it drop to the floor. He smiled as he saw her flowered, flannel pajamas and little pink socks. *How the hell can a woman look so sexy covered head to toe?*

His hands went to the buttons at her neck, slipping them loose until the top gapped opened and a hint of cleavage peeked through. Placing his hands on the soft material at her shoulders, it took little movement to have the shirt and bottoms in a flannel pile at her feet. With a quick lift, he lay her on her back, her breasts bouncing with the motion. His dick, already pressing into his jeans, was straining, leaving him to wonder if his zipper was leaving a permanent mark.

The smile on her face tugged at his heartstrings as he divested himself of his clothes as quickly as he could. Finally out of its constraints, his cock stood at attention as he ran his fist up and down its length. He knelt on the floor pulling her fuzzy covered feet toward him. Sliding her socks off, he placed a kiss on each instep.

She raised up on her elbows and watched this huge, handsome man kiss her feet and she could not contain the giggle that erupted. "I'm ticklish," she gasped, but then his mouth began to move higher and her mirth ended as her core clenched in anticipation.

Kissing her inner thighs he grasped her panties, dragging them down and tossing them into the pile of discarded clothes on the floor. Moving up again, he pulled her legs over his shoulders as he moved his lips to the prize.

With the flat of his tongue, he laved her moist folds, memorizing the taste of her. *I want this. Every night. Forever.* Plunging his tongue in, he grinned as she jumped, jerking her hips off of the bed. "Easy babe, we got all night," he said, voice like gravel.

Moving up, he latched onto her clit while moving a finger deep inside, crooking it as it hit the spot that he had been aiming for. The one that he knew would throw her over the edge. With one last suck, he was not disappointed as she screamed his name and he felt her hot sex clench his finger as he continued to move his tongue around her clit prolonging the orgasm until she fell boneless back onto the bed.

Gasping for air, she moaned, "Oh God, Tony. You're going to kill me." A giggle erupted as he kissed his way up her body. "Death by orgasm," she laughed.

"Is that such a bad way to go?" he joked, as he made his way to her breasts, latching onto one rosy nipple.

"Ummm," was her only response.

After rolling on a condom he grabbed her hands in his, pulling them over her head, exposing her beautiful body to his perusal. Moving his straining cock to her entrance, he looked down at her expectant face.

"Tell me what you want, baby," he ordered, teasing her sex with the head of his cock.

"I want you. Now," she answered, her breasts heaving with each pant.

Dipping his lips to hers, he whispered, "My pleasure," before plunging his dick into her hot, tight sex and his tongue into her warm mouth.

Moving both in rhythm, he started slowly, his dick stretching her as it hit every nerve along the way. In and out, dragging along her inner walls as the friction drove her to distraction. He moved his tongue along her neck, sucking on the tender area at the base where her pulse throbbed.

Her hands wrapped around his back as her legs entwined around his waist, opening herself up more.

She felt the power of his muscles underneath her fingertips as they moved over the ridges as they flexed with each stroke.

"More. Harder," she moaned as the friction built to a crescendo. She squeezed her eyes shut as the world around her fell away, feeling only the rocking of her body as he powered into her. She could tell she was close and suddenly felt his dick swell even larger inside.

Tony watched as her perfect teeth bit into her bottom lip, her head thrown back against the mattress as he felt his balls tighten.

"Open your eyes. I wanna see you when you come," he ordered. Her eyes popped open in obedience, their blue orbs focusing on his. Her plump lips were smiling as he felt her inner walls began to clench on his dick. Reaching down, he tweaked her clit and watched with satisfaction as she screamed his name again, feeling her milk his cock.

She watched as his normally staid expression changed as his orgasm rocked through him. With his head thrown back, she watched as the veins stood out on his neck as he powered through his orgasm. *Love. He loves me.*

He dropped his head on the mattress beside hers, as he tried to catch his breath. Rolling to the side, he pulled her along with him to keep from crushing her. Their sweat-slicked bodies cooled slowly as their heartbeats continued to pound.

Pushing her hair from her face, he watched her as

her breathing slowed. *I never thought I would have this again.* After a few seconds her eyes opened and focused lazily back at him, a slow smile crossing her face.

"Hey, you," she said sleepily.

"Hey back," he added, tucking her in tightly as he pulled the covers up over them, not wanting her to become chilled.

She drifted off to sleep, sated from sex and safe in the knowledge that he was finally here to stay. *He loves me,* she thought once again.

Tony watched her smile slowly fade away as the peace of sleep overtook her. He waited to see if the familiar tug of guilt was coming. But it did not. And for the first time in over five years, he fell into a dreamless, peaceful slumber.

CHAPTER 14

IN THE BACK of an unmarked, panel van, Gabe and Jobe sat watching the exterior of Quentin Salazar's office. The run-down apartment building attached was a hive of young people coming and going.

"He runs this dive and is able to live in the big ass house he has?" Jobe asked.

"Uh huh," Gabe grunted. "I can see why the police are looking into him. Gotta be running money through somewhere."

Jobe's eyes raised to the building next to the van. "This work for you?"

Gabe's gaze followed Jobe's. "Yeah, it's as good as any."

They moved out of the van, walking to the old, brick building across from Quentin's office and quickly made their way to the roof. The building was only three stories tall, making it perfect for the cameras they were installing. Affixing them to the edge of the roof, camouflaged by the slight overhang, they worked efficiently.

"Wish we could get inside his office." Jobe said.

"We may still be able to do something, but honestly? If we get enough visual intel, Matt may be able to get a search warrant for this guy's place."

Finishing, they glanced down as a black BMW pulled up to the front curb and watched as their suspect stepped out. Barking out warnings to the teens on the sidewalk, he moved into his building.

Noticing the teens did not lurk around, Jobe commented, "He must put the fear of God in them to keep them away from that ride of his."

Gabe nodded before answering thoughtfully, "Or the fear of something."

Finished with the installation, they called BJ to make sure the live video feed was working. Getting the all-clear from him, they moved back to the van and headed to the office to report to Tony.

SEVERAL DAYS PASSED before Sherrie tried to contact Betina again. Her text went unanswered and she finally called, but it went straight to voicemail. Walking out of her office, she went in to see Mr. Marks.

Smiling up at her, the elderly lawyer leaned back in his squeaky desk chair as he nodded for her to have a seat in one of his old, comfortable leather seats. She could not help but smile back as she commented on his furniture.

He patted the arms of his antique, wooden chair and said, "I know you've been after me to get new furniture like Simon has in his office, but I just can't make myself do it. This chair was in this office thirty-seven years ago when I first became a lawyer and old Mr. Owens took me in as a partner. I tried a new padded desk chair once when my wife came in and declared that she couldn't see how I could take the squeaking. Funny," he said as his gaze drifted away in memories, "but I never noticed the squeak. And I just couldn't get used to the new-fangled thing. It had more gears on the side than my first car. Went up, down, back, tilted. Damn near threw myself out of it one day, so I gave it to our receptionist."

Sherrie laughed at his reminiscing, then sobered as she realized he had been doing that a lot lately. Pulling her lips in, she wanted to ask him if everything was all right but hesitated, not sure she wanted to know the answer.

He looked at her thoughtfully for a moment. "You always were astute, Sherrie. You would have made an excellent lawyer."

Smiling at the compliment, she shrugged, saying, "It wasn't in the cards, Mr. Marks. But that's okay. I'm happy doing what I'm doing and I have to admit that the CASA work is very satisfying."

"Well, I know you didn't come in here to have me go on and on about office furniture. What's on your mind?"

"I don't want my work as a CASA volunteer to interfere with my duties here and that is why I have only made visits with Simon or after my hours here. But I'd really like to visit with Betina today and wondered if you would mind if I took extra time on my lunch break to do that?"

"Sherrie, you are one of the hardest working employees I have ever known and you never need to ask if you can have some extra time. But, as far as your CASA work, consider that on the clock. You are working for a child and as far as I am concerned that can easily be included in your duties here. Simon is working pro-bono on her case for DSS and that makes her part of your work. So take the time that you need and don't worry about anything."

Smiling her relief, she stood as she thanked him. Stopping at the door she turned, a question in her expression. "Mr. Marks? Are you all right?"

"Never better, my dear. I'm just an old man who enjoys his memories at times."

Nodding, she left his office but the feeling of gloom hung over her. Stopping by Simon's office, she popped in to tell him that she was heading to Betina's house for an interview. Getting his approval, she headed out of the door.

Arriving at the girl's house, she realized that Betina was still at school, but hoped to have a chance to talk to her mother. She was not disappointed when Marcella answered the door and invited her in once she had introduced herself.

Settling on the sofa, she glanced around quickly.

The small house was simply furnished, but everything was neat and clean. A few pictures on the wall showed a smiling child that she recognized as Betina at a younger age. Looking back at Marcella, she was an older version of the girl; Betina's beautiful looks were from her mother.

"I'm just checking to see how the transition has gone. How have things been since Betina came back home?"

"She's a good girl," Marcella said defensively.

"Oh, I know she is. Ms. Rodriguez, I'm not here to take her away again. I'm just checking to see how she's doing. Has she seemed glad to be back?"

Marcella looked around nervously, "She's quiet. Always been. Stays in her room a lot when she's not at school or working."

"I didn't realize she had a job. Where does she work?"

"For my husband. He has a shop and was good enough to hire her."

Sherrie knew that the man referred to as her husband was not legally Betina's stepdad since they were not married, but if Marcella wished to call him that she was not going to object.

"When does Betina usually get home from work?"

"She closes the shop with him, so about ten at night."

Looking up from her notepad, Sherrie tried to keep the irritation out of her voice, saying, "That seems rather late for her to get in. When does she get her homework done?"

Marcella's forehead crinkled as a confused look crossed her face. "She gets it done. Her grades are good," she said defensively.

"I'm sure she does," Sherrie added, deciding she would gain more information if Betina's mother were less defensive. "Can I take a look at her room?"

Marcella stood and led her to a small room behind the kitchen. It was simply furnished with a twin bed and dresser. It could have been any teen's room, but Sherrie would have known it anywhere. The walls were filled with drawings. Faces. In laughter. In sadness. In thought. The expressions that came from the drawings were so lifelike that Sherrie sucked in a deep breath in awe.

"They're beautiful. She is so talented," she gushed, not able to contain her admiration.

For the first time since entering the home, Marcella smiled in return. "She is good. Her teacher says she has talent. I don't know where she got it from. I don't draw at all."

"Maybe her father?"

A shadow passed over Marcella's face. "I don't know. He never had time to draw. He worked all the time before he died." Giving a little shrug, she turned to walk back to the living room. Sherrie took one last look around at Betina's talent before following her mother.

"I'd like to visit Betina," she said glancing at her watch. "I suppose school is over now. Can you give me the address where she works and I will visit her there?"

Jotting down the location, Sherrie stood and thanked Marcella. "I hope things work out and that Betina continues to do well. I will keep tabs on her for a while until her last court appearance." With that, she walked out and made her way down the street to the address she was given.

The neighborhood was old and slightly run down. Passing the school, she wished she had planned on talking to one of her teachers but knew that would need to wait until another time. Glancing at the school, she saw a group of young students and recognized Betina with them. She started to call out her name then hesitated, knowing that teens are often embarrassed. She walked over not wanting to intrude, hoping to catch her when her conversation was ended.

Betina was passing out cards to the other kids and Sherrie heard her say, "You can get free food here. Don't go hungry, just come by and show this card to the manager. He'll make sure you get something to eat."

As the kids wandered away, Betina turned and immediately blushed when she saw Sherrie. *That's an odd reaction.* Walking over, Sherrie greeted her and Betina returned her hug.

"What are you doing here?" the young teen asked, glancing around nervously.

"I came to see you. I've been at your house talking to your mom," Sherrie answered, noting Betina's wide eyed look. "She showed me your room and I have to say that I'm even more impressed with your talent."

Betina's face relaxed into a shy smile as she accepted the compliment. The smile left as quickly as it came as she looked at her watch. "I've got to get to work."

"I'll walk with you and you can show me the store."

Betina's expression gave Sherrie the impression that seeing where she worked was the last thing Betina wanted. Smiling, Sherrie threw out her arm saying, "Lead the way."

Without a choice, Betina began to walk down the street with Sherrie right in step. A few blocks away, they came to a grocery store. Upon entering, Sherrie noticed that a couple of the kids from the school were talking to a man behind a counter to the right. As his eyes lit upon Betina, he shouted angrily, "Did you make more contacts today?"

Betina's eyes darted to the side and Sherrie noticed that the man's eyes landed on her just then too. His angry visage disappeared behind a small scowl before a smile took its place. Coming from behind the counter, the man made his way toward them, greeting Betina with a hug.

"Betina, who is your lovely friend?" he asked, keeping his arm around the young woman.

"She's my CASA worker," came the soft answer.

"Your what?" he asked, his gaze darting between

Betina and Sherrie.

Stepping up, Sherrie extended her hand toward him, explaining, "Court Appointed Special Advocate. The judge in her case has assigned me to keep an eye on Betina, making sure her rights are being protected in court. I'm Sherrie Mullins and you are…?"

"Hernando Valesquez, her stepfather," he said smoothly. "Did you come to see where she works?"

"Yes, I did. You have a lovely store here, Mr. Valesquez. May I look around and perhaps shop a little?"

"Of course. Betina, show Ms. Mullins around." With that he moved back to the counter, continuing his conversation with the three teens.

As she and Betina walked around the aisles, she noticed that most of the workers eyed her suspiciously. *Or is that just my overactive imagination.* Glancing behind the butcher counter, she was surprised to see two young, teen boys handling the meat cutters. "They seem rather young to be working in the butcher section," she commented.

Betina's lips were tight and Sherrie noticed that her eyes continually cut over to Hernando. Wanting to prolong her visit, Sherrie grabbed a basket and began filling it with a few items as they walked. Moving to the bakery, she once again noticed very young girls working behind the counters with only one adult supervising. The woman's white uniform was pulled tightly over her large breasts and Sherrie noted the fearful look thrown her way.

"I saw some of the kids you were talking to after school up front. Do they get some free food from here?" she asked, her curiosity overflowing after seeing the teens walk out with several bags of groceries.

"Um, yeah," came the noncommittal answer.

"So, do you like working for your...Mr. Valesquez?" she queried.

"It's okay," came Betina's clipped response along with a shoulder shrug.

"Well, your mom said that you work a lot, so I guess it's nice to make some money isn't it? Are you saving for anything special?"

Sherrie could have sworn she saw a sheen of unshed tears in the young woman's eyes, before a mask of indifference fell into place.

"I've really got to get to work," Betina said, looking down at her shoes.

"Of course. I'm sorry, honey. I've taken up too much of your time," Sherrie said sincerely.

Betina's head jerked up, her eyes landing on Sherrie's. "No. No. Please come see me again sometime." The words rushed out of Betina's mouth as she threw her arms around Sherrie.

Hugging her in return, Sherrie promised she would. Walking to the cash register, she once again noted the stiff posture of the cashier who seemed to hurry the process along.

Once outside, Sherrie began walking to her car that

was still parked several blocks over. As she passed an alley, she noticed the teens with the bags of food. They had the food out and were devouring it quickly, as though they had not had a decent meal in a while. Seeing her, they quickly hustled further down the alley.

Climbing into her car, Sherrie rubbed her head as the headache that had been building began to pound. Overflowing with conflicting thoughts, she pulled out her pad and pen and began writing. It was the only way she could organize her observations as her CASA training had instructed.

She wrote about the teens receiving free food, the young age of the workers, and the change in Betina's personality at work and when she was alone with Sherrie. Her mother seemed to care and while Mr. Valesquez gave her a bad vibe, his actions had been nothing but good. *Is Betina just a troubled teen, who is rebelling from the rules in her home?* Determined to report the absolute truth to the judge the next month, she vowed to keep an eye on Betina's situation. *Something's just not right.*

TONY SAT IN his office, looking over the requests for private security. He had determined after the fiasco with a Hollywood starlet and Gabe months ago that Alvarez Security would no longer provide ongoing private security, although it was lucrative. His company did very well with the security systems they installed and monitored, as well as the occasional private security detail.

"Hey, Tony," came a soft voice from the doorway.

He looked up, smiling at Lily before nodding to the chair in front of his desk. "What's up?" he asked.

"I just wanted to know how things were going." She blushed before rushing on, "I know it's none of my business but Sherrie is a friend and well…you seem…happy today."

"I'm not usually happy?" he said dryly, trying to keep the corners of his mouth from turning up.

Rolling her eyes, Lily just smirked. "Uh, no boss. You don't usually have a goofy grin on your face."

"A goofy grin?" came another voice from the doorway. Gabe came in uninvited, but since Tony had an open door policy he could hardly keep anyone out.

"Who's got a goofy grin?" Vinny asked, walking in on the heels of his twin, with BJ right behind.

Looking at Lily, Tony quipped, "You couldn't have just come in to ask about the weather?"

"Sorry, Tony," she said with a smile. "But honestly, we just want to see you happy."

"Things are going well, thank you."

"Hell, Captain. That's not much of an answer," Gabe exclaimed. "What the hell am I supposed to tell Jennifer when she asks?"

"You telling me you don't think your wife hasn't already called Sherrie to see what is going on?"

Gabe ducked his head in embarrassment. "Yeah, she might have said something like that."

Jobe strolled in, overhearing the conversation. "You all are acting like a bunch of women," then quickly added, "Present company excepted, of course," looking at Lily.

"Well, I don't mind asking. Are you and Sherrie a couple now?" Lily countered.

Tony looked at the friends in his office, the ones he considered to be in his inner circle. His company had grown and there were numerous employees, but his former military brothers along with BJ and Lily were squarely in the friend category. And he knew they cared.

Nodding, he smiled and said, "Yes. Sherrie and I are together. And she decided to throw a party next weekend for our friends to celebrate with us. Y'all are all invited. Spouses too, of course."

Lily stood, turning to walk toward the door. Stopping, she glanced back over her shoulder with a huge smile on her beautiful face. "I'm excited for you Tony. I can't think of anyone who deserves to be happy more." With that, she and BJ left his office, leaving him with his three brothers-in-arms.

"Captain, it goes without saying but I'm gonna say it anyway. Lily's right—you deserve all the happiness in the world and we all think Sherrie is awesome for you," Jobe said, as Gabe and Vinny agreed.

Taking a deep breath, Tony nodded at his former

squad, knowing they had all been with him in his darkest hour. Now it was time for them to celebrate a new beginning.

"Okay, time for business," he drawled, motioning for the others to sit down. "I've been looking over the requests that are coming in and business is so good that we are at a point of picking and choosing what jobs we take." Glancing up at Gabe, he continued, "I know we are in agreement about no long-term security service contracts, but we have several for just one-time events or escorts."

"Got any actresses or hot female musicians?" Vinny asked, only partially joking.

Tony smiled, acknowledging, "I might have something that I think will be just down your alley, but I'm still negotiating."

"Hot damn, just what I've been waiting for," he quipped.

Tony knew Vinny's reputation with women involved consensual sex only...no strings, no complications, and rarely repeat performances. *Yeah Vinny, I may have just the job for you.* Moving on, the men discussed the upcoming security details, outlining what resources were needed.

"Jobe, anything new on those missing girls?"

Jobe shook his head in frustration. "Like they just disappeared. No one at the bus or train stations remembers them. We've checked with local schools to see if they recognized them, in case they tried to register. We looked into homeless shelters and checked with DSS."

Tony nodded. "I knew it would be a long shot, but write up what you have and I'll report to the grandparents."

Jobe looked up sharply. "Sir, I'm not giving up yet."

With the next few weeks planned out, the meeting ended. As the men filed out, they each shared a look with Tony, words unspoken. Looks of understanding. Looks of support. Tony sat for a few more minutes in his office, his surroundings the same but his feelings completely different. Instead of working until late to keep from going home to a bland, lonely apartment he could not wait to get to Sherrie.

Pulling out his cell, he called her number.

"Hi, sweetie," she greeted. "What's up?"

"I just wanted to hear your voice," he admitted honestly.

A giggle was heard from the other end of the line, shooting straight to his heart. "I think I like that," she said. "A big, strong man calling just to hear me."

"Well, it's the truth. How's your day going? You gonna be home on time?"

"It's been really weird, to be honest. Can we talk about it tonight? I've got a little more to do here in the office and then I want to take a quick drive to check out something, but I'll be home about the same time you are."

"You want me to pick up some take-out on the way to your house?"

"No, I threw some chili in the crockpot before leaving this morning. It's been slow cooking for hours and will be the perfect way to end a cold, winter day."

"I've got a better way to end a cold, winter day," he said.

His warm promise slid over her, immediately causing her nipples to pucker as well as her inner core to clench. "Oooh, promise?"

"You got it, baby," he vowed. Hanging up, he found that just talking on the phone with her and the promise of a perfect evening had his cock twitching. *Down boy, we've still got some work to do.*

SHERRIE HAD BEEN sitting at her desk, going over the report that she had typed on Betina's situation. She could face the possibility that the young teen had run away because of rebellion, but it did not fit the girl she had come to know.

When she had discussed it with Simon earlier, he warned her that as a CASA she would need to be non-biased in her dealings. Question everything, he had said. *Something is just not right, but I'll be dammed if I know what it is.*

She tried a quick internet search on Hernando Valesquez, but all that came up was information about his store and the few other businesses that he managed. *Other businesses?* Deciding to drive by to just check them out, she said her goodbyes to the others in the law office and headed to her car.

Driving back to Betina's neighborhood, she went passed the grocery store. It was only five p.m. but already getting dark. She could see activity inside the store, and knew it would be open for several more hours. Using her GPS, she drove a few blocks away to the next address, that of a laundry facility that Mr. Valesquez's managed. It appeared to be closing, but she could see lights on in the back and someone was just locking the doors. Parking in a well-lit area, she jogged over to the door and knocked loudly.

A tall, lanky teenager stood on the other side of the glass door, calling out, "We're closed. Come back tomorrow."

She hated yelling through the door, but wanted to make sure she had the right place. "Is this laundry owned by Mr. Hernando Valesquez?" The eyes of the teen grew large and he backed away from the door. "Do I have the right place?" she shouted once again.

"No speak good English. Come back tomorrow," he called before turning and running to a door behind the counter. With a quick slam of the door, the light that had come through was shut out and she knew that continuing to stand there would be pointless.

Giving a quick glance around she noted the deserted street, but was glad for the bright lights of the parking lot. Moving quickly to her car, she got in and drove down the street. A couple of blocks away, she came across the next business belonging to Hernando, but is also appeared to be closed, as were all the businesses on this street.

Coming to a dead end, she was about to turn around when a young man ran down the street, waving his arms.

"Can you help me?" he shouted.

Jumping from her car, she heard running steps from behind and before she could turn around, she was slammed forward into the car.

A large, strong body pressed up against hers, trapping her against the cold metal with her face pressed into the glass. She tried to scream but a large hand clapped over her mouth.

"Whatever you're doing here, bitch, you need to stay the fuck away," the gravelly voice commanded.

This was no teen; this was a man's voice. The teen was just a diversion. She tried to gasp for air but his thick fingers pressed against her mouth and nose. Her legs grew weak as fear and lack of oxygen made her faint. Realizing what was happening, he moved his hand from her nose while keeping her mouth covered. Inhaling deeply through her nose, her mind began to clear enough for her to feel the cold, metal blade of a knife pressing into the side of her neck.

"Keep your goddamn mouth shut or I'll slice your throat," he growled. He moved his hand from her mouth and grabbed her left arm twisting it cruelly behind her.

Agonizing pain sliced through her shoulder as she was sure it dislocated. Feeling faint again, she thought of Tony. *I'm going to die and he'll be alone again;* the thought cut through her fear.

"Don't know what the fuck you're looking for, but stay away and keep quiet. You don't, next time I'll be happy to slice you up. After I have some fun," he laughed. Pressing tighter against her, she felt his erection against her ass.

"No," she whimpered. Pain and fear had her sliding down the door, but his hand moved from her front to the middle of her back.

"Count to twenty bitch before you leave. And re-member to keep your goddamn mouth shut. Or maybe someone you care about will get hurt." With that, she suddenly felt the cold on her back, telling her that he had moved away.

After a few seconds, she managed to get her car door open and fell inside. She knew it was only a matter of seconds before the pain in her shoulder had her passing out again, so she grabbed her cell phone. Slumping over, the last thing she managed to do was dial 911.

CHAPTER 15

T URNING INTO SHERRIE'S DRIVEWAY, Tony was
disappointed to see that her car was not there yet.
Amazed at how quickly she had acclimated into his life,
he could not wait to see her. *And if our after-dinner
plans turn out the way I think they will, then—*

His cell rang and he grabbed it out of his pocket on
his way toward the front door hoping it would be her.
Seeing **Matt**, he connected, although disappointed.

"Tony, you gotta get to the hospital. Richland
General. Sherrie's here. She was attacked."

He felt his legs go weak, stumbling as he turned
and ran back down the front steps. *Oh, Jesus. Not again.*
Twenty heart-wrenching minutes later, he pounded
through the doors to the ER and was met by Matt.
Vinny, Gabe and Jennifer came in right after him.

"Where is she?" he bit out.

"She's back here. I'll fill you in as we go."

Matt told him about the call to 911 and what he
knew so far.

"What the hell was she doing there anyway?" Tony
asked.

"She said she was trying to check out some of the

businesses that her CASA child's stepfather owns."

As they arrived at the ER room, the doctor was just coming out. Assuming Tony was another policeman, the doctor reported the extent of her injuries. "She has a pulled shoulder that we've given her a sling to keep immobile, as well as some bruising around the face where her assailant held his hand over her mouth."

His knees weak again, Tony barely noticed when Gabe and Vinny moved to either side of him. "Can I see her?"

"I don't think she's up for any questioning now that she is on pain meds. She'll be ready to check out soon, once someone comes to take her home." With that the doctor moved back down the hall.

Taking a deep breath, Tony strode into the ER bay, then halted as soon as his gaze landed on his woman in the bed. Faint bruises were around her mouth and nose and her arm was in a sling. Her eyes were shut but the purple shadows were evident. A strangled sound came from his mouth, causing her eyes to jerk open.

A sloppy grin split her face as she greeted him. "Tony? Dish you come fer me? Ooooh, you brought some friensh?" she said, looking past him at Jennifer and the other men.

Crossing the room, Tony leaned over to place a kiss on her forehead, saying, "Yeah, I came for you, baby. What the hell happened?"

Her large blue eyes teared as she tried to focus on his face. "You're mad at me," she wailed.

"Tony," Jennifer admonished, moving close to her friend. Grabbing Sherrie's hand, she leaned down and said, "Oh, honey, he's not mad. He's just scared for you."

Sherrie's tears dried up as quickly as they had come, replaced by the sloppy smile once more. Looking up at Tony, she pulled his head closer and tried to whisper, "You gonna spring me from thish joint?"

He rolled his eyes as the others behind him tried to hide their smiles.

"She like this when she's drunk?" Vinny asked, as Jennifer shooed the men out of the room so that she could help Sherrie dress.

While outside, Matt showed Tony the report as he had it. "She was in a lot of pain when she came in and we didn't get a lot. Shane and I'll come by tomorrow to get the rest of her statement, if that's okay."

Tony nodded and gave them Sherrie's address. Saying goodbye to his friends, he went back in to take her home. With some difficulty, he managed to get her to lay in the back seat while he drove them to her house. Picking her up carefully, he carried her inside and up the stairs to the bedroom without her waking. Laying her down on the bed, he quickly stripped her skirt and shoes off, sliding soft flannel pajama bottoms on. Pulling the covers up, he made sure she looked comfortable before going back downstairs to secure the house.

Coming back out of the bathroom, he stood over

the bed and watched her sleep in a blissful, drug-induced slumber. Rubbing his hand over his face, he tried to still the pounding of his heart. *What did she stumble into? She wasn't robbed. Was she about to come across a crime scene and was warned off? That part of town isn't great, but it's not too bad either.*

His hand squeezed the back of his neck as a tension headache built. Forcing himself to breathe deeply, he slid under the covers on the side away from her injured shoulder. Grateful that she was not hurt worse than she was, he vowed to find whoever threatened his woman. *No one does this and gets away with it.*

She moaned in her sleep and he repositioned himself to try to make her as comfortable as possible. Knowing sleep would be impossible, he nonetheless wrapped himself around her, protecting her as much as he could, even if for tonight it was just in her dreams.

"GUYS, I KNOW I'M no help, but honestly I didn't see anything," Sherrie said, leaning back on the sofa with Tony's arm draped around her. Wearing pink pajamas and a pink flannel robe, she felt self-conscious. But Tony had insisted she be ready for bed as soon as the group meeting was over. She fingered her sling, feeling useless and angry at herself for being a victim.

Shane, taking notes, just nodded as he prodded, "Anything you give us, even tiny details, can help."

Sucking in a deep breath through her nose and

letting it out slowly to clear her mind, she agreed. Tony had wanted her to take more pain medicine this morning when they woke up, but knowing that their friends were coming she had refused. At least until she could give her statement.

Matt and Shane were there officially, but had been joined by the Alvarez inner circle of BJ, Lily, Gabe, Jobe, and Vinny. Sherrie looked around, thinking how far her life had come in the past year. From being virtually alone to having good friends who cared…she sat up straighter, determined to give a good accounting of herself.

"When I visited Betina at her stepfather's store…actually I need to make sure to call him Mr. Valesquez because he's not her legal stepfather. When I visited Mr. Valesquez's store, everything seemed fine, although I got a strange vibe from everyone. As though they didn't want me there."

"Since you actually represent the court system as her CASA worker, do you think that vibe was just a distrust of your position?" Matt asked.

"Maybe," she said slowly, "but…you know when you just get a weird feeling about something? That was how I felt." Looking around, she admitted, "I guess that's sounds very flimsy, doesn't it?"

"Not at all. Those feelings of instinct are what make a good detective," Shane added. "So what gave you some of those feelings? What did you see? You can even just list things, if that makes it easier."

Sherrie closed her eyes and let her mind drift back to the previous day. "I noticed that a lot of the workers there were teens and some looked to be young teens. I noticed that some kids from Betina's school that she had said could get some food at the store, were there talking to Mr. Valesquez and he was giving them bags. I noticed that the ones running the butcher shop carvers were young boys, not men. I noticed that no one smiled at me. One of the women that was there would stare, but then when I would turn toward her, she would dart her eyes away." Opening her eyes, Sherrie blushed, saying, "I guess that's not much to go on, but when I left I decided to drive by a couple other business that he runs."

"Why?" Matt said, still jotting on his pad.

"I...it's just that...Betina doesn't seem happy. Not at home and not at work. Her teachers say that she is smart and artistic, and that while she is quiet, she also befriends the loners. I just wanted to know more about her and since Mr. Valesquez is a big part of her life since he lives with her mother, I wanted to know more about him."

After describing the encounter and threat in detail one more time, she was showing more signs of exhaustion.

"So you don't trust Valesquez, right?" Vinny asked, leaning forward with his forearms on his knees.

"I really don't. After years of dealing with the kind of people Charisse was involved with, I developed a sense about who might be untrustworthy. So I wanted to see if his other businesses hired a lot of teens and what those businesses looked like." She leaned back into Tony's embrace.

Before Tony could comfort her, she jerked forward again, wincing at the pain in her shoulder but ignoring it.

"I've seen the underbelly of this city. I've been there. I may have been in a normal family at birth but once my parents died, I knew what it was like to be at the mercy of others. Some great foster families and some not so great. I know what it's like to do anything and everything you can to keep peace in a family that you don't really belong to. I know what it's like to go into alleys, bars, or cheap motels to drag out my drunk, high sister out of trouble. And I've looked into the eyes of the ones that were pulling her under. I worked as a waitress in a strip bar, dealing with scum. I can look at someone and tell if they are lying, cheating, or just plain mean. And I've seen evil, even when it is hiding under layers of normal."

The group watched, mesmerized, as her chest heaved with exertion and her face a mask of pain. Reaching around to try to ease her shoulder, she slumped as the fight went out of her. "I can't give you a viable reason as to why I don't trust Hernando Valesquez, but I don't."

"Darlin', that's enough for me. I trust your instincts," Shane added, as Matt flipped his notebook shut.

Lily, quiet during the questioning spoke up, "BJ and I'll start a background check on him and his businesses and see what we can dig up."

Matt winked at his wife as the meeting broke up. Leaving Sherrie comfortably reclined on the sofa, Tony walked the group outside.

"We'll push the party back a week and give her a chance to heal more," he said. The others quickly agreed and promised to come. "I want to thank you all," he said haltingly, the emotion of having caring friends overtaking him. *How many times have I sat at meetings just like this when one of their women was threatened, without realizing how overwhelmed they were?* He rubbed his hand over his jaw, feeling the stubble, before pulling his hand through his dark hair, making the waves stick up.

The men nodded, understanding the emotions behind the words, and knowing he had been there for them.

Matt and Shane left in their vehicle, leaving Tony with his crew. Jennifer slid her arms around him, hugging him while Gabe clapped him on the back. "You know we're here for you and Sherrie. You need us, just call."

Jobe moved in next. "Captain, we got your back, and I mean both of you." Turning toward his truck, he stopped and looked over his shoulder. "Tony, no one deserves that good woman more than you. Happy for you, man."

Tony just nodded, not trusting his voice. His gaze wandered over to Vinny, the only one left in the driveway.

Vinny pulled him in for a man-hug complete with slaps on the back before admitting, "Never thought you'd fall in love again, Tony. Not that I didn't want you happy, 'cause I did. But seeing you with Sherrie...well, you both deserve to be happy with each other."

Tony chuckled, saying, "Don't tell me the great Vincent is going to break hearts all over Richland by looking for love?"

Throwing his blond head back, Vinny laughed. "You got no worries on that score, boss. There is still plenty of Vinny to go around. Haven't found the woman yet who can make me want to give up my ways." With that parting shot he left as well, leaving Tony standing in the driveway.

As he turned to head back into the house, a voice came from behind.

"Lot of activity goin' on over here."

Tony saw Bernard walking over from his yard. "Yes, sir. Sherrie had a little accident and our friends were just checking on her."

Bernard's eyebrows went up in surprise. "She okay? You all need anything?"

Tony smiled at the older man's concern. "Nah, we're good." He started to move back toward the porch steps, then called to Bernard's retreating back. "Bernard?" The older neighbor turned back around. "If you don't mind, keep an eye on Sherrie's place here. I don't expect anything, but just in case."

Bernard smiled and admitted, "Always do, son. I always do."

Tony acknowledged with a nod and jogged back into the living room. Sherrie had slid sideways on the sofa, her pain medication finally taking effect. He picked her up carefully, carrying her up the stairs to her bed. Lying her down gently, he once again pulled the covers over her. Stepping back, he finally allowed the emotions of the past twelve hours to sink in. *Too fuckin close. I was too fuckin' close to losing her. That's not happening,* he vowed. *Whether she was in the wrong place at the wrong time or someone specifically after her. Not happening.*

THE NEXT DAY, Sherrie had had enough of laying around and was glad when Tony went to work, even if he had declared that he was coming home early. Running the tub full of bubbles, she sank into the warm, scented water and tried to take her mind off the past day's events.

But the pull of her assault was too strong as she became pissed again. *Focus, Sherrie. Focus. Was there anything that tied it to Valesquez?*

No. The man didn't mention Betina, or Valesquez, or

anyone. Could I have just stumbled into the wrong place at the wrong time?

Determined to take her mind off her trauma, she popped in her ear buds and finally allowed the soft music to soothe her soul as the warm water soothed her body.

THAT MORNING, TONY asked Lily and BJ what they had found on Hernando Valesquez.

Lily's face openly showed her defeat as BJ growled, "So far nothing. He runs an ethnic grocery store, a convenience store a few blocks away, and has three laundry businesses. He pays his taxes, none of his employees have ever filed a complaint, and his bank accounts look like they have the normal deposits that you would expect to find with his businesses."

Lily continued, "The businesses are all very successful, but that doesn't show criminal activity either."

"Do you think that this might not be connected to him at all?" Vinny asked.

Tony sighed, the effects of two nights with little sleep starting to show. "I don't know. I don't want to assume that Sherrie has gotten herself unwittingly in the middle of something but, sure as hell don't want to ignore her instincts."

"We'll keep after it, boss," Lily vowed.

The meeting quickly ended after the assignments

were handed out and Tony headed back to his office. He finished a few items that needed attention before driving back to Sherrie's. She was determined to get through the day without pain medication and he wanted to make sure she was all right.

Letting himself into the house, he called out but received no answer. *She must be asleep.* Heading up the stairs, he found her in the bathtub, soaking in bubbles with headphones on. The memory of weeks earlier in the cabin when he saw her just like this washed over him. His dick jumped at the sight of her naked body, breasts peeking through the bubbles.

She opened her eyes and her smile lit his world.

Pulling the earbuds out, she softly called, "Hey, sweetie."

He walked over and knelt by the tub. The bruising around her mouth was faint, but the idea of some man with his hands on her nearly choked him with anger. Tamping down the fury, he forced his voice to sound as normal as possible. "You ready to get out, baby? I'll help you."

Placing his hands under her carefully, he stood pulling her warm, wet, naked body from the tub. Trying to tell his aching cock to behave, he placed her gently on the floor being careful of her shoulder as he wrapped her in a huge towel.

She glanced down at his crotch before lifting her gaze back to his. "Got something for me, sailor?" she joked.

"Baby, don't get any ideas. You're not ready for anything strenuous and you know it," he admonished.

Pouting, she whined, "Sweetie, I can just lay there and you can do whatever you want. I don't have to do anything to hurt my shoulder. And Tony…" she purred as her hand reached out to press against his swollen cock. "It would take my mind off of things."

"Sherrie…" he growled, but before he could object, she dropped the towel, presenting herself to him.

His breath caught in his chest, staring at her beauty. Her long, blonde hair was piled into a messy knot at the top of her head but, with a quick jerk on the clip, it tumbled down. Her breasts were full and the rosy nipples peeked between the blonde strands of hair. *How can someone so short have such long legs?* Her body was toned, with a perfect hourglass shape. His fingers clasped into a fist as he held onto his control by a thread.

She lifted her uninjured arm, placing her hand on his chest…right over his heart. "Tony," she whispered. "I need you."

That was all she had to say to break his control into a thousand pieces. Sweeping her into his strong arms once again, he stalked into the bedroom laying her gently on the comforter. Her naked body, still glistening with a few water droplets, captured his gaze.

Bending quickly, he pulled one nipple deeply into his mouth, teasing the rosy bud until it was tight with need. His fingers found the other one, tugging until it stood taut as the first. His lips found it as well, and he spent several minutes feasting on her breasts.

Her fingers moved through his hair, pulling him closer. When her shoulder gave a twinge of pain she tried to hide it, but was unsuccessful. He moved off of her but she quickly objected.

"I'll lay here keeping my left arm still, I promise. Just please, don't stop Tony. I couldn't bear it if you did."

"Woman, you make me go against everything I should be doing right now."

"Don't think. Just do," she cried, her need pulsing through her core.

Rising from the bed, he gently lifted her, placing her feet on the floor. She looked at him, but he silenced her unspoken question with a kiss.

Turning her so that she was facing the bed, he gently placed his hand on the middle of her back, saying, "Bend over baby. Put your good hand on the bed and I'll do the rest of the supporting."

Holding her carefully by the hips he entered her from behind, careful to move slowly. His erection pushed against every inner muscle feeling them grab and clutch. *Shit, I gotta keep this slow and controlled.* Years in the Special Forces had taught him control and he reached down deep inside to maintain that control as his body fought to pound into her tight sex.

Slowly, torturously, he moved in and out, both feeling every inch of their body's connection. Looking down to make sure her injured arm was protected, he kept his strong arms around her to keep her from bearing too much weight on her good arm.

In just a few moments, he felt her inner muscles begin to clamp down on his aching dick as she panted, "Tony, I…need…"

Still holding her with one hand, he moved his other hand to her clit, swollen with need. Fingering it slightly, teasing it before giving it a pinch, she threw her head back, screaming his name.

That was all it took to throw him over the edge as well, his orgasm ripping from his body as he felt the tingles all the way down to his toes. Pumping until every last drop was gone, he continued to hold her sated, limp body as he pulled out reluctantly.

Carrying her to the bathroom, he cleaned between her legs with a warm washcloth. Fitting her sling over her arm again, he helped her dress before they moved downstairs. The tantalizing smell of Chinese food greeted her as she rounded the corner into the kitchen.

"Hmm, what did you bring?" she asked excitedly.

"Didn't figure either of us felt like cooking so I brought sesame chicken and fried rice."

Looking into the bag, she exclaimed, "Crab rangoons and spring rolls too. I love you!"

Laughing, he kissed her forehead before reaching for the plates. "Hell, if I'd know that was all it took to get you to love me, I'd have brought you Chinese a long time ago."

Stopping him with a hand on his arm, she looked into his eyes, a soft smile on her face and said, "All I need is you."

Dropping the food back to the counter, he took her face in his large hands kissing her once more. "Same here, babe. All I need is you."

HERNANDO VALESQUEZ SAT in his small grocery office, listening to the man babble on the other end of the phone. He could not believe the fucking moron had threatened Ms. Mullins. The last thing he needed was for the police to start poking around his businesses. He had worked hard to make sure they were legitimate. Rubbing his hand over his face, he knew what he had to do. Get rid of the mistake and report to his superiors. Getting rid of the mistake would be easy. Telling his superiors? That would take some finesse, but if the man was taken out first…then it would make the news easier to explain.

Cutting off the babbling, he kept his voice steady and even. Setting up a meeting behind a local bar, giving the excuse of needing to talk where no one was around was the bait. Hanging up his cell, he headed out into the night to catch the rat.

Slipping into the alley early, he waited behind the dumpsters. He did not have to wait long. The punk who had taken it upon himself to go after Ms. Mullins after seeing her outside the laundry was walking down the alley. Why she was there was something that he intended to get Betina to find out tomorrow. But for now?

With a quick movement, the man's neck was slit. Fast, without a squeak from the victim. Tossing the body forward so that none of the blood touched him. Eyeing the security cameras he smiled. He was outside their viewing perimeters.

Slipping back through the night, he grinned to himself. He had not worked his way up to be a successful businessman to allow anyone to threaten that.

Now, to keep Ms. Mullins from suspecting him. The smile left his face. That may take more thought.

The next morning, he walked into Quentin's office, glancing around nervously. Quentin looked up, coal-black eyes boring into him. Hernando licked his lips nervously, wiping his sweaty palms on his pants.

"You seen coming here?"

"No, no. I came in the back way. No one saw me. No one at all," Hernando babbled, but Quentin had already looked back down at some papers on his desk.

Unsure if he should talk, Hernando stood shifting from one foot to the other.

"You got something to say, then say it. Otherwise, get the fuck out of my office." Before Hernando could begin speaking, Quentin interrupted, "And, I don't want any fucking bad news."

"No, no. It's all good. The idiot that tried to assault the court worker has been taken care of. I did it myself."

Quentin's gaze looked at him steadily. Unblinking. "Any blowback?"

"Oh no, sir. No blowback. She's got no idea who threatened her and he'll never talk," Hernando chuckled, his eyes imploring Quentin to share the joke with him. Silence was all that greeted him.

"What about the court worker?" Quentin asked. "She gonna be a problem?"

"I'm keeping an eye on her and I'll make sure she's no worry to you or me. It'll all be good. You've got my word on that."

Quentin quirked an eyebrow as he continued to stare. "You're word? What the fuck makes you think that your word is worth anything?"

"I've never done you wrong, sir. That ought to count for something," Hernando protested.

Nodding, Quentin agreed. "So far, you're right. Make sure you keep it up. I want to know the instant that court bitch is a problem."

"Yes, sir," Hernando said, turning to hurry out of the room. Taking a deep breath, he willed his nervousness to go away. Sucking in another deep breath, he walked out of the front door of the building before realizing that he parked on the back block. "Damn," he muttered. "Gotta walk around."

TERRANCE CALLED INTO TONY'S office. "Chief, been watching Quentin's building and I'm seeing some people come out that never went in and others go in that don't come out. You think there's some other entrance?"

Tony immediately called BJ and asked him to pull up the floor plans to the old building. Thanking Terrance, he headed out to the main room to see what BJ could find.

"This block of old buildings have been around for a long time, but it looks like they may have some connections underground."

Several of the others gathered around, watching the screen. BJ showed underground connections between several of the buildings in a two block area. Lily walked over, having quickly pulled up more information. "The buildings didn't have large passageways but did have tunnels large enough for men to install and work on the water and steam pipes, so they're plenty big enough for a man to walk through."

BJ confirmed, "Yeah, it looks like there are possible tunnels between the building where Quentin's office is located, the old apartment buildings down the street and then the club in the back."

Tony called Shane, reporting what they had found.

While he was on the phone, the others traced the path of the tunnels to see what else they may be connected to, before looking up when Tony approached them again.

"Police can't get a search warrant without probable cause, so…looks like we may have a black op mission," Tony announced with a grin.

The whoops sounded as Gabe, Jobe, and Vinny broke out in shouting and fist bumping. Lily rolled her eyes, as BJ smiled knowing he would be able to be on his first clandestine assignment. Tony headed to the conference area saying, "Let's go. We've got planning to do."

DRESSED IN SKIN-TIGHT, black, long-sleeved shirts and black cargo pants, the men slipped out of the van heading toward their destination. Terrance, as driver, and BJ, as computer expert, stayed in the van making sure everything from their end would go like clockwork.

Tony, Gabe, Vinny, and Jobe moved silently down the alley two blocks over from Quentin's building. The dark, rainy night provided the best cover, keeping most people indoors, while these men barely noticed the rain.

Making their way into one of the buildings, they quickly found the entrance leading down to the steam tunnels. The tunnel initially appeared unused for many years but, as they made their way toward their destination, the evidence of use was easily seen.

Coming to Quentin's building, they easily determined which set of stairs went to his office area. Gabe secured a small camera, checking with BJ to make sure it was operational. Moving along, following the tunnel map that Lily had discovered, they made their way to the entrance of the strip club that the police were watching.

Giving a curt nod, Tony motioned for Vinny to secure another camera at that junction. Noticing the next turn of the tunnel, he wanted to see where it led as well, since it was apparent that it was being used.

Within several hundred feet, they came to several run-down apartment buildings with two entrances to the steam tunnels. This time, Jobe secured the camera, before he and Tony re-traced their steps. Picking up Vinny and then making their way back to Gabe, the four men exited the tunnels as stealthily as they had entered.

Within minutes the six men were heading back to the agency building. Vinny looked over, asking, "What do you think, Tony?"

"Quentin's definitely using the tunnels to move some people around. Could be people he doesn't want coming in his front door. Could be his way of keeping his involvement in the club secret since his name isn't actually on the ownership papers. The apartment building has me concerned. Don't know why that part of the tunnel appears to be used."

"When we get back, I'll patch these three camera into the main feed and add them to the bank of cameras for the surveillance crews."

Terrance chuckled, adding, "Looks like I just got more to watch." The others grinned, having put their own time in front of the bank of cameras. Tony always started new hires, even licensed Private Investigators, in the surveillance room. It was a good lesson in weeding out the ones just looking for glory jobs and gave everyone a chance to share in the duties.

Pulling into the underground garage, the men piled out, securing the van and the equipment. BJ immediately went in to set up the camera feeds while Tony called Shane, letting him know of their success.

Driving home in the early hours of the morning, he looked forward to just that—driving *home.* For years after calling the Army home, he had simply driven to his empty apartment, stripped and gone to bed. Now there was someone, in a little blue Victorian house, waiting for him. She had asked if he wanted to stay. *"It seems silly for you to keep paying rent on an impersonal apartment when you are here most of the time."* Chuckling to himself, he realized that he never thought he would be living in what looked like a life-sized doll house. Turning into the driveway, he parked, but stayed in the vehicle staring at the vision in front of him. *Yeah,* he thought, warmth flooding through him. *This is home.*

CHAPTER 16

SINCE PUTTING OFF the party for another week, Tony decided to take Sherrie on a little trip; she was definitely tired of being indoors and coddled. She had gone back to work on Thursday but Mr. Marks has fussed over her so much that she felt strangled there as well.

Bundled into the truck, she asked where the secret trip was headed.

"If I told you then it wouldn't be a surprise, would it?" he teased.

Several miles out of town, they meandered down a small lane near the river. Turning onto a long, gravel driveway, she saw a small house at the top of a hill. Partially out of stone, it looked as though it had been transported here from another time and place.

"Where are we?" she asked in curiosity.

"This used to be our family vacation home and my father lives here now."

"Your father? You didn't tell me we were meeting your father!" she exclaimed. Looking down at her jeans and sweater, with the arm sling still on, she immediately fretted over her appearance.

Tony glanced sideways, chuckling. "Baby, you're gorgeous. And this is just my dad. Nothing fancy. Hell, my dad wouldn't know fancy if it bit him in the ass."

A giggle escaped as she relaxed. Looking around, she was enchanted by the old fishing cabin. "This looks so old, as though it could be from an ancient fishing village in Europe."

"It was built by my grandfather when he was very young and first married. He and his brothers hauled some of the stone from the river to make the foundation. My father was born here, but the family eventually moved closer to the city. They kept this place though, for vacations and just as a getaway."

Before she could ask any more questions, they pulled up to the front where an older version of Tony stood to greet them. Hailing them from the porch, he called for them to come inside and get warm. They hurried in and Sherrie was immediately struck by the hominess of the cabin.

The main room boasted a vaulted ceiling and she could see a small loft over half of the area. An old, scarred dining table stood at one end and the other end of the room sported a comfortable sofa and a well-used recliner. The coffee table and end tables were also old and scarred, but seemed perfect for the place. A stone fireplace sat at the end of the room and with spring still a month away, the crackling fire gave off warmth, as well as lending ambiance to the quaint home. The only modern intrusion was a flat screen TV sitting on an old cabinet.

A quick glance told her that the kitchen was behind the dining table and with a small hall dividing the back area, she assumed the bedrooms and bathroom were there.

Tony pulled her in close, still careful of her shoulder and made the introductions.

"Dad, I'd like you to meet my girlfriend, Sherrie Mullins. Sherrie, this is my dad, Ed Alvarez."

Before she could get her greeting out, she found herself in a bear hug by the elder Mr. Alvarez.

"Dad, don't break her," Tony admonished, pulling her back into his embrace.

She laughed at his father's enthusiasm, but her mirth stilled when she looked into his face and saw tears in his eyes.

"Forgive an old man, my dear," he explained. "I've wanted my Tony to find happiness and despaired that he was never going to do that. But seeing you here today, makes my heart full again."

Tony felt her body tremble and he knew her tears would come if he did not intervene. "Baby, can I get you something to drink? Dad, you got anything other than beer?"

"You make your old man sound like a drunk, son," his father joked. "As it is, I have some hot tea in a pot just for you." Leaning toward Sherrie, he said, "I heard you like tea."

Smiling her beautiful smile, she agreed saying, "I

would love some."

Settling on the sofa next to Tony, with Ed in the recliner, they talked and laughed through the afternoon. Ed told stories of Tony growing up and the many fishing vacations they had in the cabin.

She glanced sideways at the handsome man laughing with his father. His face relaxed into a smile, caramel eyes twinkling. The Tony she had met a year ago was always somber, but she realized that with time he had relaxed…letting life back in to touch him again. He turned his head, looking down at her with a questioning expression on his face, but she just smiled as she tucked her head back into his shoulder.

Later, in the kitchen, she was staring out of the window over the sink at the dock leading out into the edge of the river. The water meandered slowly in the tributary, cedar trees lining the far side. It was easy to imagine Tony's family vacations spent here by the water. Ed came up behind her with another cup from the table and looked out as well.

"I love your view from here, Mr. Alvarez," she said.

"Call me Ed, my dear. And yes, it is a magnificent view." The two of them watched silently as Tony shoveled snow from the back porch toward the dock.

With the last dish washed and placed in the drying rack, she found herself unable to move away from the scene in front of her. Even bundled up, she could imagine Tony's strong muscles bunch and cord as they lifted the heavy snow. He had not waited for his dad to ask for help, but saw a need and immediately, quietly set to the task.

"He was a good boy, who's turned into a good man," Ed said quietly, watching his son.

Tears pricked the backs of her eyes as she nodded, afraid to trust her voice to speak.

"A parent wants to see their children happy. Damn near broke me and my Ruthie's heart when we watched him at the funeral of Marla and Sofia. No man should bury a child, and sure as hell not at the same time as burying his wife."

The older man's voice cracked as he spoke and she was no longer able to hold back the tear that escaped down her cheek. She glanced at his face, devastated by the ravaged look etched into his expression.

"Thought we'd lost our son." Seeing her surprise, he quickly added, "Not literally, but what was left was just a shell of a man. Know this sounds crazy, but we were glad he headed back to his squad. Being in the military gave him something to fight for, a reason to keep living. For his men. For the mission."

Ed gripped the sink, his gnarled hands clutching for support. She reached out, placing her hand over his. He looked down for a moment, at their touch. She watched as his face transformed as a small smile replaced the haggard expression.

Clearing his throat, he looked up into her face. "He may have gone back to the mission, but he wasn't the same. Some life experiences change us. My Ruthie died knowing that her son's heart was damaged and her last words to him were for him to find life again. He may have nodded to her just to ease her passing, but he didn't feel it in here," he said, touching his chest.

"We met when he saved me," she whispered. "I wouldn't be here today if it weren't for him."

"My dear, you may have been a mission when you met, but you're no longer that. You've brought him back to life and my only regret is that Ruthie didn't live to see this day. You've given him life again. Hope. Love. You've brought my son back to me."

She choked back a sob as the older man pulled her in for a hug. As she clung to Tony's father, she could feel his arms doing the same. Both hanging on as the emotions overtook them.

Hearing Tony approaching the house, the two in the kitchen broke apart, both wiping tears from their faces.

"Lordy, look at us," his father laughed. "We should be celebrating instead of crying."

She smiled back, wiping her eyes. "Sometimes tears are good," she admitted.

Ed looked at her benevolently. "Yes, ma'am. You're right." With one last pat on her hand, he turned to head out to the garage to meet Tony as he stowed the shovel.

Sherrie dashed into the bathroom to repair her makeup, but when she reappeared Tony's concerned expression met hers. Walking straight into his arms, she lay her head on his massive chest as his arms enveloped her. Answering his unasked question, she whispered, "I'm fine. Your dad and I just had a nice talk."

He pulled her away from his chest so that he could peer into her eyes. What he saw nearly felled him…trust, happiness, and love.

After saying goodbye to Ed, with promises to visit again soon, they drove back to the city. Tony glanced over at the profile of Sherrie's beautiful face, stoically staring out of the window.

"You okay, babe? Dad didn't upset you, did he?"

She heard the tentative tremor in his voice, recognizing the concern emanating from him.

"Of course your dad didn't upset me, sweetie. He's wonderful." After a brief pause, she continued, "He loves you very much. He thinks you're…happy now." The last part sounded more like a question than a statement.

Tony jerked the truck over to the side of the road and Sherrie looked around quickly, glad there were no other cars around.

"What—"

"Babe," he interrupted. "You've got to know that I'm happy. With you. With what we've got."

She turned, smiling as her hand reached over to cup his strong jaw. "I know. It's just that I couldn't seem to get over the feeling of you rescuing me one more time, but your dad said something."

He lifted his eyebrow in question, but she continued quickly. "He said that I saved you." She so desperately wanted the words to be true, but now that they were out, they sounded presumptuous. Ducking her head, she wished she could pull the words back in.

He captured her face with his large hand pulling it back around to his. "Oh no, baby girl. You don't get to hide from me. Ever." Leaning over, he placed a gentle kiss on her trembling lips. "Dad's right. You did save me. Never doubt that, baby."

He angled her head for a more intimate kiss, taking this one deeper, wetter. A claiming kiss. One that spoke of love. Hope. Forever.

After a few minutes they pulled apart, both breathless. Eyes locking, warm caramel meeting sky blue. Slow smiles began.

"Let's get home, baby. I want to show you just how much you've saved me and I sure as hell can't do it on the side of the road."

Later that night, he showed her exactly what he thought of her saving him. Over and over, long into the night.

BETINA LAY ON her bed, sleep eluding her once again. Turning on the lamp by her bed, she reached for her art pad, but halted as she heard footsteps in the hall. Quickly shoving it back under her mattress, she pulled the covers up knowing her stepdad was coming.

Stepdad. Miss Sherrie told me that he has no legal authority over me since he isn't married to mom. But he has other authority. One that I can't ignore.

The door opened quietly and his presence filled the small room. No small talk. Just down to business.

"How many did you contact today?" growled softly.

She hated this feeling. Helpless. Used. No control. Sighing, she answered, "There were two, but only one came to the store." She saw his questioning expression and continued, "The skinny girl with the dirty hair. She hasn't eaten lunch this week at school."

Hernando nodded, making a notation in his notebook. Flipping it closed, he leaned against the doorframe. "I need more. We will be running laundry on a twenty-four-hour schedule, so you need to step it up and get me more."

"I'm doing the best I can," she said. "There haven't been any new kids in school lately."

"Then look on the streets. You do what you are told and get me more," he growled, slightly more loudly this time.

Tears pricked the back of her eyes, but she forced them away. *They won't help. Nothing helps.*

"And make sure you keep that snoopy court worker away from here. I catch her somewhere she's not supposed to be and it won't go good for you. Or your mother."

Her eyes darted up to his quickly. "I'll do it."

"Yeah," he chuckled. "You do that." Turning, he

left the room, closing the door behind him.

Betina sat very still until she was sure he was not coming back. Pulling her art pad out, she began sketching again. It was the only thing that made her feel any better about her life. Her fucked-up, out of control life.

TONY, SITTING AT the head of his main conference room, went over the weekly assignments with his employees. After the larger staff meeting was over, he dismissed everyone except his inner crew.

They looked at the relaxed man in front of them, seeing the effects of his relationship with Sherrie clearly on his face.

"Boss?" BJ asked. "What's up?"

Tony looked at his former brothers-in-arms—Jobe, Vinny, and Gabe—as well as BJ and Lily. He lay a folder on the table in front of him, announcing, "I've had an offer from another…security type firm for us to collaborate with when possible and I'd like to take them up on it."

Gabe let out a huge breath saying, "Damn, Tony. You had me worried that you were going to sell the company."

The others grinned sheepishly, admitting they thought the same thing. Tony shook his head, "You all know this business means everything to me. No way I'd sell out. But I do have a way that we can work with another company at times and I think the partnership will be beneficial."

"So who's the company?" Vinny asked.

"I was contacted by Jacques Bryant, our former Chief Warrant Officer—"

"Jack?" Jobe asked, a grin on his face. "Ol' French-ie, himself," he added at Tony's nod. Seeing Lily's look of confusion, he explained, "His mom was French and named him Jacques, but we knew him as Jack."

"Yeah, until Vinny found out his real name and gave him the nickname Frenchie," Gabe laughed.

"What has he been up to?" Vinny asked.

"Seems he continued in Special Forces for a couple of years beyond us and then, when he got out, started his own business."

"What kind of business?" Lily asked, astute enough to see Tony's hesitation in naming the company.

"I'll call it a security business, but it's a little different than ours. It's more...covert."

"Covert?" BJ asked.

This had the attention of Vinny, Gabe, and Jobe immediately; having served with Jack they knew his penchant for covert operation planning and gadgets.

"He's created a team of people with diverse backgrounds and specialties. They're still pretty new, but are having some real successes with their missions."

"And Jack wants to work with us?" Gabe asked.

Tony nodded before continuing. "Right now, we

have just verbally agreed to help each other out on cases where we think sharing will be beneficial. We'll consider the details at a later time." Looking over at Vinny, he added, "Don't worry, Vinny. You'll still get to provide security for your starlets and rocker girls when they come into town."

"Thank God," Vinny quipped. "Which reminds me, when am I going to get one of those assignments?"

The others chuckled as Tony replied, "Got something in the works right now. I'll let you know as soon as the details are worked out."

Lily headed back toward her office with a smile, patting Vinny on the shoulders as she went by. "One day, Vinny, love's going to hit you when you least expect and I am going to sit back and enjoy watching it knock you for a loop." With a wink, she left the conference room.

Gabe turned toward his twin saying, "I'm telling you bro. Don't mix work and pleasure. I did and it was a fuckin' disaster."

Vinny reared back in his seat smiling. "That's 'cause you forgot to let 'em know it was only for one night."

As the meeting broke up, Tony felt lighter than he had in a long time. Business was good. Sherrie was good. *Maybe, just maybe things are looking up.*

SHERRIE WAS BACK at work and more determined than

ever to check up on Betina. She called her school and made an appointment to meet with one of her teachers. Finishing her work for Mr. Marks, she headed to the school during lunchtime. Once she checked in with the front office, she was escorted to Mrs. Rushmore's English classroom, where the teacher agreed to meet with her during her planning time.

"Thank you so much for seeing me on such short notice," Sherrie greeted, sitting down with the friendly teacher.

"It's my pleasure. I want to help Betina as much as I can."

"I have some questions that go beyond the ordinary ones that I can easily get elsewhere, if you don't mind," she said.

Mrs. Rushmore acquiesced and Sherrie pulled her pad and pen from her purse. "When I ask Betina about friends, she indicates that she doesn't really have any. Is this true? Do you see her hanging out with any other students? Girlfriends? A boyfriend?"

The teacher shook her head, answering, "She really is a quiet, good student. I was shocked when I heard that she ran away—she definitely is not a behavior problem here at school. Being a rather poor inner-city school, we have our share of problem students, but she's not one of them. Unfortunately, we lose some kids to the streets and gangs every day, but again, she's never been a problem. I don't see her walking in the halls with other students consistently. She does meet and greet almost everyone. I know she would be embarrassed if she realized that someone had noticed this, but she really has the most giving personality."

Sherrie lifted her gaze from her notes to the teacher. "How so? In what way?"

"Well, when I have cafeteria duty, I see her hanging back, watching the other students. And the ones that don't have lunch money, she casually goes to them and gives them lunch money."

Gives them money? Where does she get that money from if her work at the grocery doesn't pay much?

Mrs. Rushmore continued, "She always talks to them for a few minutes and then they head up to the line where they get lunch. A few of these kids have left our school, but I'm sure they'll always remember her kindness."

Filing that information away, she asked about Betina's classwork and once again found the teacher with nothing but praise. Standing at the end of the interview, Sherrie gave her a business card and asked if she would call or email if she thought of anything else.

Walking back to her car, her mind was filled with Mrs. Rushmore's words. *Always gives lunch money to the kids who can't afford it.* She remembered Betina talking to the kids after school, telling them they could get food at the Valesquez store.

Walking back into the law office, she went directly to see Simon. He looked up, a smile on his face as he greeted her, and she noticed Mr. Marks was sitting in there as well. She started to back out of the room, but they beckoned her in.

"I hate to be a bother, but I had a question and perhaps you two are the perfect ones to ask." Taking a deep breath, hoping her employers would not think her ridiculous, she asked, "Do you ever get a feeling that something just doesn't add up when you are talking to a client?"

Both men looked surprised and confused, so she rushed to explain. "I'm still working on Betina's case and while I have no evidence, I just *feel* like something isn't adding up."

"Intuition, my dear," Mr. Marks said. "You must look at facts, but never fail to listen to your intuition."

Simon added, "You'd make a good lawyer, Sherrie. You're book smart, but you're very people smart as well. I'd say keep digging."

"But carefully," Mr. Marks called as she was walking out of the office.

"I will," she agreed. "No more dark street investigations for me. You never know who you'll meet!"

Back in her office, she pulled her notes out as she began to type them into a semblance of a report that would eventually go to the judge. *Betina, I know there is something going on. I can just feel it. Maybe a surprise visit is what is needed.* She knew the grocery wasn't open on Sunday so she hoped that would provide the perfect time to see how Betina was with both her mom and Mr. Valesquez around.

The vibrating of her cell phone pulled her out of her musings and with a smile on her face she answered, "Hey, sweetie."

"You got plans for dinner tonight?" Tony asked.

"Not really. I think there is some leftover meatloaf from the other night."

"Then let's go out. I've got some news and I thought we'd hit that new steak house downtown."

"Oohh, you know the way to my heart," she laughed.

"Darlin', you're already in mine," he replied. "I'll pick you up in about twenty minutes."

Hanging up, she headed to the restroom to freshen up. Looking into the mirror over the sink, she patted her hair in place then re-applied her lipstick. Staring at her reflection, she could not help but smile. *Girl, you've come a long way since cocktail waitressing in a strip joint to keep an eye on Charisse. A good job. A good man...who is drop-dead gorgeous.* For a second, a flash of doubt crossed her face. *Can it stay this good?* Sucking in a huge breath before letting it out slowly, she squared her shoulders and held her head up. *Just because everything always went to shit before doesn't mean it still will. Things have changed. My life has changed.*

Her pep talk over, she headed out to wait for Tony.

CHAPTER 17

THE RESTAURANT WAS dimly lit, the candlelight flickering on the table between them giving off a romantic air, as Tony and Sherrie finished their meal. Her pale blue, figure-hugging jersey dress with a scooped neck had captured his attention all night. Her dress offered him a hint of the luscious cleavage he planned on partaking of tonight, as soon as he could get her home. Her blonde hair floated around her shoulders, and the thought of running his hands through the silken tresses as he took her had him shifting in his chair.

Sherrie was equally perusing from her side of the table. His muscular arms and chest stretched the material of his navy shirt and the plan of popping one button at a time until she could peel it off revealing the prize underneath, had her core clenching. He had just shared his news about collaborating with an old Special Forces buddy and she could see the excitement in his eyes.

"I never ask about your time in the Army," she confessed, trying to think of something besides the ache deep inside her core. "I suppose I just assume that if you want to talk about it, you will. But it seems that you are very close to those you served with."

He nodded as he looked at her eyes, seeing in their depths an interest in him. Not his war stories. Not tales of glory. But interest in him.

"When you spend that much time together as a team, you have to know each other's movement, thoughts, actions…anything less could mean at best a failed mission or at the worst, death."

Her eyes shined with tears as she whispered, "I hate that you had to face that, but so glad you had men at your back that have become your brothers."

He looked down at his plate, realizing that for so long the memories of his days in the Army were tainted by his grief, but those men stood by him when he fell apart. And put him back together again. Raising his eyes, he stared at the beautiful woman across from him. Life had not been easy on her either, but here they were—stronger together than they had been apart.

I want this woman in my life forever. He had not bought a ring, although the idea of asking her to marry him had been on his mind lately. *Fuck it, who needs a ring right now anyway. At least I can tell her what I want.*

"Sherrie?" he said softly, reaching across the table grasping her hand. "You know I love you. Will you—"

"Tony? I thought that was you!" came an excited voice from the right.

Jerking his head around, he saw Marla's parents walking toward their table. *Shit timing.* He had always had a good relationship with her parents but they'd lost contact over the past couple of years. Their grief was as profound as his, but in their case shared grief did not seem to give him comfort.

He stood quickly, reaching out his hand in greeting. "Ted, Vivian. Nice to see you again."

Vivian bypassed his outstretched hand and came in for a hug instead. He returned the embrace, but felt ill at ease when she would not let go. Glancing behind her at Ted, his eyes must have given a pleading look because Ted moved in to gently pull his wife from Tony's arms.

Shaking Tony's hand, Ted said, "Now, now, Viv. Let the man breathe."

Sherrie looked on in curiosity at the tall, handsome man in front of their table. His gray hair was neatly trimmed and his suit appeared expensive. The woman at his side was also tall, reed-thin, and elegantly dressed as well. She saw their eyes dart toward her and she shot a glance at Tony.

Tony introduced the couple to Sherrie. Vivian as she smiled down at Sherrie and said, "I see you're just ready for dessert. We won't keep you." She stood awkwardly, as though she wanted to stay, but knew she should not.

Ted quickly placed his hand on his wife's shoulder and said, "My dear, let's move on. I'm sure they'd rather be alone—"

Vivian's eyes frosted over, but as Sherrie realized…not with anger, but with grief. *This woman buried her daughter and her granddaughter. I'm sure seeing Tony brings painful memories to the forefront.*

Sherrie reached her hand out and placed it on Vivian's arm. "I'm so sorry for your loss," she said sincerely. Vivian's watery eyes lifted and found hers. "I recently lost my sister and while my grief is not like yours, I still sympathize."

"Oh, I am sorry about your sister," Vivian admitted.

It appeared that she wanted to say more, but the words never came. Ted wrapped his arm around his wife as they quickly said their goodbyes, leaving a frustrated Tony looking over the dwindling candlelight at a very reserved Sherrie. *Shit,* he thought ruefully. He scraped his chair back, rising as he held out his hand. She placed hers in his gently and moved toward him.

Tucking her into his side, he escorted her to his truck. Neither speaking out of fear of what the other was thinking. By the time they entered her house, he could stand the silence no more.

"Baby, we gotta talk," he growled, frustration pouring out in his words.

Her gaze shot up toward his, fearful of his tone. "Oh…okay."

"I am so sorry about that. I haven't seen them in a long time and well…that was awkward.

Her lips trembling, she approached him, placing her hands on his strong chest, feeling his heartbeat pounding against her fingertips. "Tony, it's okay, really. You've shown me that I'm not a replacement for Marla, and you've been able to open yourself up to love again. Viv…has nothing to be open for." Giving a little shrug, she admitted, "Grief, in some form or another, lasts forever."

Looking down at the woman who taught him to love again, he cupped her face in his large hands, running his thumbs over her petal-soft cheeks. "I love you, baby."

Smiling up at his warm eyes, she said, "I love you, too."

"You're being really understanding about tonight, but you gotta know that I was frustrated as hell. I wanted tonight to be just about us."

Pulling him down, she touched her lips to his. Just as he was taking the kiss deeper, she moved away, a teasing grin on her face. Growling, he swatted her ass before scooping her up in his arms. Climbing the stairs, she pulled him back in for a kiss, this time letting him take it as deep as he wanted. And he wanted it deep.

Later, their breaths came in gasps as their erratic heartbeats pounded in an ancient rhythm from their lovemaking. Slowly as their bodies cooled, their breathing evened out and their hearts began to beat as one.

Tony lay with her in his arms, marveling at the strength of this woman. Strong and independent, but willing to give it all to him in the bedroom. She could have been pissy about Vivian but instead was kind and understanding. *I wanted to ask her to marry me. But she deserves wine and roses. She deserves to have the ring right there.*

Looking down, he saw her face relaxed in slumber. He snagged the covers and pulled them over their cooling bodies, keeping her tucked closely to his side. Smiling, he drifted off to a peaceful sleep.

HERNANDO PEERED OUT of his second-floor office window overlooking the laundry that was in full swing despite the late hour. With the extra teen labor he had been able to increase his business and now added two more hotels as his clients. Quentin indicated that he was very pleased with Hernando's work.

His sharp eyes scanned the operation, checking to see that everyone was working. The two new girls were still learning and it showed—their actions were clumsy. The woman in charge of their training was not paying enough attention.

Opening the small window, he whistled and saw her stiffen before turning his way. *Yes, she knows what will happen.* Without another word, he shut the window and waited for her to appear at his door. She hurried in and started to shut the door.

"Leave it open," he ordered. "It may serve as a deterrent for the others." With a jerk of his head, he ordered, "Go out by the railing. You know what to do."

Eyes wide with fright, she hesitantly made her way back to the railing that overlooked the facility. The two young teens looked up in fear, their gazes joined by the others. Placing her hands on the rail, she bent over as tears welled in the anxiety of the coming punishment.

Hernando looked at her ass, his crotch growing tighter as his dick swelled in anticipation. He loved the cruel dominance. The control. The power. The rush of adrenaline fed his cock as he pulled his belt out of his pants.

The woman's trembling legs barely held her up but she knew not to move. With a swift downward swing, his belt slapped against her bottom. Four more in quick succession finished her punishment.

Ordering her inside of his office, he followed her, a cruel smile on his face as he unzipped his pants. Pulling out his erection, he placed his cock at her entrance and slammed into her from behind, palming her blistered cheeks. As horny as he was, it did not take long to finish and tuck himself back into his trousers.

"Now get back to work and get those girls up to speed," he growled at the crying woman. She pulled her pants back on hurrying to get out, trying to avert her eyes to those below. The ones she did glance at looked at her in sympathy, except for a few of the men who palmed their crotches. She knew what that meant. They would wait until after work and then demand her services.

She wanted out but knew there was no way. Hernando gave them a place to stay rent free, but the four dollars an hour she made only went so far. To get away meant she would have to live on the streets. Her chest heaving with frustration, she moved back over to the two teenage girls, showing them once again how to quickly bleach the towels before putting them in the large laundry equipment. Their fear had them speeding up the process.

Hernando watched with satisfaction as all of the workers processed the laundry quicker. *Nothing like fear to keep the workers in line.* Chuckling to himself, he moved back to his desk, turned out the light and headed to Quentin's place.

TONY WALKED INTO WORK the next morning, greeted by Doug.

"Sir, I've been watching the tunnel cameras. Not much happens other than there are some people that enter through one of the back buildings and go to Salazar's office. We don't have bugs in his office, so all I got is visual. You wanted to know if anyone seemed to make multiple trips and I've seen about six or seven. I gave those photos to Lily to process."

Tony nodded, saying, "Thanks. Good job. Go home and get some sleep and I'll have you on just one more night shift before you switch with Terrance."

Calling out to Lily, he asked for an update as soon as she could get one to him.

An hour later, she walked into his office with her reports. I ran the images that Doug gave me. Nothing interesting actually. A couple of them have police records but nothing recent. One appears to be coming and going several times, but he has his face hidden so I don't have a good image to process. I'll have Doug keep me posted on any newer ones."

SHERRIE WAS TAKING a rare sick day to have a follow-up appointment with her doctor about her shoulder. When the doctor asked her if it was impeding her normal activities she choked out her answer, thinking about the activities of the previous evening. Her flaming face gave away her thoughts and her doctor laughed, saying that she was glad there was no hindrance.

Back at the house, she was cleaning to get ready for the party that weekend. Turning the music up loudly on the TV, she began to dance as she cleaned. Dressed in old, faded yoga pants and a sweatshirt that had seen better days, she vacuumed, dusted, scrubbed the kitchen and the bathrooms. All while listening to the oldies station. Hearing a familiar song, she stopped while mopping. It was a song her mother used to dance to before her father left. *She would twirl Charisse and me around in circles until we were dizzy.* Sighing at the memory, she walked over and changed the channel on her TV.

Before she had time to pick the mop up again, she heard Tony's truck pull into the driveway. Glancing at her watch, she wondered why he was home in the middle of the morning. His footsteps pounded up the porch and through the door, quickly taking in the scene in front of him.

"What's up, Tony?" she asked.

He stalked forward, a sexy grin on his face. "Babe, you cleaning this house, dancing around singing in these tight pants while shaking your gorgeous ass...I've been wanting to get back here for hours." Reaching her, he pulled her close, capturing her lips in a possessive, wet kiss.

Dazed when she came up for air, she smiled dreamily at him. Then awareness of his words slowly dawned on her. As he started in for another kiss, she threw up her hand, halting his lips.

"Oh, no," she warned, poking him in the chest. "I want to know how you knew what I was doing."

He nodded toward her security camera in the hall-way, near the door. "I have this place watched."

"You...you have...what the hell are you talking about? Who's watching?" she sputtered.

"A live feed goes into my place. We have a bank of videos of various residents who pay us to keep an eye on their property. I employ several people who monitor the video feeds. It's only on the doors and windows, but I got a call from Vinny, who's at the monitors, that every once in a while he could see you dancing by with a mop."

"Tony, you didn't ask my permission! What if I was prancing around naked?" she asked, suddenly horrified at what someone could have seen.

"Honey, with the business I'm in, I need to make sure our residence is monitored. Gabe and Jennifer as well as Matt and Lily have one too. Vinny and Jobe still live in their secure condo, so they don't have direct feeds, but their places are secure as well."

"That still doesn't answer my naked question," she declared, her foot tapping against the wooden floor.

The thought of her doing housework in the buff had his blood rushing to his dick and out of his head. Turning her way, he began to stalk toward her as she backed up. Her back hit the wall and he trapped her with both hands on either side of her head.

"Tony…" she warned.

"Babe, they are only aimed on the doors and windows. If you were dancing around naked, the only way you'd be seen by the cameras was if you were standing naked in front of the door or a window. And somehow I don't believe you'd ever do that. Believe me, I'm the only one that will ever see you dancing naked in this house." With that he leaned down, capturing her mouth in a searing kiss.

All thoughts of being angry flew out of her head as

his kiss took on a life-force of its own. Tongues tangling, hands exploring, she allowed him to ravage her mouth in expectation of him ravaging other parts of her body.

His mind was going in the same direction, so he broke the kiss to scoop her up and toss her over his shoulder. She smacked his back but his hand came down hard on her ass, quieting her. He took the stairs two at a time, rubbing where he had spanked.

Giggling as she dangled over his shoulder, she could not help but give a little wave toward the camera as they disappeared up the stairs.

CHAPTER 18

AFTER A LATE MORNING round of amazing sex, Sherrie found herself driving to Betina's house for another visit after Tony left to go back to work.

After an enthusiastic hug from Betina, they settled at the kitchen table. Her mother bustled around as though afraid to leave them alone, finally moving to the other room after serving them tea.

"How's school?" she asked the young teen, hoping to put her at ease. Betina was always more relaxed when they saw each other without anyone else around. *Does her mother make her nervous?*

"It's fine. I've made up all of the work I missed when I was out for a few days before going to the foster home. My teachers told me my grades are back to where they should be."

"I talked to your English teacher and your art teacher the other day. They have nothing but good things to say about you."

Betina smiled shyly, the pride shining in her eyes as she tried to contain her pleasure at the compliment.

"In fact, your art teacher told me that if you keep up the good work, she thinks you could get a scholarship to an art college if you wanted."

The girl's eyes grew wide, shining with tears as she clutched Sherrie's hand. "That would be such a dream."

Giving her hand a squeeze, Sherrie asked if she had any new drawings. Nodding, Betina jumped up from the table and ran back to her room. Marcella came in from the living room, obviously having heard the conversation, and she asked, "Do you think she could go to college?"

"I don't see why not. She can apply for financial aid and with scholarships, should be able to cover the costs. It would be a way for her to have a good paying job."

Marcella seemed to waiver, her eyes darting toward the door. "She has a job with her step-father. She doesn't have to go away to college for that."

"But don't you want more for Betina than to work all hours in the store or laundry?"

Before her mother could answer, the back door opened and Hernando strolled in. Seeing Sherrie, he plastered a smile on his face making a big production of kissing Marcella. "Hello, Ms. Mullins. Here to talk to our Betina?"

Our Betina, my ass.

Smiling back, just as insincerely, she said, "Yes. She's just gone to show me some more of her artwork."

Marcella turned toward Hernando saying, "Ms. Mullins and her art teacher think that Betina could go to college."

"Bah, who needs college? I have no college and I

manage three laundries and a grocery store," he scoffed.

Choosing her words carefully, Sherrie acquiesced. "I agree that not everyone needs to go to college, but Betina could have the chance to choose whatever career she would like to have and not just work for hourly wages."

She caught the steel glint in his eyes as he said, "There is nothing wrong with working for wages. My workers are well compensated and they are happy."

Just then Betina walked back into the room, her art pad dangling in her hand, as her eyes moved between the three adults in the room.

"Don't you agree, Betina? Working for me is a good thing. Who would need college?"

"Yes," she answered meekly.

"There," Hernando said, effectively closing the conversation.

"Well, Betina, let's sit and go over some more questions I have…about school," she added quickly, hoping to have a chance to continue her conversation alone.

Satisfied, Hernando and Marcella headed to the den, but Sherrie noticed that he sat in the chair nearest to the kitchen door, making it easy for him to hear their conversation. Keeping the questions light, she was disappointed to see the glow go out of Betina's eyes. The excited teen, eager to consider college, was now sullen and giving short answers to Sherrie's questions.

As the meeting came to a close, Betina seemed deep in thought before stealing a glance into the den to see

Hernando and her mother watching TV. As the girl's gaze moved back to Sherrie's, she placed the art pad on the kitchen table and slowly pushed it toward her. Licking her lips nervously, she looked at Sherrie and said, "I want you to have this."

"Oh, honey, I can't take your drawings," Sherrie protested.

Betina's hand stayed firm, not allowing Sherrie to push the drawing back. "I *need* you to have them," she said.

Sherrie considered Betina's intent expression, feeling that she was trying to tell her something, but not knowing what it was.

"Okay," she said slowly. "If you're sure."

"Yes, I'm sure," Betina stated firmly. "My life, my world is in these drawings. I need you to understand that."

The intense expression on the teen's face had Sherrie's heart pounding. Glancing down at the drawings, she wondered what she was supposed to understand.

"My world," Betina repeated, her eyes pleading.

Hearing Hernando getting up from his chair, Betina jerked her hand back and Sherrie found herself sliding the pad into her oversized bag. Not knowing why she felt the need to hide it from him, it seemed important to keep him from knowing that Betina had shared anything of consequence.

Wanting to end on a positive note, Sherrie said, "Betina, your teachers mention that you are really kind to others also. You offer food money to some of the kids that don't have lunch money and I saw you talking to some students about getting food at the grocery. It seems that you really look out for others and I'll be sure to put that in my report."

Betina's eyes grew large as she licked her lips nervously. Hernando walked into the room, placing his hand on Betina's shoulder, slightly squeezing.

"Yes, she's a real sweetheart, isn't she?" he said.

Sherrie kept the smile on her face while her mind was racing. *He's not happy about something. What the hell did I say that he didn't like?*

"Yes," she agreed. "It seems you are too with the offer of food."

"No one should go hungry. Betina and I just help out some kids. No obligation of course. I'd hate for you to put something in your report that would give the grocery any undue publicity."

His words were taut and his eyes were cold. Glancing back at Betina, Sherrie could see his fingers flexing into the girl's shoulder.

"Of course. I understand," she said with a forced smile that was beginning to hurt her cheeks.

"Ms. Mullins, can you stay for dinner?" he asked.

While his question was welcoming, his tone was not. Smiling, she shook her head saying,

"Thank you but I must be going. Betina, you're hearing will be coming up soon and we'll need to meet at least one more time before that."

The girl nodded nervously and headed back to her room as Marcella showed Sherrie to the door. Walking back to her car she could feel eyes boring holes in the back of her. Climbing into the driver's seat, she saw Hernando standing at the window. His expression chilled her. *I know something's up. I just don't know what. Yet...*

SATURDAY DAWNED CLEAR and the freezing weather gave them a small break, with the high reaching the mid-forties. Tony had insisted that they could grill out for their party, but she had been sure that the cold winter would never allow for that.

"I told you so," Tony teased, as he reached around her in the kitchen, seasoning the steaks and chicken.

"I don't see how you stand being out there," she exclaimed. "I hate the cold weather."

"But babe, cold weather is what brought us together."

She could not help but giggle at the reminder of their winter storm cabin adventures. "Well, you men can go grill outdoors in the cold while us women keep warm inside."

The house soon began to fill up with their friends as Gabe, Jennifer, Shane, Annie, Matt, Lily, BJ, and Suzanne came in bearing platters of food. Jobe came by himself and said that Vinny was picking up his date.

The men headed out to the patio to begin the grilling. After a few minutes of small talk, Tony asked Shane and Matt if there was anything new they were working on.

Sharing a look, Matt admitted that they had been pulled into some missing children investigations.

"What's that got to do with vice?" Jobe asked.

"Maybe nothing," Shane answered. "But ever since the Department of Justice gave a presentation on Human Trafficking, vice is now looking into missing child cases, especially if teens are involved."

"I hate to ask a stupid question, but isn't that the same as smuggling kids across the borders?" Gabe asked.

"Nah. That's human smuggling. Human trafficking is exploiting persons for sex or labor." Seeing the looks of confusion, he continued. "Basically, it's luring someone into working for you, whether sex or just labor. You pay them shit and they are trapped."

Shane picked up the explanation. "Could be sex or it could be working in someone's sweatshop. Problem is that statistics show that there are a lot of kids and teens involved. Believe it or not, human trafficking is the fastest growing criminal industry in the world."

"Damn," Tony growled. "We can't even keep our kids safe."

"Richland is a huge area for it, with the crossroads of three major Interstate highways. We are on a connection from New York to Miami," Matt added.

"So, we are starting to patrol the bus stations and train stations."

"And when the detectives working missing children cases think there might be a problem, they contact us," Shane added. "We try to get the pictures up of the kids, so that the cops on the street will have something to look at."

Matt added, "I've looked at those pictures so much in the last few weeks, I see them in my dreams."

The men quieted as the back door opened and Sherrie poked her head out. "Hey sweetie, just checking on the grilling."

"About another ten minutes, babe," Tony called back.

"Vinny's just pulled up," she called. "I'll send him out."

A few minutes later, Vinny came out with his flavor of the day—a tall blonde with fake boobs showcased in a tight sweater, looking extremely out of place at the gathering. Vinny tried to convince her to go inside but she insisted that she wanted to stay with him. Frustrated, he went back inside with her to keep her from interfering with the men's conversation, finally settling in the living room with a ballgame on the large screen TV.

Gabe shook his head saying, "I swear, even on my worst day I wasn't as big a horndog as Vinny."

The others laughed as Tony shook his head and said, "It seems like he goes for the same type every time.

I can't tell the difference between this girl and the last twenty women I've seen him with."

Jobe moaned, "You all are married or," looking at Tony, "almost married. I'm the one he drags along to his bar nights. Jesus, the women flock to him but I swear he only goes for bimbos. Any other woman there? Nope. Just the bimbos."

"That way he doesn't have to think. Or talk. Or anything other than buy them a drink, dance with them on the floor then take them back to their place and dance with them in their bed," Shane added.

"Y'all have nice apartments. Does he ever take them to his place?" Matt asked.

"Oh no," Gabe and Jobe said simultaneously. Jobe continued, "No way. He wants to get them off, get himself off and get the hell out of there. He'll never bring someone back to his place."

"Well, if he ever does end up with someone there, then send out the invitations 'cause he'll be getting married," Tony quipped as the others laughed.

WHILE THE MEN grilled outside the women worked in the kitchen, side by side, moving seamlessly around each other as only friends can do.

Annie and Suzanne talked about the new veterinary clinic Annie had opened just outside the city. Annie was the veterinarian and Suzanne was the vet tech.

"I need to make an appointment for Pippi," Lily remembered, referring to her little dog.

"Just remind me before we leave today and I will put it on our automatic call list," Annie said. "At least everyone loves Pippi. You should see it when I have to bring my own cats in. They're horrible."

Suzanne agreed, adding, "Annie's cat, Rags, is especially naughty. He howls the entire time."

Jennifer got off her cell phone, apologizing to the others. "Sorry, I had to take that call from Ross." She was the guardian of her young brother. "He's with Gabe's parents for the weekend and had to tell me about the outing they had on the boat this morning."

The conversation continued to flow and the women tried to include Vinny's date when she came in, but she insisted on plastering herself to Vinny's side. Rolling their eyes, the women finished up the preparations quickly.

As the men came in with the meat from the grill, they were just setting everything out. Picking up an art pad, Jennifer flipped though it admiring the drawings.

"Sherrie, where did you get this?" Jennifer asked. "These drawings are so lifelike."

"They are amazing, aren't they?" she replied. "My CASA case draws them and she gave the pad to me. I think those are drawings of her friends from school."

Lily looked over Jennifer's shoulder, admiring the pictures. "Wow, these are fabulous."

The other women circled around as Jennifer flipped

the pages over, each revealing another beautifully detailed face.

"It's as though I'm looking right at their faces," Annie exclaimed. "I have no artistic ability at all, so I'm always amazed when I see something like this."

Matt walked by, kissing his wife's neck as she closed the art pad, placing it back on the table. Suzanne laid it on the kitchen counter out of the way of the table.

Everyone filled their plates with an abundance of food that was brought. At times like this, Sherrie was still in awe of how her life had changed. For the better. Good food. Good times. Good friends. Glancing up at Tony's profile as he sat with his legs touching hers, she could not help but think of the best change of all. A good man at her side.

"Is SHE GOING to be a problem?" Quentin asked.

"No, no," Hernando assured his boss. "I've got her under control."

"Really? I don't give a shit about details, just make sure you do."

"No worries, boss. I'm not letting a piece of pussy ruin us."

Quentin chuckled. "Speaking of pussy, I've got some news and need your help. You got a chance to really step into the big time here if you play your cards right."

Hernando eagerly awaited, always on the lookout to impress the higher ups and make more money. Managing the grocery and laundries was fine, but he knew more money could be made as long as he played his cards right.

"Need new girls for the upper rooms in the clubs," Quentin replied.

"New girls?"

"Yeah. We want 'em young. Got men that are wanting young."

Hernando licked his lips, his mind already planning what would need to be done. "How young we talkin'?"

Quentin chuckled again. "Mostly teens. We got some customers that'll take 'em younger, but most just want young pussy. You think you can accommodate? It'll be worth your time. You do good on this and you got a good shot at being the manager of one of the clubs down on the river."

The idea of being a strip club manager instead of spending his days in the grocery and his nights in the hot laundry made his mouth water. "I got this, don't worry. I got a girl thats good at recruiting. She'll do what I say 'cause I got her mother as bait." Smiling to himself, he could see the money piling up. "Oh, yeah, I got this."

"Good. I'll be in touch. Just make sure your recruiter doesn't make any mistakes. There's been a shit ton of money we've missed out on 'cause we weren't in the market. Those days are gone. I want those girls and

I want that money."

"You got it boss," Hernando said, hanging up. Sitting back in his chair, he pondered how to get Betina to continue to recruit without knowing what she was recruiting for. Licking his lips again, he knew just how to convince her. Either she keeps recruiting...or she goes into the stable. Palming his dick, he wondered how tight her virgin pussy would be. He had not touched her since he had been living in Marcella's home, but if she ended up in the stable? He would make sure to be one of her customers.

CHAPTER 19

THE WINTER SUN peeked through the blinds, sending shards of light toward the bed. Tony woke first, staring at the woman curled up into his side. Her long blonde hair, spread across the pillow, tempted his fingers to curl in their silky tresses. He shifted slightly, rolling more toward her while keeping her firmly in his embrace. Her face, angelic in sleep, was too much to resist and he moved his forefinger softly over her cheek.

Her eyes fluttered as she was pulled from her dreams, finally opening and settling on his gaze. Watching a smile spread across her face he felt his heart stumble. *How did I get so lucky?* Smiling back, he vowed to do whatever he could to keep her looking at him that way every morning.

Her hand, warm on his bicep, smoothed over the corded muscles as she moved it lower. Down his rigged abdomen. His eyes widened as her hand continued its path, ending as it encircled his already engorged cock.

"Hey, you," she greeted, licking her lips as she began to move her hand up and down his hardness, rubbing the pre-cum around the head.

His voice, rough as broken glass replied, "Hey

back," before he pulled her over, latching his lips onto hers. *I'll never get enough of her*, was the last conscious thought he had as he breathed her in, consuming her mouth.

Immediately awake she felt the onslaught of his lips right down to her core, as she felt his cock swell in her hand.

"Tony," she pleaded, but anticipating both of their needs, he was already rolling on a condom before pulling her over. With her back tucked to his front, he slid his hands to her breasts, tweaking and tugging her nipples. The jolt shot straight to her core as it clenched in need.

His dick, with a mind of its own, moved straight toward her drenched entrance and he seated himself in one push. "You okay, baby?" he groaned, knowing they had little foreplay.

"Go. Now!" she cried out, craving the friction that only he could provide.

"Yes, ma'am," he chuckled, pumping in and out, faster and faster. Moving as a piston he held her tightly, loving the moans emanating from deep inside of her. While keeping one hand on her breast he slid the other hand down, giving her swollen clit a squeeze.

That was all it took for her to fly apart, calling out his name as her inner walls squeezed him and he neared his climax. He felt his balls tighten just before roaring out his own release. Pouring himself into her waiting body, he tightened his grip on her breasts, only too late hoping he was not leaving bruises. Loosening his fingers, she reached up to clasp his hands, stilling them.

"Don't want to hurt you, baby," he growled into her ear.

"Mmmm, the only way you would hurt me now is if you let go," she purred back, relaxed and sated. "What a way to wake up."

Chuckling, he pulled out but kept her tucked in tightly, kissing her ear. She settled deep into his embrace, luxuriating in the warmth.

"How did I get so lucky?" she whispered.

He stilled, not sure he had heard her. *Lucky? Her?*

She whispered again, "I wanted a hero. I waited for a hero. I knew the minute I looked into your eyes the first time you rescued me that I'd found a true man. One who also was a hero. I don't know how I got so lucky."

He rolled her over to face him, brushing the hair from her eyes. "Oh, baby. I'm no hero. It took me so fuckin' long to get my head outta my ass and go for you. I'm the lucky one that you didn't give up on me a long time ago."

Her blue eyes held his caramel ones as she smiled, reaching her hand up to the rough stubble on his jaw. "I'll never give up on you, Tony. I love you. You'll always be my hero," she admitted, a tear sliding down her face.

Leaning down, he touched his lips to hers. A whisper of a kiss. But one with meaning. Heart. Soul. Forever.

TONY WENT INTO WORK to watch the cameras for a couple of hours after one of his employees had a family emergency. Sherrie hated that he worked so hard, but since the company was his she knew he felt responsible for every aspect.

After cleaning the house, she settled onto the sofa and flipped through the TV channels. Finding nothing, she clicked it off tossing the remote onto the end table. Seeing Betina's art pad lying next to it, she picked it up and began to flip through the pages again.

The faces on each page were so lifelike. Their expressions reached out to her as though she were sitting in front of the actual person instead of an impression on the page. Girls. Boys. Some adults. Some with smiles, sitting at school desks. Others with a strangely blank look on their faces. Some of the eyes seemed haunted.

Rubbing her hand on her forehead she stared, trying to have a subliminal message come through. *What was it she said?* "My life, my world is in these drawings. I need you to understand that." *Your world? What did you want me to understand?*

Feelings of frustration poured over her as the secret meaning was lost. Near the back of the art pad were drawings of places...the grocery, the laundry. Several of them were of the inside of the buildings depicting people at work. A few others were the outside, the details of her drawings overwhelming. She could see every brick on the outsides and every item on the insides.

Nothing. I'm getting nothing other than she is an incredibly talented artist. Maybe that was all she meant? Maybe she just meant that art is her world?

Giving in to the frustration, she heard Tony's truck pulling back into the driveway so she tossed the art pad back to the end table.

Marcella left for work, kissing Betina goodbye before walking out of the door. Betina hated when her mother went in early leaving her in the house alone with Hernando. Throwing her books into her back-pack, she tried to hurry in an effort to avoid him.

No such luck.

"Betina, sit down," he ordered walking into the kitchen. "We need to go over your new assignments."

New assignments? She did not like the sound of that, but his expression brooked no disobedience. *Fourteen more months and I'll be eighteen years old. Graduated. Out of this house. Out of his life. If I live that long.*

"Are you listening," he growled, grabbing her upper arm, pushing her into a chair.

"Yes," she replied, knowing she would have a bruise the next day. *What's one more?*

"Keep up with the kids at school, but I want you more in the field as well."

"I...where?" she asked in confusion.

"Bus station, for one. After school, you don't go to the grocery store anymore. I want you to go to the downtown bus station. Watch for the young ones. Girls. The ones that look lost. Or alone." Chuckling, he said, "Especially the ones that look scared and try not to show it. They'll be best."

"Best for what?" she asked.

His gaze was steel as he stared at her across the table. "Your job isn't to know a fuckin' thing. Your job is to do what I order, when I order, and exactly how I order. You got that?"

Her chest heaving with hate, she kept her expression steady. "Yeah, I got that. But what do I say?"

"Same as always. See if they need food. Direct them to the store. Once there, I or someone else will take care of them."

"What's different? Won't they work in one of your shops?" she asked, dangerously curious.

"You don't tell 'em shit. You just get their trust. Give 'em the address. Offer 'em food. Leave the rest to me."

Almost shaking with hate, she sat stoically for a moment, desperately trying to find a way to escape. This home. This man. This life.

His chair scraped across the floor as he jerked himself to a stand. He leaned over, his face right in hers, and snarled, "Don't even think it. I can see you trying to think of a way to not do this, but bitch, you want your mama safe? Then you do what I say, when I say it. You mess this up and not only will you go in a pimp's stable of whores, but your mama will too. You got me?"

"Yeah, I got it," she whispered, trying to still her erratic heartbeat.

"Good. See that you do. You start today." With that, he moved into the other room, calling out behind him, "Have a good day at school."

She heard him chuckling to himself, amused at his own joke. She hated him. This was her life. Her world. *If it's the last thing I do, I'm getting out.*

TONY SAT AT his desk studying the man sitting in front of him. Jacques "Jack" Bryant, his former Chief Warrant Officer. Jack, a big man at over six feet of pure muscle, had been leaner than the twins when they were in the service, but now Tony saw that he had put on weight…and none of it looked like fat.

"Jesus, you got bigger," Tony laughed.

"It's my mom's fuckin' cooking," he exclaimed. "When I got home two years ago from the Army, I moved back to the farm with her to help out since my dad had passed."

"I'm sorry," Tony admitted, realizing how out of touch he had been. There had been a time when the squad members knew every detail of each other's lives. "I had no idea your dad died."

"That's okay," Jack assured. "He got cancer and by the time they found out, he only had a few months to live. But man, I'd forgotten how my mom can cook. I'd be fat as a cow if it weren't for the farm work."

"You still there and trying to run a business?"

"Nah, she's renting out the farmland. It works good for her 'cause she lives in the house but doesn't have the farm responsibilities anymore. So how's the men?"

"Gabe got married several months ago and—"

"Married? Gabe? That horndog? Damn, I have been out of the loop. Tell me Vinny and Jobe haven't fallen under the spell?"

"Nah, Vinny's still the worst of them all and Jobe? You know him…he's waiting on someone special."

Tony smiled then noticed Jack's gaze intently staring at him. "Something on your mind?"

Jack rubbed his hand over his chin, pondering for a moment. "You seem…I don't know…happy."

Tony chuckled, knowing that being in love again really did show. "I found someone, Jack. Someone special and if she'll have me, I plan on asking her to marry me."

"I knew there was something going on with you. Captain, I'm happy for you. I thought you'd never get over…uh…well, not get over, but move on. I'm real glad you found someone. Tell me about her."

"Her name is Sherrie. She's a paralegal here in town."

"Is that how you met?" Jack asked.

Tony laughed, saying, "No. She was actually a rescue mission. She had some trouble and I went in. I wish I could say that I immediately went for her, but...well, I had some issues to deal with, and sometimes us guys can be dumb-shits."

"Ain't it the truth!" Jack agreed. The silence stretched for a moment before Jack added, "You deserve to be happy again, Captain."

Tony smiled his thanks before glancing at the garage monitors, Tony noticed his crew arriving at work. "Let's go meet the gang."

As Gabe, Vinny, and Jobe greeted Jack, the whoops and hollars could be heard around the building. Settling in Tony introduced Lily and BJ, identifying the assembly as his core group.

"I've been telling Jack about our operation here and he's interested in collaborating with us at times when needed. Our businesses are different enough that we can easily provide each other with our diverse skill set."

The others listened as Jack explained what he had assembled. "I had the opportunity during the last two years in the Special Forces to belong to a task force made up of multidisciplinary persons. I decided that with my government contacts, I could do something similar on the outside. I have someone from the CIA, FBI, DEA, and ATF as well as several from Homeland Security. We take jobs that often need us to um...fly under the radar, so to speak."

After a few more minutes discussing the various

scenarios with which the two companies could benefit each other, Tony asked for a report from Lily and BJ on Hernando.

"I have finally found something interesting. It seems that he has a high turnover of employees and I have also noticed that most of them live in the same apartment building. I share Sherrie's suspicions and am looking to see who owns the building and who pays the rent."

BJ added, "Boss, I drove by the grocery and laundry and found good spots for security cameras to keep an eye on the coming and goings. Jobe and I can use the utility company uniforms and appear to be working on the lights while installing the cameras."

Tony nodded in agreement and after a few more minutes of business, Lily and BJ left, leaving the former squad members a chance to catch up.

Finally, Jack stood and shook their hands goodbye. Tony walked him to his vehicle and the two old friends promised to get together soon.

"I'd like you to meet Sherrie," Tony added.

"I'd like that very much." Clapping his former Captain on the back, he said, "I never knew anyone who deserved happiness more than you, sir. If Sherrie's brought you back to life, then she will have my eternal gratitude."

THIS IS WHAT BETINA hated. Recruiting. Getting lonely, outcast girls to trust her. *So that I could get them shit jobs in a shit laundry for shit money.*

She walked down the hall toward the cafeteria, seeing a new student standing to the side, looking around trying to not stand out. *But you stand out to me. I can spot you a mile away.* Old clothes, worn backpack. A hungry look...not only for food but for company.

Betina casually walked over to the student, with a small smile on her face. Too big a smile and she would look insincere. No smile would make her look unfriendly.

"Hi. You new here?" she asked.

The girl nodded, her eyes darting around as though she did not want anyone to know she was new.

"I've been here a while. I can sit with you during lunch if you'd like," she added. "You want to get your lunch first?"

"I...um...don't eat lunch. I'm not hungry," came the reply, the girl's chin lifting in slight defense.

"I've got extra if you want," Betina offered, sitting next to the girl and offering an abundance of food from her backpack.

The girl's eyes grew wide as she looked at the food, but gratefully dug in. Betina made small talk for a few minutes, carefully gaining the girl's trust, while loathing herself.

"If you ever want more food my...step dad runs a grocery and he's always giving away some food to my friends. He might even get you a job there sometime if you want."

She knew the instant she had the unsuspecting girl hooked. It was the look in her eyes. The way she smiled at Betina like she were a saint. She handed the girl a card with the grocery's name and address printed on it. "When you go, just show them this card and they'll fix you up."

The bell rung and Betina stood, saying her good-byes. The other girl stopped her with her hand on Betina's arm.

"Thank you so much," she said. "This means so much to me that you would help me out. I really owe you," she added.

Tears hit the back of Betina's eyes as she battled to keep them at bay. "No problem," she croaked out then turned quickly to hurry back down the hall. She bypassed her English class and bolted out of the back door. Jogging down the street to an alley she crouched down behind a dumpster, finally letting the tears flow.

Cursing Hernando and whoever he worked for. Cursing her mother for being weak and not seeing what was going on in her own home. Cursing herself for being afraid to get out from under Hernando's control.

The tears finally abated and she sat a few more minutes in misery. *If I think this is bad, what about when I start recruiting at a bus stop.* She gritted her teeth and screamed out in frustration. Shaking with fury, she felt her tears flow again. Down the alley, a back door opened as a man came out trying to identify the scream. She hurried around the corner out of sight, wiping her tears away once more.

Taking a deep breath, she made her way to the nearest bus stop, knowing that she had no choice but to start Hernando's new assignment as soon as possible. *One more year until I graduate. One more year, mom, and then you're on your own. One more year and I'll leave Hernando forever. Please...just one more year.*

CHAPTER 20

TONY, GABE, BJ, AND JOBE parked their panel van across from the laundry, eyeing the building.

"Figured we could get one wide screen camera on this old apartment building here on this side of the road and it would capture the entire front of the laundry. Then we've got lots of places for the alley to get the back door. That would give us maximum vision on the exits," Jobe stated.

Tony nodded his agreement, saying, "Let's get going."

With the three men in nondescript uniforms they went to work, giving off the impression to any onlooker that they were from a utility company checking lights.

While Gabe and Jobe secured the hardware, Tony watched the front of the building for any observers, pleased to see that they did not appear to be attracting any unwanted attention. BJ worked in the back of the van with his computers, making sure of the connections and the visibility on his screens.

"Looks good, boss," he reported as Gabe and Jobe climbed back into the van.

Driving around to the back they repeated the operation. "What do you think is going on, Captain?" Jobe asked.

"Don't really know. That's why I haven't called in Matt or Shane yet. But Sherrie was attacked near here. Lily says there is a high turnover of employees and when she dug deeper, she wasn't too sure about the tax records for the laundry. If Sherrie is working with this guy's stepdaughter, then I want to know what's happening."

Gabe and Jobe made quick work of installing the camera in the alley and as soon as BJ cleared it as operational, they headed to Hernando's grocery store to do the same.

Tony sat in the driver's seat watching as Hernando walked out of the front of the building and waited on the sidewalk. After a few minutes, two teenage girls with a younger boy with them came around the corner. They approached Hernando cautiously before handing him a card. Hernando made a grandiose gesture of bringing them inside.

To the outside world, he looked like a generous neighborhood businessman, but the hairs on Tony's neck stood up. Too many years trained to notice every detail of his surroundings, including people, had him distrusting the man instantly. *Fucker's up to something.* The idea of Sherrie having to be in the man's presence at all had him gritting his teeth so hard he thought they would break.

His attention was diverted when Gabe and Jobe

joined them in the van again.

"Job's done," Gabe announced. "By the way, did you see that guy out front? Is that him, 'cause I wouldn't trust that guy for nothing."

Before Tony could agree, Jobe spoke up. "Got a bad vibe, Captain."

Nodding, Tony pulled the van away from the curb. He always trusted his instincts, but knowing that his men had the same thoughts...*oh yeah, we'll be watching you.*

FRIDAY NIGHT FOUND SHERRIE AND JENNIFER sitting on bar stools at Cantina's, a new Mexican restaurant in town that advertised early-bird Happy Hour drink specials for women. They had decided to take advantage of the deal and Sherrie and Jennifer were already into their second Aquatini.

"When are the guys getting here?" Sherri asked, feeling the effects of the strong drink. Blinking several times, she tried to glare at the bartender. "I think he's trying to get me drunk. This thing is potent."

Sherrie looked resplendent in an emerald green dress with a tight bodice and flowing, short skirt. The bodice was low enough to offer a tantalizing glimpse of the tops of her breasts, while the skirt swayed with each step she took.

Jennifer, looking like a fairy princess in her blue,

off-the-shoulder dress, rounded out the duo of beauties. The women talked and laughed for several minutes before the waitress brought several drinks over, pointing to the two men from the bar who sent them. Sherrie shook her head and said, "We'll pay for our own drinks, thank you." The bartender nodded and moved to serve the next customer.

"So how's Ross doing?" Sherrie asked about Jennifer's brother.

"God, he's growing like a weed. None of his clothes seem to fit so I threatened to drag him shopping the other day. Ross grumbled, so Gabe stepped in and took him. I was so grateful until they got back home."

Already giggling, Sherrie asked, "What'd they buy?"

"Black t-shirts and cargo pants," Jennifer clipped.

Her forehead wrinkled in confusion, she said, "What's wrong with that?"

"Because that was all they bought. He told Gabe he wanted to dress like him so he got five black t-shirts and three pairs of cargo pants. He's going to look like a ten-year-old security agent!"

The ladies giggled again at the idea of a little mini-Gabe running around. "I do have to tell you something," Jennifer said softly.

Cutting her eyes quickly to her friend, Sherrie asked, "What?"

"We're buying a house. We'll move into it in about a month."

Throwing her arms around her friend, Sherrie

exclaimed, "Oh my God, that's wonderful." Knowing how much Jennifer wanted to raise her brother in a house with room for a dog had her squeezing Jennifer tightly, while tears hit the back of her eyes.

"So…" Jennifer said, "Tell me about you. What's new with the CASA case you're working on."

Sherrie quickly filled Jennifer in on Betina's case. Jennifer's background as a social worker had her on alert instantly with the new information Sherrie was giving her.

"I don't know what's going on, Sherrie, but be careful. Trust your instincts. If it doesn't seem right, then go with that gut feeling."

Sherrie nodded slowly, her mind going back to the art pad. "I keep getting the feeling that there is something there."

"Then keep digging."

By the time their third drinks were placed in front of the girls, they pushed them back simultaneously. "Oh, no. No more. I've gotta move or I'll fall off this stool."

Jennifer slid off her seat and pulled Sherrie down as well. "Let's hit the ladies' room, then hopefully the men will show up soon."

Sherrie stifled a yawn. "If they're not here soon, let's catch a cab home and call it a night."

Pouting, Jennifer agreed. "And we looked so good, too. Just for them."

Slightly swaying as she made her way to the bathroom down the hall next to the bar, Sherrie said, "Well then, we'll just tell them about the men that wanted to buy us drinks so they'll think twice about missing our dates."

Finishing their business and touching up their makeup, the two friends walked out of the restroom, arm in arm. Hearing a whimper, they turned toward the sound, seeing a large man with his hand clamped around a woman's wrist, pulling her through the back exit door.

"You accepted the drinks I sent and you drank them. Seems like I should get some thanks," he was saying as the door slammed behind them.

Without hesitation, the two women ran to the door pushing it open. The man was several feet away, his hands now on the woman's shoulders as he pushed her against the brick wall. She was crying and struggling, but to no avail. He had at least six inches and fifty pounds of pure muscle on her. Off to the side was another man, much smaller, with a weaselly look on his face as his hands were unzipping his pants.

Sherrie screamed, "Back off—"

"Get outta here, bitches. This ain't your business," the larger man growled.

Jennifer immediately barked, "We're making it our business," as she pulled out her cell phone and took a quick picture of the men assaulting the woman.

"Goddamn it," he shouted as he let go of the still whimpering woman and barked at his friend. "Get her."

The weasel stalked toward Jennifer as she shoved her phone back into her purse and looked toward the bar door.

"You ain't getting away with my picture, bitch," he sneered as he grabbed her arm. She managed to kick him with her stiletto heels in the shin and he bent over howling. While he was hopping around on one foot, she kneed him in the crotch.

"Dammit, you're worthless," the large man growled as he left the whimpering woman and reached for Jennifer.

Sherrie whirled, then jumped on the back of the man before he could grab her. She wrapped her arms around his neck and tried to squeeze, realizing too late that she had no idea how to take him down.

As he reached up to her arms, Jennifer ran over and kicked him in the shins also, infuriating him further. Slapping her across the face, he backed up quickly slamming Sherrie in the wall behind him. The impact pounded right through her, but she refused to let go of his neck. He slammed her once again. As he prepared to do it one more time, she knew she could not stand another hit.

Jennifer's face, filled with rage, came at him from the front with a trash can lid, hitting him in the legs as she aimed for his crotch.

Sherrie squeezed her eyes shut, trying to prepare for the next bone-jarring assault.

TONY PUSHED HIS WAY through the crowd, moving toward the bar since Sherrie's last text said that they were waiting there. Gabe, right beside him, scanned the area not seeing the women at all.

Vinny chuckled. "Looks like they may have given up and gone home. Sucks for you, but the rest of us may have some luck," he said, his eyes scanning the room at the obviously available women hungrily looking back at him.

The air crackled in the bar as the four men made their way forward. Tall, built, confident—the crowd parted as they shouldered their way through. Making it to the bar, Tony nodded toward the bartender who immediately hustled over.

"You see two beautiful blondes here together?"

"Yeah, man. They attracted a lot of attention; a couple of men sent them drinks but they insisted on keeping their own tab. They waitin' on you?"

At Gabe's nod, the bartender glanced around. "They headed to the ladies' room a while back. Come to think of it, I haven't seen them since."

The hair prickled on the back of Tony's neck as it always did when a mission was not going well. He stalked toward the hall behind the bar, Gabe on his heels. Vinny, in tune as always to not only his twin but his former commander, immediately followed.

Seeing the exit sign over the door beyond the restrooms, Tony slammed through, the sight outside stopping his blood cold. Instantly, the situation was assessed and the men went into action. Like years before on mission, but now? It was personal.

Sherrie suddenly felt a rush of air hit her front as she began to fall, only to be grabbed before hitting the ground. But these arms were gentle. Throwing her eyes open, she tried to escape, but a soft voice whispered in her ear.

"Relax, honey. I've got you," Jobe's voice soothed.

Breathing heavily, she twisted around to see what was happening. Oh my God. The man who had her pressed against the wall, was now being held up against the wall, Tony's hand on his throat as the only thing holding him up. The man was gurgling and gasping as the fight was leaving him. Eyes darting to the side, she saw Vinny cradling a crying Jennifer as Gabe was in the process of pummeling the man who had been on his wife.

Shaking, she looked back to Tony who had not let go of her assailant's neck and screamed, "Stop!" Twisting in Jobe's arms, she cried, "He'll kill him and go to jail."

"Shhh, darlin'. Tony's got it. He knows what he's doing."

Tony's eyes were black as he easily held the squirming man. "You touched my woman, any woman, without their permission?" he growled.

Heedless of the man's gasping, he held him firmly

with one arm of steel. The only other sound was Gabe's fist hitting the other man.

Sherrie continued to shake despite the gentle hold Jobe had on her. She was dimly aware of the shushing noise he made but all she could see was Tony's fury.

"Tony," she heard Jobe's voice call out. "See to her." Instantly the man against the wall crumpled to the ground as Tony's hand left his throat. Turning quickly, he pulled Sherrie from Jobe's embrace, his face stone hard but his eyes caramel warm.

"Are you all right? Did he hurt you, baby? You gotta tell me," he pleaded, not sure he would be able to contain himself if the answer were 'yes'.

With her head pressed tightly against his chest, she could only mumble. He lifted her chin to peer into her eyes, seeing tear streaks down her cheeks.

"No. No, he was going to," she panted. "Jennifer? Is she—"

"She's fine. Gabe's got her," he said, kissing her hair. His military training taught him to regulate his breathing but nothing was helping now. Heartbeat pounding, he could not seem to let her go.

The police arrived and took the statement of the young woman, still crying with Vinny's arms around her. Sherrie made her way over to Jennifer throwing her arms around her. Now that the danger had passed what was left was anger and both women now shook with rage.

The woman they rescued made her way over before

the police drove her home. Her tear stained face looked up at them as she gave her heartfelt thanks.

"I'm so ashamed. I did accept the drinks they were sending over, but never meant for any of this to happen."

"No man should ever put his hands on you that you don't agree go," Jobe spoke up behind her, his eyes cold and dark.

Sherrie hugged her, but could not help but throw out some advice. "Stick with the buddy system, sweetie," she said, winking at Jennifer. "It helps."

The police detective made his way over to the two women. "So according to the young woman, you didn't know her before and hadn't noticed her at the bar?"

"No," Sherrie admitted. "We were just coming out of the bathroom, when we saw him grab her."

"I didn't like the way he was kind of pulling her along. You could tell she didn't want to go," Jennifer added.

"Did you call for help or try to get the attention of anyone from the bar?" he asked.

Eyes flashing, Sherrie placed her hand on her hip and began tapping her foot. "There wasn't a whole lot of time to think about what to do, you know? We just ran out here to see what we could do to help."

"And when you got out here, you found not one but two men assaulting the woman. So you two did what?"

"We...um..." Sherrie's eyes cut over to Tony

standing with his men. Arms crossed over his chest. Legs apart. His stance was…foreboding. And his expression…*oh dear.*

Jennifer was staring at Gabe and Vinny as well. Their expressions were like Tony's. Pissed. "We…well, I got my phone out and took his picture—"

"You what?" exploded Gabe, uncrossing his massive arms and placing them on his hips.

"You know? For evidence?" Jennifer stuttered.

"What happened then?" the detective continued.

Sherrie took pity on Jennifer and jumped in to defend her. "The big one holding the woman told the weasel to go after Jennifer."

"The weasel?"

"Yeah, he looked kind of like a weasel."

At this point Tony felt as though his head was going to explode. Jobe was now grinning and Vinny was trying to hold on to his anger, although it seemed to be a losing battle. Gabe was still furious and the more the girls talked, the angrier he became.

The detective looked at his partner as he wrote her statement down. "Okay, so what did the weasel do?"

Jennifer continued, "He tried to grab me but I kicked him in the…um…down there," she whispered. The detective's pen hovered over his pad as his gaze lifted back to hers.

Vinny, unable to contain his laughter, slapped Gabe on the back. "Your woman just kicked a man in the nuts and you're pissed." Walking over to her, he leaned down, kissing the top of her head.

"Don't encourage her," Gabe bit out.

The detective wanting to finish the statements turned to Sherrie asking, "And what did you do during this?"

Avoiding Tony's glare, she answered, "When Mr. Big went after Jennifer I jumped on his back." Ignoring the growl emanating from him, she continued. "He couldn't shake me off, so he kept running backward into the wall to try to jar me loose. I held on for two of them, but I was kind of scared that when he did it again, then I wouldn't be able to hang on." She smiled then, saying, "But then they showed up and finished them off." She hoped her smile would lessen the fury on Tony's face. It didn't.

The detective snapped his notebook shut, saying, "If you think of anything else, give us a call." With that, they left, leaving the two girls surrounded by four large men.

"Tony," Sherrie began. "I jus—"

He threw his hand up, saying, "I don't want to hear it."

"But—"

Stalking toward her, he towered over her and growled, "Do you know how stupid it was for you to jump on a man his size? You should have called the police. You should have run into the bar. You should have—"

Stamping her foot in anger, she poked her finger in

his chest. "Don't you dare lecture me! You go out all the time and rescue people. I do it one time and you get pissy."

Tony looked down at the small finger being shook at him. *One snap and that man could have broken her hand. Or knocked her out. Or...*

Sherrie, with her arm around Jennifer, continued her rant. "We saw a woman being dragged out of a building and we just acted on instinct."

Looking up at her husband, Jennifer added, "Kind of like you did when you ran out here and saw us."

Gabe walked over, pulling Jennifer from Sherrie's hold. Kissing the top of her head, he sighed. "Babe, not happy. But all I want to do right now is get you home, let you soak in the tub and then hold you all night until my heart stops pounding in fear."

Smiling up at him, she leaned into him. He turned and headed out of the alley with her tucked under his arm. The rest of the group then heard him say, "And then I'll spank your ass red."

Vinny and Jobe chuckled as they headed back into the bar, leaving Tony and Sherrie standing in the alley by themselves. She lifted her face to his, fighting back the tears that threatened to fall. He stepped forward, enveloping her in his embrace once more, pressing her face into his chest. She could hear his heartbeat. Solid. Strong. They said nothing. The anger drained from him as he cradled her to his chest. Several minutes passed in silence as they both drew strength from each other. Together, stronger than apart.

"I'm sorry I scared you," her small voice said.

His arms tightened. "I'm sorry I yelled," he admitted. Taking his hand from the back of her head, he slid his fingers to her chin, lifting it up. Peering into her tear filled eyes, remorse struck him. "I am sorry, baby. I'm proud that you jumped in to help someone. I just...I never want to feel that feeling I had when I came through the door and saw that fucker slamming you against a wall. All I could think of was choking the life out of him."

"I know. I was scared too. We should have called for help, but honestly Tony? The adrenaline took over and we just jumped in." They were silent again for a moment, then she asked, "Is that what it is for you? When you have a mission?"

"Yes," he admitted, "but I'm trained. Trained to fight. Trained to kill. Trained to assess my enemy in an instant. You, my sweet, are not."

She nodded, knowing he was right. Looking back up, she suddenly felt utterly exhausted. "Take me home?" she asked.

"No place else I'd rather be, darlin'," he said, tucking her in his embrace as they headed toward his truck. One hand slid down to her hips as they walked. "And I'm thinking that Gabe's got the right idea," he said, giving her ass a sharp pat.

CHAPTER 21

VINNY AND GABE were in the main Alvarez area working on a new security system when BJ walked by, calling out to Vinny.

"Boss wants to see you. He's in his office."

Vinny immediately headed to Tony's office, finding him at his desk with files spread in front of him. "You called for me, sir?"

Tony looked up at one of his most trusted friends. Vinny was smart, quick, intelligent, the best sharpshooter he had ever seen, and Gabe's backup medic. Vinny might joke and screw around during down time, but when the mission was in full swing, there was no one he trusted more to have his back than him.

"Business has been steady and we've got a good reputation in Richland and now in Virginia as a whole. But I've got a new request from someone who needs us in another state. That kind of recognition has come from hard work and dedication and I'd like you to take it. This could take our company to a whole new level."

Vinny's interest was piqued and he waited to hear more about it.

"Got a request for a security detail to escort someone from Los Angeles to Richland." Before he could continue, he saw the flash of interest as well as concern in Vinny's eyes. Gabe had gotten tangled up with a diva actress on an assignment before meeting Jennifer, and it had turned out to be a cock-up situation.

"Nope, not an actress. A musician," Tony clarified.

"Just an escort detail?" Vinny asked, willing to take any mission assigned, but curiosity getting the better of him.

"Yes, they'll have a concert in LA where you will meet them. You'll escort them on their flight to Richland."

"Concert?" Vinny asked, not able to keep the idea of spending a couple of days with a female musician, preferably a beautiful rock star, out of his mind. "Who is it?"

Tony sat quietly for a moment, staring at the file in front of him. Rubbing his chin in thought, he finally looked up at Vinny and said succinctly, "Not saying."

Vinny's eyebrows pulled together in confusion. "Not...saying? Sir?"

Tony looked deeply at Vinny before continuing. "Vincent, you're one of my best. Ever since the first time I laid eyes on you and your twin, I couldn't have asked for better. One thing about you was that when you were on a mission, you gave me one-hundred percent. Off mission, if you thought with your dick it didn't matter. You still work just as hard for me as when we were in the Special Forces, but I need your head on this mission and not thinking with your dick."

Vinny started to protest, but Tony put up his hand. "I want you in this mission, regardless of who it is."

Vinny, understanding what was at stake, agreed. Male, female, old, young—it did not matter to the mission. Standing, he nodded to the leader he trusted with his life. "When do I leave?"

"I'll have the details by the end of the week and you need to be ready to fly to California in a couple of weeks."

His cocky grin back in place, he nodded as he said, "You got it, Sir."

Tony looked back to the file in front of him, a slow smile beginning to spread across his face. *This mission will be good for Vinny. Good for the agency, but good for Vinny.*

SHERRIE ENDED HER MEETING with her bosses and organized her files on her desk. Looking at them, she realizes that Mr. Marks' needs for her had decreased while Simon's had increased. As she continued to ponder the workload, she realized that Mr. Marks was definitely taking on less and less. *I've been so busy with my CASA case, I hadn't even noticed. Is he ill?* The more she thought about it, the more concerned she became.

She checked the time and hurried down the hall to his office, wanting to catch him before he left. His door was opened, but she knocked on the door frame anyway. He looked up, smiling, and invited her in.

"Did we forget something at our meeting?" he asked.

"No, sir. I just...um." Now that she was there, she was not sure what to say.

Laughing, he pointed to the old, comfortable leather chair in front of his desk. "My dear, just come right out with it. I think we've grown familiar enough with each other that you can just ask me what is on your mind."

She settled in the seat, resisting the urge to lean back in the soft leather, instead perching at the edge. "Sir, I've noticed that you're not giving me as many assignments as before and I was, well...are you still satisfied with my work?"

"Sherrie, of course I'm satisfied. You are one of the best paralegals I have ever worked with in my *long* career."

Noticing he emphasized the word 'long', she was unable to ascertain what he meant by that. She watched as he took off his glasses and rubbed his eyes, then brought out a cloth from his jacket pocket to clean his spectacles off before replacing them. Sighing, he said, "I've been thinking of something for a while now, but until I talked to Simon to get things settled, I hadn't wanted to say anything."

"Are you well?" she could not help but burst out.

His eyes widened in surprise and he quickly said,

"Oh, yes. I'm fine. I'm so sorry that you worried. I never thought that you would think of illness." He looked over at her with a gentle, fatherly look on his face and said simply, "I'm retiring, my dear. It's been a long career in law that I have loved. But now, I'm feeling my age. My wife's mother needs more care. My wife and I would like to travel more and see the grandkids. The time is right."

Sherrie did not know what to say. The idea of him leaving the office filled her with sadness, but the idea that he could be free to do what he needed or wanted certainly was deserved. "I…I'll miss you so much," she admitted, "But I can see why you want to retire."

"Thank you, Sherrie. I've been slowing down, turning more over to Simon but I realize that I'll need to have someone replace me. Simon and I have talked. He'll buy out my share of the business and then will hire another lawyer since it will be important for him to have a say in who he works with. As far as you and the receptionist, of course your jobs are safe."

She was grateful, especially since she had not even considered that her job might be in jeopardy. "Do you know when you'll retire?"

"I was thinking in about another two months. That will give the office a chance to make more changes and time for us to make all of the arrangements. My wife and I will sell our home here and be moving to North Carolina to be nearer her mother and our daughter. And it will satisfy my need to get out on the water and do some fishing," he added, a smile on his face.

"Um…what about your cabin?" she asked hesitantly, wondering if they would keep it so that she and Tony could return sometime.

"I've got a buyer for it and will have it off my hands soon. My wife and I are trying to simplify everything."

Nodding, she tried to keep the disappointed look off of her face. Lifting her gaze back to his, she said honestly, "I'll miss you, Mr. Marks. You gave me a chance when no one else would."

He rose from his seat and walked over to her, taking her hand and pulling her from her chair. Holding both of her hands, he said warmly, "You have been like another daughter to me these past two years. I appreciate everything you do and wish you nothing but the best." With that, he lifted her right hand to his lips, giving a soft kiss.

SITTING IN HER CAR, Sherrie watched Betina as she left school and hopped on a Richland Transport bus. She followed her, noting that she did not get off at the grocery or the laundry. In fact, she followed her all the way to the large, downtown bus station. Parking, she quickly found Betina standing near the edge of the building talking to two young women, their luggage at their feet.

What the hell is she doing? Sherrie moved closer so

that she could hear, but not be readily seen. A group of tall lockers stood between her and Betina and she prayed that they stayed on the other side.

"You don't have any family here?" Betina asked. The two others must have indicated they did not, because Betina continued. "I was like you too. Came into town not knowing anyone and was on the streets in no time. Costs a ton of money to rent an apartment. And food? Totally outrageous."

"So how'd you make it," another girl's voice asked.

"Finally met a great guy who runs a grocery. He likes to hire teens because it helps them and keeps his costs down too. Plus I get some food every day and he'll help find you roommates to share an apartment with."

"How lucky you are," came another female voice. "You think he's looking for more help?"

"He's always looking," Betina answered. "I hear he's opening a club and he'll need help there as well. How old are you?"

"I'm eighteen and she's sixteen," was the answer.

"That's perfect. He'll train you as a cocktail waitress and you can make a ton of money in tips."

"What about me?" the younger voice asked.

Sherrie heard a hesitation in Betina's response. Leaning closer to the end of the row of lockers, she strained to hear.

"He'll...take care of you too. He's got...um...different jobs he can give for...

um…different stuff."

"Well, we just got off the bus with nowhere to go. How do we get in touch with him?"

"I've got a card with the grocery's address on it. You can stop by there anytime and if he's not there, just ask for the assistant manager, Juan."

"What about now? Can you show us?"

Sherrie heard the soft sigh coming from Betina. *What is she doing? It's like she's recruiting them for jobs. There's no way Hernando can take all of these kids to work. And club? What club?* Her mind racing with thoughts, she almost missed the fact that they had walked over to one of the buses. Peeking around the lockers, she saw Betina buy the tickets before handing them to the other two girls. Getting a good look at them now, she could see that the older one had auburn hair pulled into a ponytail with a top-heavy figure showcased in a tight t-shirt. The younger girl had stringy blonde hair and was very slim.

What kind of club is she talking about? Having worked as a cocktail waitress before, Sherrie knew that if it was a slimy place like she had been in, the expectation was that the waitresses would perform any service just like the strippers on stage. Sherrie had resisted, but she was in her early twenties at the time and capable of making her own decisions. These girls? They looked tired, hungry and willing to take what was given.

She quickly got back into her car, now that she

knew they were heading to the grocery. Getting there before the city transit, she parked close enough to see what was going on without being intrusive.

She saw when the three girls alighted from the bus and walked to the store. Juan was outside placing new sales signs on the windows when they approached. *Damn, I wish I could hear what they are saying.* She rolled her window down and strained to hear anything from the conversation.

TONY'S PHONE RANG and as he glanced at the identification, he saw it came from his surveillance room. "Yeah?"

"Got a visual of Sherrie sitting in her car outside the grocery. That girl she works with is standing outside also with two other girls and a man, not Hernando. She's not in trouble, but just thought I'd let you know. She's obviously trying to see what's going on." Chuck, the newest hire for Alvarez Security, laughed. "Yeah, she has her window down and is half hanging out of the car trying to listen. I'm not sure her surveillance skills are quite up to your standards, boss."

"Shit," Tony said, rubbing his hand over his face. "Keep watching and let me know when she leaves."

"Got it," came the affirmative.

Tony sat back in his chair, thoughts of Sherrie filling his mind. Lily walked in to hand him some information on a case and noticed his pensiveness.

"You okay, Tony?" she asked.

Starting to just agree, he hesitated.

"It is work or Sherrie?" she prodded, then smiled. "I know business is good, it must be Sherrie."

Chuckling, he nodded. "It seems…harder. Or different. I…" He knew he was not making sense, but had difficulty putting into words the emotions swirling around.

Lily sat in the chair across from him and asked, "Tony, were you around much with your first wife?"

"Truthfully? No. I was usually away on duty."

"So, even though you loved your wife and she must have not minded being alone while you served overseas, you were removed from a lot of the day to day annoyances. You know, like who squeezes the tooth-paste from the bottom, kind of stuff."

He sat, thoughtful. *Did Marla resent me being gone? She always seemed so in control of everything and when I was home, we just enjoyed each other.* His mind rolled to Sherrie and the corners of his mouth began to turn up.

"Living with someone, day in and day out, isn't easy. It's not all naked fun," Lily giggled. Then her face sobered as she thought of the issues she and Matt had had to work on. "I guess what I'm saying is that the relationship you have with Sherrie is nothing like what you had with your wife years before."

Tony nodded as he turned his gaze to the wise woman sitting in front of him. "You're right," he agreed, knowing that Marla had been easy-tempered and complacent, exactly what he needed then. But Sherrie? She was fire and ice...and he love it.

Lily stood, nodding to the papers on his desk. "That's some of the work I've been helping Matt and Shane with. I've done some digging on the missing girls that Gabe and Jobe are working on as well. There may be a link, Tony. Give me another day and I think we may need to meet."

Trusting Lily's instinct, he nodded as she left.

FINALLY, THE MAN outside the grocery walked inside with the two girls from the bus station. They were all smiling, but Sherrie could not get the feeling that something untoward was happening and it directly involved Betina. The young girl started walking down the street, so Sherrie jumped out of her car and called to her.

A startled looked appeared on Betina's face instead of the usual smile that Sherrie received.

"Um...hey," Betina said, adopting an air of non-chalance.

Not wasting time, Sherrie approached her. "You want to tell me what that was all about?"

"What?" Betina asked. "I don't know what you mean."

"Those girls. The bus station. Hernando being such

an altruistic guy. The club. Talk to me, Betina. What is going on?"

Eyes wide with fright, Betina glanced around quickly to see if anyone was around. Grabbing Sherrie's arm she pulled her over toward the parking lot. "You shouldn't be following me," she hissed.

"What's going on?" Sherrie repeated. "You can't tell me that something's not happening and I've got a bad feeling." She saw tears in Betina's eyes and a look of agony.

"I'm just trying to help," she answered. "That's all." Glancing around nervously, she said, "We really can't talk here. I'm fine. I promise."

Betina turned to walk back down the street, then stopped when she heard Sherrie call, "I care about you. Please let me help." Twisting around, she said once again, "My life is in my art."

"Betina, I don't know what you mean by that," Sherrie admitted, her frustration at an all-time high.

Glancing around once more, she leaned in slightly toward Sherrie and said, "The eyes are the mirror of my soul." Her quote was accompanied with her eyes filled with pleading.

With that, Betina hurried around the corner, leaving Sherrie standing on the street, as perplexed as ever. Getting into her car, she drove home, determined to re-examine the art pad and not stop until she discovered what Betina was talking about.

SHE MISSED THE MAN in the car, listening to their conversation. Hernando had driven up and saw Betina and the nosy bitch having what looked like an argument. Betina was his best recruiter, easily manipulated by threats against her mother. *Maybe it's time to move her to the club. A few nights being used by the men looking for young pussy would go a long way to keeping her under control.* The idea had merit, but then he watched the bitch drive away. *But if Betina disappears, Ms. Mullins would be looking for her, and that could get messy. Unless,* he thought with a smile, *Ms. Mullins is taken care of. After all, there are more clubs than just his that can always use pussy. She would bring a good price.* Smiling, he left his car and walked into the store to meet the two new recruits.

THAT EVENING TONY found Sherrie sitting at the kitchen table, an art pad in front of her as she poured over each picture. She looked up guiltily as he walked in.

"Oh, no. I lost track of time and didn't even think about dinner."

Walking over, he pulled out his phone and quickly ordered pizza to be delivered before leaning down to kiss her. Taking her face in his hands, he deepened the kiss, determined to take away the look of fatigue on her face.

"You never have to worry about fixing dinner for me, babe. I'm just as capable of getting us something. Anyway, you look like you are hard at work." He leaned back in for another taste. His dick reared to life as his hand slid down to cup her breast. Rubbing his thumb over her nipple, he captured her moan in his mouth.

"Food's not gonna be here for at least twenty minutes," he pointed out.

Her answer to his unasked question was to suck his tongue into her mouth while palming the straining erection pressing against his jean zipper.

Lifting her in his arms, he felt her legs wrap around his waist. Backing her a few feet, he carried her to the stairs before laying her down. Pulling her yoga pants over her hips, dragging her panties along with them, he tossed them to the bottom of the stairs. She leaned up and fumbled with his zipper, trying to get it over his swollen cock.

"Thank God you don't go commando or I'd be afraid of zipping your dick," she said between breathless kisses.

"Don't even joke about a zipped dick, baby," he warned, pushing her hands away and taking care of his jeans himself. He watched as she lifted her shirt over her head and threw it across the banister to land somewhere in the hall below. He grabbed the front of her bra and with a flip of his wrist had it unsnapped and tossed it somewhere behind him.

Laid back against the stairs, she was perfect. Toned figure with her natural breasts free and her legs parted, her glistening sex bared for his perusal. Not able to wait, he pulled her legs over his shoulders and dove in, latching his mouth on her clit before licking her folds. *God, I love the taste of her.*

The mini explosions sent her head back against the stairs as her hands grabbed his hair, holding on for the ride. It did not take long for her inner core to tighten like a spring ready to snap. Lifting his hands to her breasts while keeping his tongue deep inside, he tweaked and pulled each nipple. Moving quickly back to suck her clit deeply into his mouth, he felt her shatter as he lapped her juices.

Screaming her release, she pushed her hips up keeping them in contact with his face. Not that he was going anywhere; at least, not until he had ridden out her orgasm. Gently pulling her legs from his shoulders, he watched as her satisfied smile filled him. Feeling more connected with her than with anyone ever in his life, he knew what Lily meant. This woman was worth everything to him.

"Over baby," he ordered, assisting her in turning over to face the stairs, her gorgeous ass in the air. Dragging the end of his straining cock through her juices, he knew she was ready. Plunging to the hilt, he pushed as deeply as he could. "You okay?" he asked, loving the feel of her tight core already grabbing his dick, but wanting to make sure she was comfortable.

A moan and the backward push of her hips, further impaling his erection into her, was her answer.

Grabbing her hips, he pounded into her. The time for slow and easy had passed. With the slapping of his balls against her ass sounding in the stairwell, he reached around finding her breasts bouncing with each thrust. Pinching first one nipple and then the other quickly had her panting, trying to find her release again.

He looked down at the woman in front of him. Her back, smooth and silky, ending in a lusciously curved ass just perfect for his hands. He moved his thumb over her rosebud opening and, expecting her to stiffen, was surprised to find her pushing herself back toward him even further.

"You'd like that sometime, baby?" he asked, applying slight pressure to her opening without penetrating.

"Yes, anything with you," she admitted between breaths.

Smiling, he glanced at the mirror on the hall opposite of the stairs, catching a glimpse of their bodies. Seeing her breasts bouncing up and down as he pulled out and pushed back made him even harder, if that was possible. She quickly reached the peak again and screamed his name out once more as the explosion rocketed from her sex outwards to her whole being. Within a few more strokes, he felt his balls tighten as he released deep inside of her. Throwing his head back, he roared as he powered through his own orgasm.

This time, she glanced to the mirror on the wall, watching in fascination at their coupling. Smiling, she saw him as he collapsed on top of her, both falling to the stairs.

Before they had time to catch their breath, the doorbell rang. Sherrie's eyes grew wide as she searched in vain for her clothes.

"Babe, run upstairs. I'll get the door."

She obeyed and grabbed new clothes to put on. As she came down the stairs, she saw Tony holding the pizza box and her bra. Giving him a questioning look, he grinned, saying, "This was at the front door. The delivery boy noticed it and handed it to my while I got my money."

Eyes wide, with a blush blistering her face, she exclaimed, "Oh my God. We can never order from there again!"

Kissing the top of her head while he moved toward the kitchen, "No worries, babe. I gave him a big tip."

Groaning, she made her way into the kitchen be-hind him. *Men!*

CHAPTER 22

SUNDAY MORNING DAWNED and just as they were enjoying their coffee, Tony received a call. A security system they had installed in the home of one of Richland's wealthiest neighborhoods had gone off, indicating an intruder. Tony and Jobe were heading there to reset the system after the police were finished.

After he left, Sherrie pulled out the art pad and began looking at the pictures again. The detail of the faces was amazing. *The eyes are the mirror of my soul. Not 'the soul' as the quote goes, but she said, 'my soul'. What did she mean?*

The eyes of the faces were filled in with swirls of her art pen. Sort of like a script if one looked closely. *Script?* She hurried to the kitchen and rummaged around in her junk drawer, pulling out a magnifying glass. Hustling back to the table, she grabbed a small lamp from the end table and brought it over as well. With the extra light focused directly on the faces and the magnifying glass on the eyes, she could see...*Oh my God, writing. Tiny, miniscule writing.*

Grabbing a pen and notebook, she wrote out the first word she saw. Patrick. *Was that the name of the boy in the picture?*

Turning to the next page, she used the magnifying glass to peer into the eyes of the young girl depicted. Linda.

Excited, she moved through the art pad, finding names scripted in each of the eyes of the drawings. Not knowing what it meant, she knew she had latched onto something. Wanting to call Tony, she looked at her watch. He had only been gone an hour. *I can't disturb him now.*

Flipping over to the drawings of the grocery and laundry, she marveled once again at the detail of Betina's talent. The bricks in the buildings, the signs in the windows—as though she was looking at a photograph. Glancing at the magnifying glass lying on the table she grabbed it. *Maybe there's more script.*

Not finding any, she felt her frustration return. Refusing to give up, she rubbed her eyes before bending to the task once again. Moving from the grocery store drawing to the laundry, she slowly slid the glass over the building. As the window came into view, she jumped. What had looked like circular squiggles over the windows giving them a dirty look at a quick glance were...*faces.*

Her heart pounded as she looked at the tiny faces peering out of the window. Not distinct features, but definitely faces.

Laying the glass down, she put her shaking hand on her mouth. *What is going on in that building? Are those the faces of people being held there?*

A glance at her watch again indicated that Tony would not be home for hours. Sending him a quick text, she headed out of the door. Sunday in the middle of the day would be the best time for sleuthing she thought. Daylight. No one working on a Sunday. *Perfect.*

Thirty minutes later she pulled into the well-lit alley behind the laundry. Her phone beeped an incoming message from Tony. He had received her message and told her under no circumstances was she to go alone.

Sitting in her car, she quickly called the Alvarez Security. When Doug answered, she immediately told him where she was.

"Girl, stay in that vehicle until one of us gets there and if anything looks weird, get the fuck out of there."

She was just agreeing when she heard a commotion in the background. "Doug? What's going on?"

Doug got back on the phone, saying, "Girl, there's gonna be hell to pay. Tony just called to have us check on you, but I told him we were on our way since you'd called in first."

Pursing her lips, she knew Tony would be mad, but she had followed his directions. *I called first and I'm waiting.*

Seeing Vinny pull into the alley, she got out of her car and was able to hear noise from inside the building that her car had muffled. *Damn, I thought it would be shut down for the day.* Metal stairs zig-zagged up the back of the building with a pile of crates underneath. Looking around before waving to Vinny as he parked, she quickly climbed up the crates and pulled herself up the metal ladder.

Making her way to the nearest window, she peeked in.

"BOSS, SHE'S GOOD," Doug called out as soon as Tony and Jobe reached the agency.

The re-setting of the complicated system had taken longer than he wanted and as much as he wanted to get home, he knew he needed to check on the materials for the next install. He hurried into the surveillance room, Jobe on his heels.

"Vinny was closest, so I have already sent him and Terrance to help her."

Tony looked at the computer screen that Doug was pointing to. The one outside of the alley of the laundry. Where Sherrie was heading up the fire stairs in the alley. With Vinny scrambling quickly behind.

"What the fuck is she doing?" he exploded.

"Vinny's there, boss. He's got her and Terrance is on watch too."

Tony saw Vinny stealthily climbing the stairs and grabbing Sherrie from behind with one hand over her mouth and the other protectively around her waist. He could see Vinny speaking to her and she nodded before he let her go. Then Vinny looked into the window as well. They carefully made their way back down the stairs, where Vinny assisted her from the crates.

"I want her ass here instantly," Tony growled into the radio connected to Vinny's earpiece. "In your car. Get her keys and if she gives you any problems, tell her I'll deal with her when she gets here."

Doug looked at his boss, knowing the next part of the intel was not going to make his boss happy. "Sir, there's more. We got a clear identification on one of the men in Quentin's tunnels. It's Hernando. He works for Quentin. And for the first time last night, there were some girls going from one of the outer buildings through the tunnels to the club. We think this may be how they move some of the younger girls into the club."

SHERRIE STARTED TO WALK back toward her car when Vinny snatched the keys from her hand and tossed them to the other man coming from behind a dumpster. Before she could protest, Vinny clipped, "Terrance'll drive your car. You're to come with me."

"But—"

Vinny took her arm gently, steering her toward his truck parked at the end of the alley. "Darlin', I don't think I'd test Tony on this."

Pursing her lips, she looked into Terrance's smiling face, his white teeth in contrast to his dark skin giving his handsome face even more stunning looks. Allowing Vinny to assist her up, she wisely kept quiet during the ride to the agency. All the while, steaming. *I was careful. I followed his directions. I texted him first and then I called the office. I waited in my car until someone came before looking in a window.* Giving an angry snort, she thought, *Just let him try to pick a fight with me!*

THE YELLING FROM TONY'S office had continued for the past ten minutes. Terrance, Doug, Jobe, Gabe and Vinny waited patiently, but when the arguing did not seem to end, Jobe looked over at the others to see if he should step in.

Before he could speak, Tony threw open the door and shouted, "Terrance. You got her bag?"

Terrance nodded and handed the large purse that was in Sherrie's car to his boss. Tony took it and said, "Show me." Since he had not closed his door, the group outside could hear sniffles inside and papers being shuffled.

"You can't see them without some help," Sherrie said, wiping her tears. Tony had ripped her a new one with some of his team right outside the door. She was furious and hated crying when she was mad, thinking it made her look weak.

Tony took the art pad from her hand and walked out of the room with it. Not knowing if he wanted her to follow or not, she decided that she did not care. *I know what I saw and want to see his face when I'm right.*

Looking up, she realized that the group had grown; Gabe and BJ were there as well. Her face flaming, she held her head high and stormed over to the table where Tony had taken the pad. He had laid it flat against a white tabletop, with a strong light above. BJ sat at a computer station and with a few clicks had the pad projected up on one of the whiteboards on the wall. The group, intrigued, moved closer.

Determined to not give in to her tears again, she asked BJ to focus on the eyes and enlarge. He did so and the script came into focus. "I don't know what it means other than possibly the names of the kids she was drawing."

During the argument with Tony in his office, where he alternated between hugging her and threatening to paddle her ass, she had explained what she had discovered and why she had gone to the laundry.

Tony rubbed his hand over his face, torn between being furious at her for trying to play detective, and impressed at what she had found. He turned the pages slowly as BJ enlarged and focused on the eyes. Coming to the name Alecia, he stopped immediately, his heart rate zooming.

Sherrie looked around in confusion as the air in the room began to crackle. "What…what is it?"

BJ pulled the focus off of the eyes and the full face of the young girl filled the screen. "Goddamn," Vinny exclaimed.

"Is there one of Elizabeth in here?" Tony asked, his voice forced.

Licking her lips nervously, she nodded as she leaned forward to flip several pages ahead. Another young girl's face appeared on the wall. "Tony?" she asked tentatively. "Please tell me what's going on."

He turned his face to her but before he answered, he growled, "Get Matt and Shane."

From the side, she saw BJ pick up his phone and make a call. After the call was placed, Tony said in a gentler voice, "Sherrie, where is the picture of the laundry?"

With now shaking fingers, she flipped through the pages until she came to the one she was looking for. Tony still had not answered her question, but she knew that he would when the time was right. Something major was happening and she wisely let it happen without pelting him with questions. She pointed to the window.

With the high illumination and magnification of BJ's program, it was clear to see that the swirls in the window pane were actually tiny, nondescript faces peering out.

"I...I thought maybe she was trying to tell me that someone was trying to escape or get out or...I don't know." Her words sounded silly to her now. If there was someone there, their presence would have been seen as intrusive and Tony had been right—she would have been in danger. Tears threatened to fall and she swallowed hard several times to hold them at bay.

Tony took two steps and enveloped her in his arms. Cradling her head against his chest, he breathed her in.

Her voice caught in her throat as she tried to speak. "I'm sorry. I just wanted to help."

Pulling her tighter into his powerful body, he kissed the top of her hair, letting his actions speak volumes. Tony saw Shane and Matt arrive with Lily and take in the scene, before moving toward Gabe and Jobe to find out what was going on.

Sherrie quickly wiped her tears and spared a glance up. Tony's eyes were no longer angry but caramel warm again. Giving her a squeeze, he let her go and they walked over to the screen again.

"Baby, you'd better fill them in on everything you've told me and then we'll let you know what's going on."

Sherrie told about her CASA work and Betina, starting from the first time she met her to her latest contact. She left out nothing, telling of her suspicions of Hernando, to following Betina to the bus stop, to her analyzing the art pad for clues.

When she stopped, Tony picked up the discussion as he described the cameras they had installed knowing that Sherrie would sometimes be there.

"That's how you knew where I was?" she asked

incredulously.

"Babe. Later," he said tersely.

Pulling her lips in, she kept quiet, but knew that the conversation was only tabled for now—definitely not over.

Then he landed his bombshell and all other thoughts flew out of her head. "We've been looking for an Elizabeth and Alecia for the police because their grandparents came to us and asked for help. They have been missing for about three months. The grandparents admit that the girls ran away after their dad was abusive."

Matt quickly had BJ flip through the other drawings, several he recognized. He and the others began to talk excitedly, comparing notes. Sherrie sat in the middle of the group feeling lost.

Tony felt her fear before he glanced over to see it written on her face. He had been so angry before, but only out of fear. "Babe," he said softly in her ear. "I think you're onto something that's a helluva lot bigger than you bargained for."

She turned her pale face towards his and pleaded, "Please tell me."

Sitting at the large conference table, Matt began by bringing them up to date on their investigation into human trafficking. Stunned, Sherrie listened, each word making her feel sicker.

"I talked to you all about human trafficking earlier, but some of you weren't there?" Matt asked.

The shocked looks from those around the table only matched the silence that greeted the detectives.

"Isn't that where women are kidnapped and then sent to foreign countries for sex slaves?" Vinny asked.

"It's modern slavery, but is more than just sex slavery," Matt countered, "and it's happening right here in Virginia. What we're investigating is the child trafficking."

This statement captured the attention of the group.

Shane picked up the report in front of him, reading, "It can be child sex trafficking or child labor trafficking. Children make up twenty-six percent of the trafficking in the United States and many of them are in our schools."

"Then why can't they get out? Get help? Tell someone?" Vinny asked.

"These victims are kept in bondage through a combination of fear, intimidation, abuse, and even psychological control."

Lily spoke up again, "Like the children who are kidnapped and stay with their captors even when it's physically possible for them to walk away?"

"Exactly," Matt agreed.

"We've gotten some intelligence that there is a large ring here in Richland, but we're not getting very far in finding out much. We've been tasked to investigate, but so far these kids have really disappeared. I know Lily was looking into the disappearance of the two girls whose grandparents contacted you. With Sherrie's information, this may all be linked."

"Seems they do a lot of recruitment in the schools. We've got a school counselor in a downtown high school that's working with us. She's had some suspicions and after hearing about this in a conference she went to, made contact with us."

The group nodded, the idea of children being systematically used and abused not sitting well with any of them.

"Fuck," Gabe exploded. "I thought getting out of the Army would be boring. At least over there I felt like I knew who the hell the enemy was. But here? Goddamnit, the depravity of some people."

The others nodded, but it was Tony that spoke. "That's why we do what we do. We protect those who can't protect themselves."

Sherrie had been quiet during the entire discussion, but could no longer hold back. "Betina. She's the recruiter, isn't she?"

"From what you're telling us, it sounds like she is. But remember, she's a victim too," Matt answered.

Her breath caught in her throat as she gasped out loud. "The club. Oh my God, the club. Do you think that's what Hernando is holding over her head? If she recruits, then she stays out of the club? But the dancers and waitresses have to be over eighteen years old. I mean I know club owners can do what they want, but there's enough adult girls who want the jobs, they're not going to risk hiring young teens."

Sherrie noticed the men around the table all look-ing at each other as they avoided looking at her. "What? What am I not getting?"

"The sex clubs will have rooms," Tony said gently. "Rooms upstairs or in the back where underage girls…and boys…will be kept for…um…customers." He started to take her hand but she was faster.

Jumping up, she knocked her chair over. "Oh, Jesus," she said, clasping her hand over her mouth. "No, no," she cried as she bolted from the table.

This time Tony was faster, wrapping his arm around her waist he picked her up and cradled her against his front. "Shhh," he murmured against her neck.

"I thought I'd seen it all in the dives I was around and even though Charisse sold her body to whoever would buy her drugs at least she was never held captive. Oh my God." She began to struggle to get loose, but Tony held her tight.

"Let me go!" she screamed. "I want to kick his ass! How dare he use Betina like that. She tried to escape but was described as a troubled teen and sent back to the viper's den. Tony, let me go."

"Not doing it, baby. You've got to calm down. You're no good to her like this. That's why we're here. Baby, listen to me," he said, giving her a little squeeze. "We have to get all our intel and then plan. We go in half-cocked and we lose the kids."

She was no longer struggling but her breasts heaved

with fury as he continued to hold on to her until she was under control. Nodding, she felt his arms loosen slightly, but he held her until she was steady on her feet. Turning to the group she blushed at her outburst, but Vinny just walked over and gave her a hug.

"Darlin', that kind of passion to right a wrong is what we do."

Turning to Tony, she said, "I want to help. What can I do?"

"Nothing, baby. It's too dangerous. Watching Vinny pluck you from the side of the wall today was enough for my heart to take."

"Tony, you can't keep me out of this. It's too important. And anyway, I'm the only one she trusts. She won't talk to any of you," Sherrie argued.

Tony's patience blew again and forgetting they had an audience, he shouted, "No! I'm not going to fuckin' lose another woman in my life!"

The words hung out there as everyone in the room froze. No one moved. No one spoke. No one breathed.

Sherrie began to shake as she looked into Tony's ravaged face, feeling the weight of what just happened. She knew he never spoke publicly about his loss. Her next words could make or break the man in front of her.

She put one foot in front of the other until she was toe to toe with him, her head leaned way back. His eyes were dark and she longed for the warmth in them that she always saw when he looked at her. Reaching up to cup his jaw, she said, "Okay. I won't do anything that you don't want me to do. You've rescued me twice and I never want to put you through that again. I love you."

His black eyes warmed to caramel as his breathing slowed down. "I love you too, baby," he said, wrapping his arms around her as he pulled her into his chest, wishing she could be even closer.

The group stayed still for another moment, allowing the couple to have their healing, then began to talk softly about the investigation. She lifted her head from his chest as he wiped her tears. Leaning down, he captured her lips in a gentle kiss. One that spoke of forever.

They turned back toward the group and resumed their seats. In control, Tony took charge, determined to erase the look of fear from Sherrie's eyes.

CHAPTER 23

TONY LAY IN BED the next morning, staring at the woman who held his heart as she rested in his arms. Her long, blonde hair spread across the pillow as her hand rested under her cheek. When she dressed for work, she looked every inch the professional woman that she was. But asleep? She looked like a china doll with porcelain skin and rosy cheeks.

He smiled at her sleepwear, his large t-shirt hanging off one shoulder. She had abandoned the flannel pajamas and stole his t-shirts now to sleep in. *Nothin' sexier,* he thought, as he leaned over to kiss her shoulder. She made a small moan, but stayed asleep. *She was exhausted last night.* After a long meeting in his conference room, the group had finally created a plan.

He knew that the wheels of justice could turn slowly, but Sherrie had had a hard time being patient. Matt and Shane, with Betina's art pad and BJ's enlargements, were going to report to their chief and see if they could get search warrants for the grocery, the laundry, and the club. They were also going to see if they could get one for Hernando's house. They wanted him, but only because he was just one more cog in the wheel. If they could get him to roll over on the men above him, it would help shut down at least a part of the organized human trafficking in Richland.

Sherrie had wanted them to go immediately last night. Becoming frustrated, the only way she gave in was when Shane finally told her that going in now meant that nothing would hold up in court and Hernando would get away and hide his evidence. Pursing her lips she had remained quiet, but Tony knew it had been hard. *Hell, it'd been hard for all of them.*

Not knowing where the club was had them at a distinct disadvantage. They had no idea if it was already established or not yet opened. Lily and BJ were working around the clock to try to find out more. Jobe and Gabe were working with some of the new employees on surveillance to keep track of where Hernando was going at all times.

Sherrie stirred and her eyes fluttered open. Crystal blue ones met his and he leaned in for a kiss.

"Hey, you," she said sleepily.

"Hey back," he replied.

"You let me sleep late," she accused, glancing at the clock.

"You needed it, baby. I don't figure Mr. Marks is going to fire you for being late for the first time ever."

Sherrie sat up in bed suddenly, and said, "I forgot to tell you. He's retiring in a month and moving away."

Tony sat up, propped himself against the headboard and pulled her back against him. "Retiring?"

"Yes," she lamented. "I like Simon well enough and Mr. Marks said that my job was secure, but…he's been kind of a father to me for the past year." She twisted around to look at him. "Not only that, he's selling the mountain cottage. I wanted to be able to go there again with you."

Tony tucked her into his side again, brushing her hair from her face. "I'm sorry, babe. We'll find another cabin to visit sometime. I promise."

She nodded against his chest, but knew that nothing would ever hold the memories of the Marks' cabin. Sighing, she looked over at the clock. "I've got to get ready for work. I may be late, but I've been working so much overtime, I don't think they'll mind."

"I'm going to be at the office today, Sherrie, waiting to see what comes from Matt and Shane. I need you to be safe and promise me to stay out of trouble."

She saw the fear once again in his eyes and never wanted it to be there again. "I promise. I'm going to the office and seeing what I can do to help Mr. Marks' retirement transition go smoothly for Simon and the office. Believe me, I'll be busy." She started to get out of the bed, but then turned back. "Tony?" she said tentatively. "Will you let me know what's happening? I'm really scared for Betina."

"Absolutely, baby. I promise."

BETINA WOKE, ONLY able to open her swollen eye to a slit and she could feel her lip just as puffy. She tried to sit but found nausea forced her to lay back down. Memories of the previous evening filled her mind.

The house was empty when she got home after work. Her mother must still be at work, but Betina did not mind. In fact, alone time was welcome. She could read, listen to music, or draw. Anything to pretend for just a little while that she was not the recruiter that sent other girls to their bondage.

She spent so much time self-loathing, that the few minutes of respite were the only time she did not want to either run away again or kill herself. But neither would help the girls; the clues she had slipped to Sherrie would have to work. Please let them work.

Hearing the door open, she hoped it was her mother, but it was Hernando's angry presence that filled her doorway. Stalking into her room, he backhanded her before she could react. Falling back on the bed, he grabbed her by the front of her shirt and backhanded her again. This time her head snapped to the side and she saw stars before her vision became so blurry she saw nothing.

Screaming, she tried to scramble away from him, but he was too strong.

"You stupid bitch. I have given you everything. All you had to do to keep living here with your mom was recruit for me. But no, you had to run off and get the police and court services involved. Now you got that Mullins bitch snooping around. What did you tell her?" he screamed.

"*Nothing. I told her nothing!*" Betina cried, holding her face.

"*Well, she's been snooping around the laundry, I saw her follow you the other day. She looked upset, so I want to know what she knows.*" He walked toward her, his hand raised again.

"*Nothing, I swear,*" she cried again.

Hernando stopped, his mind working. Looking at her split lip and seeing that her eye was already swelling, he knew that he had to get her out of the house. "*Come with me,*" he ordered. Before she could protest, he added, "*Your mama will be here soon. If you don't want me to hurt her then come with me and I'll keep you somewhere overnight. I'll tell her you are spending the night with a friend.*"

Once again the threat against her mom was all it took and Betina stumbled out of the bed and followed him to his car. Her mind numb, she barely paid attention to where he was taking her. He pulled into an alley that was barely lit and they walked through a back door. Taking her up a back stairwell, he left her in a small room with a bed and a dresser. There was a small bathroom with just a toilet and sink through a door. No closet. No window. No escape.

He locked her in and as she sat, overwhelmed at her life, the tears began to flow.

And now it was the next day and she had lost all sense of time. Hernando had not come back. She was hungry, but at least could drink using her hand from the sink faucet. With no mirror, she could not even see what she looked like.

The lock on the door sounded and she turned to the bedroom. In walked a large man wearing a cowboy hat, jeans with a leather belt and huge buckle, as well as cowboy boots on his feet. Not understanding what he was doing there, she stood numbly for a moment. *Is he here to rescue me?*

That notion was quickly disbanded when he lunged for her, a leer on his face. "I paid extra for a virgin, but didn't expect her face to be all smashed up. I aughtta get some of my money back."

He grabbed her, pinning her arms as she began to scream and struggle to gain freedom. As large as he was he had no problem ripping her shirt as he pushed her back on the bed and threw his large frame down on top of her. Her shirt in rags, he began assaulting her as he tried to get his hands down her pants. Squirming, she was doing nothing but inflaming him even more as the large bulge in his jeans was indicating.

Her mind racing, she quieted, laying completely still. He looked down in surprise before grinning. "You can't wait to get holda' my cock, can you girlie? Well, ol' Bobby's gonna give it to you good."

She tried not to move as he leered at her naked breasts just a few inches from his face. Seeing the fight go out of her, he stood and tossed his hat to the side. Unbuttoning his shirt, he quickly discarded it as well. Pulling his leather belt out of his jeans he snapped the leather, making a popping sound.

"We might use this later, little lady. Your little ass may just need tanning by my belt." He tossed the belt on the bed beside her and her eyes latched onto the large, heavy metal buckle.

He bent over to remove his boots when she moved like lightening, kicking at his crotch when his pants were halfway down. He hit the floor, clutching his dick as she flew off of the bed. She had the belt in one hand and swung it down toward his head. The metal buckle cracked against his skull and he stilled. Heart pounding, she grabbed his shirt, throwing it over her torn one and then saw his cell phone lying on the floor. Scooping it up, she fled the room, running down the back stairs and out into the alley. She did not stop running until she finally collapsed in an unfamiliar neighborhood near the river.

She pulled out the cell phone and called the only person she knew she could trust.

SHERRIE WAS ALMOST finished with the work day and ready to head home. Tony had only texted her once to say that 'things were progressing'. *What the hell does that mean?* she wondered, but did not want to ask too many questions.

Her phone buzzed and she slid it out of her purse as she was walking out of the building. Not recognizing the number, she almost let it go to voicemail, but then thought that maybe Tony was calling from a different phone.

"Hello?"

"Ms. Mullins?" came a timid, shaky voice.

"Betina? Is that you?" she asked, her blood turning cold. "Where are you?"

"He hurt me," she cried. "The man…he…"

"Oh, Jesus," Sherrie said. "Where are you?"

"I don't know. I ran away from him. I…I was…locked up."

"Can you get to somewhere safe? Can you call 911? Find a policeman," Sherrie's voice began to rise with fear.

"No, no police. He said he'd hurt mama."

"Okay, baby, listen to me. I'm going to come get you, but you have to help me find you. Do you see a street sign or business?"

"Um, I'm peeking around a corner and I see 81St SW on the street sign."

"That's good, Betina. Now are there any businesses or store signs around?"

"Across the street it has a closed up sign on the door, but above the door it says Club Edge."

Club Edge. Oh my God. The name of the club where Sherrie and her sister used to work. Locked up now, it was in one of the seedier areas of town. "Keep hiding, honey. I'll be there in about twenty minutes."

Jumping in her car, she called Tony. Quickly telling him what was happening, she knew what he was going to say and she was ready.

"No, Tony I can't let you go in. She won't trust anyone but me. It sounds like she was assaulted and I'm not having her more traumatized. Can you meet me there?"

Coordinating, she drove as fast as she could to the familiar location. As she rounded the corner where her old workplace was, she looked across the street seeing the alley that Betina had called from. Scanning the area, she bit her lip wondering how long it would take Tony to get there. Just then a dark SUV came from the other direction and she could see Jobe as the driver.

Heaving a sigh of relief, she jumped from her car and ran, pointing to the alley. "Betina?" she cried out. "Oh, thank God," she muttered as she saw the girl hiding behind a dumpster. Running to the frightened teen, she threw herself at her, wrapping her arms around Betina as protectively as Tony held her. Betina's tears flowed freely before she started gasping, jerking from Sherrie's arms.

Twisting her neck to see what was wrong, she saw Jobe cautiously coming behind her. "It's okay, honey. He's with me. He's here to help us."

Jobe came up quietly and said, "Sherrie, we need to get her to the hospital. Why don't you let me drive?"

Betina was shaking her head violently from side to side, so Sherrie looked up at Jobe and pleaded, "I've got to be the one to take her." Sherrie stood, pulling the girl up with her. They started out of the alley when

Betina tripped over her feet. Jobe stepped up and carefully scooped the injured girl into his arms. Making soft, comforting noises, he carried her to Sherrie's car and placed her in the passenger side.

"I'm following right behind," he informed Sherrie as she quickly hopped into the driver's seat.

"I'm taking her to Richland General and will call her social worker so she can meet us there."

Making the trip as quickly as possible, Sherrie was pleased to see not only the social worker, but also Tony as well as Matt with a female detective. Jobe carried Betina in and she was whisked back into the ER bays. The social worker and detectives went back with her, leaving the others in the waiting room.

Tony enveloped Sherrie in his embrace, seeing the shock on her face. "You did good, baby," he murmured into her hair. "You called me, followed the directions that kept you and her safe, and you got her here."

"I wasn't scared until I saw her and then, it hit me...this was real," she said, looking up into his face. "Does that make sense?"

Nodding, he said, "Absolutely. Sometimes a mission doesn't seem real until you are right into the thick of things."

They did not have to wait long before Matt and the female detective came out. Matt gave a quick report to an anxious Sherrie. "She gave us a lot. Told about Hernando, how he got her to recruit for cheap labor for his store and the laundries. Then she admitted that he had coerced her into recruiting for the club. The underage girls he wanted her to get would be held in the upper rooms as essentially sex slaves. When he caught her talking to you, she defied him and he threatened her mom again and got her to the club. He had a customer that wanted a virgin and that was when she finally fought back and escaped."

Tony took her weight as she leaned heavily against him. "Oh my God," she said, tears in her eyes. "I, of all people, know the depravity of some, but…this just seems like a bad dream."

The female detective spoke up and said, "It doesn't appear that she was sexually assaulted, but only because she managed to get away."

"What now?" Jobe asked.

"For Betina," the detective said, "the social worker will stay and then they will put her in a protective, therapeutic foster home. Ms. Mullins, she said she'll call you tomorrow."

Matt spoke up, looking at Tony, "For us? We've got a raid to plan. We shouldn't need you for the raid, but we'd love your intel in the planning."

"Anything you need, you got," Tony said.

"I'll head home then?" Sherrie asked.

"Yeah, baby, that'd be good. Lock yourself in, take a bubble bath, have a glass of wine and relax. You deserve it," he said with a kiss.

Looking into his eyes, she smiled. "That sounds amazing," she admitted. Walking out together, she left in her car, seeing Tony standing by his SUV until he was out of sight.

With a quick prayer for Betina and the other girls trapped in that life, she headed home.

TONY AND HIS CREW were circled around the conference table looking over the information that Lily and BJ had been able to pull together. Matt and Shane were on a conference call with their police chief.

Lily said, "I've traced Hernando's money beyond the grocery and laundry. It seems that he's able to fly under the IRS radar by using workers that don't get paid, so they never show up on any of his filings. That's how he uses so many workers—he doesn't pay them."

"What do they work for if not to get paid?" Gabe asked. "Who'd want to work for free?"

"It looks like Quentin rents some low-rent apartments that were meant for a small family and he has about eight workers stay there. Hernando gives them enough food for one meal a day," she added.

Shane agreed, "With this setup, Hernando gets loner kids, ones who are ready to hit the streets if they aren't already on the streets and offers them a deal. They work for him and he and Quentin take care of them in their own way. Then Quentin launders his club money through the businesses that Hernando and others like him run."

"And Hernando doesn't have to follow any child welfare laws as to hours per day or week worked," Matt said.

"A modern-day Fagan," Tony said. "They do his dirty work and he takes care of them in the most minimalistic way possible."

"Hernando's laundries have expanded to twenty-four-hour service and have multiple hotel contracts. He's rolling in the money and doesn't have to pay most of his employees. He's now moving into supplying girls for Quentin's clubs."

"Quentin runs the club legitimately with legal aged girls to serve and dance, but gets some underage girls to be in the upstairs rooms," Matt said.

"And with the underground tunnels, they can get the younger girls in the back rooms without anyone noticing from the streets."

"No way Quentin's a one-man show," Tony stated.

Matt spoke up, "Hell, he's only one man in a whole industry, but we haven't identified his immediate boss yet. We just know Hernando works for him, but no idea, as of yet, who Quentin reports to."

"We're getting search warrants right now to hit the grocery, laundry, and the club simultaneously. Best we can tell this is a huge operation and the DA was willing to let the investigation continue on its course so we could get the higher-ups but, now that we have Betina's statement, we've got to hit them hard and fast."

"Surprise is essential," the Chief said, and then

signed off as Tony's group wished them luck.

Jobe looked around the table, "This one feels weird, Captain. We just provided some information that the police didn't have and yet we're not going after the bad guys."

Gabe nodded, "I was just thinking the same thing."

"How do you all think I feel every time you go out after all I've done is give intel?" Lily piped up.

"We did our job and we did it well. This time it's up to the police to go after their mission," Tony said.

Tony looked at his watch, seeing that it was just after noon. He walked out of the main conference room and toward his office as he called Sherrie. It went to voice mail but then he grinned...*maybe she took my advice and is having that bubble bath.*

JOGGING UP THE club stairs, Hernando relished seeing Betina used, knowing that she'd be perfect for servicing men now. Seeing the door open, he assumed the client had left, but hoped that Betina had not escaped. Stunned, he looked down seeing the man barely lifting himself off of the floor with his pants around his ankles and Betina nowhere to be found. "You dumb fuck!" he screamed at the man trying to pull his pants up. "You let her get away."

"Me, a dumb fuck? I paid for a scared virgin and you promised me that! Instead, I got my balls shoved up to my throat! Someone's gonna pay," the man growled, looking down on Hernando.

"She shows up with the police and no one's gonna get paid, you asshole. You can't even subdue and fuck a kid?" Hernando's panic was rising. Where could she have gone? Would she have gone to the police? No, then she would have to admit her part in recruiting.

Looking around wildly, his mind furiously worked to think of where she would be.

"Fuck!," the man bit out. "The thieving bitch took my cell phone."

Hernando's heart sunk. With a cell phone she could have called someone to pick her—Ms. Mullins. Goddammit! That's exactly who she would have called.

Turning, he bolted out of the room and ran down the stairs with the yells of the dissatisfied client ringing in his ears.

Driving home quickly, he ran into the house, heading back to Betina's room. Marcella walked out of the kitchen. "What are you looking for?" she asked as he rummaged through papers on Betina's desk.

"Quiet, woman. That bitch daughter of yours is going to get me in trouble and if she does, your meal ticket is gone."

"Betina? What has she done?" Marcella asked, her curiosity overriding the angry vibes pouring off of Hernando. She pulled his arm from the desk, "Tell me what you are doing!"

He whirled, backhanding her across the face. "I told

you to be quiet. I offered her a chance to make money for helping me and she's trying to get me arrested."

Her face stinging, Marcella stood dumbly looking at the man in front of her. The one she hoped would marry her. And now, he appeared ready to kill her daughter.

Seeing Betina's backpack sitting next to the desk, he dumped the contents on the bed, watching as papers fell out in disarray. Shuffling through them, he saw one with Court Services at the top. It had Sherrie Mullin's name and phone number on the form. Pulling out his cell phone, he quickly input her information and easily pulled up Sherrie's address.

Smiling at his ingenuity, he turned once again, this time to see Marcella standing in the doorway blocking his path.

"I don't know what you want with Betina, but I won't let you hurt her," she said, her voice shaking with anger and fear.

He charged her, knocking her out of the way. She fell back, hitting her head against the doorframe. Slumping to the floor, tears streamed from her face as she saw him run out of the house. *What have I done?*

CHAPTER 24

I T HAD BEEN a long evening and Tony was anxious to get home. The group was moving toward the back door of the offices leading to the parking garage when Doug leaned his head out of the security monitor door.

"Tony, wait," he yelled. "Looks like movement outside of Sherrie's house on the back side. Can't pick it up very well, but it appears to be a—"

Just then the sound of an alarm went off inside the room, causing Tony, Gabe, Vinny, and Jobe to hustle inside.

Fuck—someone's broken in! And they're there with Sherrie.

SINKING INTO THE hot bubbles had been the perfect way to end her day. Sherrie grinned, thinking back to when Tony surprised her at the cabin when she had been soaking in the tub. *Hmmm, I wish he could come home now.*

Deciding she had become a wrinkled prune, she rose from the tub and donned her flannel pajamas

341

bottoms and one of Tony's t-shirts. Sliding her feet into socks, she padded back into the bathroom. After brushing out her hair, she went downstairs to her kitchen. *What was it Tony suggested next? Wine? Oh, yeah.*

Pouring a glass of wine, she made her way toward the living room. A loud crash from her sliding-glass door triggered the alarm and as she whirled around, tossing the glass, she saw Hernando stalking toward her. Her feet rooted to the floor, she watched as he moved closer. As her eyes dropped from his angry face, she saw what was in his hand. A gun.

"You bitch," he shouted over the screaming of the alarm.

Jolted out of her surprise, she darted toward the front door, only to find her escape thwarted as he clamped her arm in his vise grip.

"Where is she?" he growled, squeezing her arm. "Give her up and I'll leave."

"Go to hell," she said, gritting her teeth at the pain in her arm. "She's where you'll never find her." Her head jerked to the side as his free hand slapped her face. Stars danced behind her eyes as she tried to regain her balance.

"Then you're coming with me, bitch," he yelled, backhanding her on the other side of her face. He started dragging her through the house toward the shattered door.

Her feet hit the broken glass and she screamed as

she began to fall. Still dragging her behind him, her legs and knees went through the glass. The sound of sirens filled the night air, even interrupting the sounds of her alarms.

"Goddamnit," he screamed again, dragging her backward. Shoving her toward the sofa, he growled, "You're gonna be my ticket outta here."

The piercing alarm continued to shatter what was left of Sherrie's nerves and one look at Hernando showed same. "Let me shut off the alarm. Please," she begged, watching him pace waving the gun wildly.

His eyes landed back on her and he lifted his hand with the gun pointing straight to her, saying, "Do it. But one step outta line, bitch, and you won't make it outta here alive."

Her rubbery legs and cut feet barely held her as she made her way over to the panel by the front door. *Can I make it? Can I get outside?* A cold metallic object pressed into her side.

"Don't even think about it," he said as though reading her mind.

Her hands shaking, she quickly pressed the code into the panel, silencing the alarm. The sudden quiet was as jarring as the alarm. Only now she could hear her heart beat erratically inside her chest.

By now, the flashing lights of the police were illuminating through her blinds. Keeping her head still, she glanced upwards at the security camera. Tony's words ran through her mind. *I have this placed watched.*

A live feed goes into my place. I employ several people who monitor the video feeds.

Hernando threw open the front door, holding Sherrie in front of him, the tip of the gun pressed to her head. "Back off," he shouted. "You get any closer and she's dead."

With his arm around her in a vise, her gaze darted out of the door trying to see in the dark. Movement. Police cars. Flashing lights. *Tony? Are you there too?*

"Mr. Velasquez, this is the Richland Police. You need to lay down your weapon and let Ms. Mullins go. Once she is free—"

Hernando's answer was to slam the door, dragging Sherrie behind him as he moved away from the windows in the front of her house. Sweat pouring off of his face, he pushed her down on the floor in the hallway between the kitchen and the stairs. "Sit there bitch and don't move. I know how this'll work. They'll call and talk, wanting me to give up. But I'll outsmart them all. You'll be my ticket outta here."

Sitting on the floor with her knees pulled up to her chin, she looked up, her heart pounding in her chest. *Tony'll come, I just know it.* Staring at the man in front of her, fear still kept her immobilized. *Hernando's crazy. How will Tony fight crazy?*

A slight movement to her left caught her eye. *Tony?* she hoped. A face moved slightly from the laundry room giving her a glimpse of...*Bernard? Holy shit, what is he doing here? And in his hand...a gun?* Seeing a barely perceptible shake of his head, she quickly looked back in the opposite direction, not wanting to give away his location.

TONY'S MEN, IN military precision, quickly grabbed their mission gear that was always within ready reach and jumped into the SUVs. Gabe drove one with Tony as shotgun rider. Jobe in the back seat had Matt on the phone following what the police were doing. Vinny driving the other, had BJ on his laptop pulling up the floorplans of Sherrie's little Victorian house.

"Jesus, Tony. Her old house has twists and turns and little rooms," BJ groused, knowing that could impair access.

Jobe reported from Matt, "Back glass door at the dining room was shattered, setting off the alarm. Hernando surprised her and has her hostage. The police verbally engaged him but he's back in the house, holding her hostage."

BJ pulled up the security camera footage, then clipped, "There's a second man inside. Snuck in while the police were just pulling into the front. Looks like he went from the dining room door through the kitchen and is hiding in the laundry room."

"What the hell?" Tony roared. "There's someone with Hernando?"

"Don't think so. Looks like he came in and is hiding. And Tony? He's armed. And swear to God, it looks like a little old man."

"Goddamn it," Tony cursed. "Get Matt on the phone."

Jobe patched back through to Matt and handed the phone to Tony. "Matt? Have someone go next door and see if Bernard Kotowski is home. He's a neighbor. Former military from the Vietnam era and we think he's snuck into Sherrie's house and is hiding. May be armed."

He could hear Matt shouting orders and cursing at the same time. "We don't need some rogue old man reliving his glory days with an attempted hostage rescue," he growled.

Tony tossed the phone back to Jobe. His stomach churned. *I should have kept a man on her. I should have not let her go home alone. I should have—*

"Tony?" Gabe's voice broke through his tortured thoughts. Tony's gaze jerked toward him as the lights of the night passed the windows, casting shadows over the face of his friend.

"Stop. Whatever the hell's going through your mind right now, just stop. This isn't your fault. You gotta get your head back into the mission, sir, or I'll personally sideline you," Gabe continued.

Tony lifted an eyebrow at the threat, but knew enough about successful missions to know if he went in half-cocked, Sherrie's life could be compromised. So a nod was his only response as he turned back to Jobe to ask about an update.

"ETA is three minutes, boss," came Vinny's voice over the radio. BJ chimed in, "Tony? Looks like Sherrie's house has a partial basement and partial crawl space. You ever been down there?"

"Crawl space, no. The basement is little more than a cellar. It's about ten by twenty and is used for storage. Door is off of the kitchen near mid-hall."

Gabe added, "It's only got two small crawl-through windows that we alarmed when we were at her house."

"What about the attic?" BJ asked. "Where do the attic stairs come down into?"

"The hall outside the bedrooms. Never been up there." *Shit, how could I have not checked out the attic?*

"Then, sir, it looks like the attic is still the best entrance into the house," BJ added.

Tony nodded and, glancing back at Jobe, growled, "Get Matt and call it in."

Parking away from the driveway Tony and his men jumped out of their vehicles, grabbing their gear. Kevlar under tight, black, long-sleeved shirts, black cargo pants, night vision goggles and armed to the teeth, they headed over to meet Matt and Shane.

Shane nodded his greeting, then said, "Hostage negotiator isn't happy about you being here, but the chief gives his support."

"Fuck the negotiator," Tony bit out.

Matt placed his arm on his friend, saying, "Easy, man. His job is to get everyone out alive, including the neighbor who you say may be in there."

"Don't give a damn about Hernando and I hate to see Bernard get hurt, but damnit it, he put himself in harm's way when he snuck in wanting to play the hero." Turning to stare Matt, and then Shane, directly in their eyes, he continued. "Got one plan. Get Sherrie out alive. Anything else? Don't give a fuck."

Matt and Shane having both rescued their wives from dangerous situations just nodded. They got it. Family first. And Sherrie was family.

SHERRIE'S MIND RACED, trying to decide what to do. Bernard was hiding in the laundry room and was armed. *Tony has a gun in the nightstand by his bed, but that's upstairs. No way could she get to it.* She wiped her sweaty palms on her pajama bottoms, trying to still her pounding heart.

I know Tony's outside. I know he's planning something. Think. Think. Her eyes darted around, desperate to help. Closing her eyes for a moment, she quickly thought of her house. *What would Tony do? Attic?* Her eyes popped open as she thought about the stairs to the attic from the upstairs hallway. Her breasts heaved in panic as she thought it through. *No, he's never been up there...he'd never chance it.*

Her gaze moved to Hernando as he stood over her, shifting his gaze between the front door and the back.

Her cell phone rang, the sound coming from the kitchen counter.

"Get it," he ordered. "Might be the police ready to make a deal."

Licking her lips nervously she stood, her feet bleeding as she walked to the counter. Her gaze went to the kitchen window, but she could not see out. Wondering if the police had surrounded the house and were watching her now, she picked up her phone.

"Hello?"

"Ms. Mullins? This is Sergeant Levin and I'm here to help get you and Mr. Velazquez out safely. Are you all right?"

"Ye...yes," she answered.

"Does he have a weapon on you now?"

Glancing back at the barrel of the gun pointed directly at her, she nodded, forgetting to speak out loud.

"Ms. Mullins, we have a visual on you from the kitchen window and see you nodding. Is he behind the kitchen wall?"

Before she could answer, Hernando barked, "Give me the phone, bitch." She handed it to him and he motioned for her to sit down in the hall again.

"You want to talk, pig? You talk to me," Hernando said. "I want out and you're gonna help me get out or this bitch is dead."

The negotiator and Hernando continued to talk for a few minutes; he kept the gun trained on her as he rattled off his demands.

Her eyes darted once again toward the laundry room where she could see Benard now squatting on the floor, trying to aim his gun around the corner. Her eyes grew round as she tried to indicate that he needed to stay quiet and with the barest shake of her head, he moved back a bit.

Her mind racing again, she glanced at the door next to the laundry room. *The basement! Tony could come through there. He'd been down there when she had asked for help storing some boxes.* Closing her eyes again, she thought of the two small windows. *Can he get through?* Wiping her hands on her pajamas again, she swallowed back the bile that threatened to come up. Her gaze sought out Bernard's once more. *It may just be up to us,* she thought. *Oh, Jesus help us.*

MATT AND SHANE kept vigil outside hidden by the bushes, their eyes trained on the two men as Tony and Vinny ascended the ladder placed against the house. The placement of the ladder allowed them to be unseen by anyone on the inside of the house and it lead to the small attic window. The two men were so silent, not a sound was heard.

"Damn, I'm good, but not that good," Matt admitted.

Jobe nodded his appreciation of their feats. "Special

Forces training. Most missions we went on, absolute silence and surprise was essential." Nodding toward the now closed attic window, he added, "And Captain Alvarez was the best. Never seen a man train so hard."

Gabe added, pride in his voice, "And Vinny? Best sniper we had."

The four of them silently spread out among the police that had their eyes on the house. Always trained to keep their focus one-hundred percent on the mission, a look passed between Jobe and Gabe, each knowing what flashed through the other's mind. *Let Sherrie be safe, 'cause their boss—and friend—couldn't survive another loss.*

The darkness of the attic appeared illuminated in a green hue as Tony moved stealthily from the window to the stairs. Vinny's image appeared by his as they stopped. Both with audio amplifiers, they could hear the voices coming from below. No words were needed as they both assessed the risks. *If Sherrie and Hernando were in the hall where the stairs were located, they'd never get a shot off without endangering her.*

Speaking softly into his radio, Tony ordered, "Keep him away from the stairs." Gabe relayed that to Shane who headed off to the negotiator.

The phone rang again and Hernando picked it up this time. "You gettin' my transportation?"

"We're working on it, Mr. Valesquez. The chief won't agree if we can't have visual of Ms. Mullins to confirm that she is still alive."

"How stupid do you think I am? I let this bitch get near a window, then you'll have a shot at me," Hernando bit out, his gaze darting around at the windows in the house.

"We'd just like to see her. You can move toward the living room and stay behind her if you like, but then we could see her easily."

"Not happening. Not going toward the front of the house." Hernando looked down at Sherrie, still sitting on the floor, a smile crossing his face. "You look at the little window in the back door and you'll see her, but not me."

No! she thought. The back door led to the patio from the laundry room. *We head toward the back door, he'll see Bernard.* Her legs refused to obey, but several swift kicks to her hips had her crying out as she stood.

Tony and Vinny slipped down the attic stairs and quickly passed through the hall by the bedrooms. They stopped at the top of the stairs leading down to the first floor, listening to the sounds below. Pulling off their night-vision goggles, they set them gently on the floor.

"Target?" Tony whispered.

BJ, still monitoring the inside security cameras, reported, "Sherrie and Hernando are moving toward laundry room off of kitchen. Neighbor is in there but have no visual on him."

Sherrie now stood in the doorway of the laundry room, visible from the window in the outside door. She saw nothing but blackness in the yard, but knew someone was watching. It gave no comfort. Her stomach in knots, her gaze drifted down seeing Bernard squatting next to the washing machine.

Bernard lunged forward, pushing Sherrie down while taking a shot at Hernando. The shot rang out as BJ shouted "Go!" into the radio, sending Tony racing toward the sound. Escaping harm, Hernando shot over Sherrie's head, hitting Bernard in the side, immediately dropping him to the floor.

Sherrie tried to move out from under the bleeding man, her hands pressing against his wound. Twisting her head around, she stared into the barrel of the gun, anger fueling her being.

Hearing a noise from the dining room, Hernando screamed out, "Come any closer and the bitch dies."

Tony and Vinny halted, just out of sight. Tony stepped back slightly, allowing Vinny to move into place. As much as he wanted to spill Hernando's blood himself, he would only place Sherrie's safety in his best sniper.

Her heart beating out of her chest, Sherrie glanced down at Bernard, seeing his eyes looking up at her. *Get the gun*, he mouthed.

Glancing to the side, she saw his gun laying right next to her. She recognized the same type of pistol that Tony had used when teaching her to shoot. Sliding her gaze back up, she saw Hernando pointing his gun at her, but looking behind him at the dining room, listening for another sound.

Tony must be in there. He came. As relief resonated through her, the sickening feeling of his being hurt cut into her solace. Eyes moving back to the gun, she slowly slid her hand forward until it curled around the grip. Lifting it, she tucked it into her front, hidden from Hernando's eyes should he turn back around.

Tony crept down the hall by the stairs and with Vinny in the dining room, both were ready to take Hernando down. Receiving the all-clear from BJ, Vinny prepared to move around the corner and shoot as soon as Tony distracted him.

A shot rang out, Hernando's cry screaming in the hall. Both Tony and Vinny instantly knew the sound did not come from either of their firearms. Rounding the corner, weapons drawn, they saw Hernando on the floor, his body jerking in the throes of death. Several feet away lay Bernard, blood still seeping from his wound. And in between the two men knelt Sherrie, covered in blood, the pistol still in her shaking hand, pointed at the man dying on the floor.

Her face bruised and eyes wild, Tony knew she was in shock. Her pajamas were covered with blood. *How bad is she hurt?* "Sherrie," he called out softly, as Vinny radioed for help. Within a few seconds, the house filled with policemen as well as Gabe, Jobe, and BJ. Gabe looked at his twin for confirmation that he was all right before glancing down the hall, seeing Tony trying to approach Sherrie.

"Baby, look at me," Tony said again, this time with

a little more force. Her eyes slowly raised to his. "Give me the pistol, baby." He moved another step forward, his hand outstretched. No one moved, afraid to startle her. He watched her chest heave as her breathing increased. "Eyes, baby. Eyes on me."

The sound of gunfire still resonated in her ears as all other sounds seemed muffled. Staring at the man lying on the floor, she focused on the dark stain on the carpet. Her vision blurred as her mind tried to make sense of what she was seeing. Far away voices crept into her consciousness. Becoming louder. Clearer.

Her gaze moved up toward the voice that seemed to be calling to her. Someone calling her *baby*. Eyes landing on Tony she saw his outstretched hand.

Confusion filled her expression as she looked at him. "Baby," he said again. "Drop the gun, sweetheart." Tony watched as her gaze drifted to the gun in her hand, recognition flaring in her eyes.

Gasping, she tried to open her fingers, but they were locked. Tony rushed forward, gently prying the gun from her frozen grip, wrapping one arm around her and handing the weapon behind him, feeling it taken from his hand.

Vinny quickly secured the weapon as he rushed past Hernando to Sherrie. Gabe and Jobe had pushed past both of them to get to Bernard, calling for the EMTs.

"Tony, let me see her," he ordered, knowing his boss would not willingly let Sherrie go. Tony, arms shaking, only released her enough to see to her injuries.

Vinny quickly motioned for BJ to assist. "Watch the back door," he ordered, wanting BJ to help preserve Sherrie's privacy. With Tony holding her up, Vinny pulled her pajama bottoms off, quickly assessing her injuries. Dark bruises from being kicked covered her thighs and hips. Her legs and feet were covered in cuts from the glass.

He lifted his gaze to Tony, saying, "She's got some glass in these cuts. The hospital will be able to get it out and get them cleaned. She may need some stitches."

So much blood was on her shirt, but Vinny's hands hesitated as his eyes sought Tony's silent permission.

Tony nodded, trusting his men completely. Tony turned Sherrie so that she was facing him and Vinny slid her shirt off while standing behind her. He quickly ascertained no injuries from the back and with a swift eye on her chest was able to see that none of the blood on her shirt had come from her. She had another large bruise on her side and on her face. By then, BJ was handing Tony a sweatshirt he found lying on the washing machine and Sherrie was quickly covered again.

Tony looked down, realizing that she was totally unaware of having been checked out. Only when Gabe yelled for the EMTs to enter did she snap out of her trance.

"Bernard? Oh my God, he tried to save me," she cried, trying to move toward him.

"No, no, baby. Let them do their job," Tony admonished gently, pulling her back. As Bernard was being taken out of the house on a stretcher, the group moved out of the laundry room.

"I have to go with him," Sherrie said, her gaze still unfocused.

"Baby, you're going to the hospital yourself. Just because you weren't shot doesn't mean you're not hurt. We've got to get you checked out as well."

Hernando was being lifted onto a stretcher, his breath raspy from the hole in his chest. His eyes landed on Sherrie, pinning her with his expression. "Y...you...ruined... every...thing," he gurgled.

Her whole body began to shake as her numbness left instantly. Thoughts of Betina and the host of other children coerced into being held captive flew through her mind. Chest heaving with anger, she looked down at his pasty face, recognizing imminent death. "Good," she said simply.

His eyes rolled back into his head as death claimed him. The realization that she had killed another human slammed into her. She began to drop to the floor but never hit as Tony's arms swept her up into his. Her head drooped back as she slipped into unconsciousness.

"Now," he barked to his men, all falling into action. Once again Gabe drove, but this time Tony held Sherrie in the back seat as Jobe rode shotgun. Vinny drove the other vehicle as BJ called Jennifer. Quickly telling her the basic information, she knew to call the other women.

Looking down at the unconscious woman in his arms, Tony thanked God she was safe. And cursed himself that it was her and not him that pulled the trigger.

CHAPTER 25

THE WAITING ROOM was filled with friends and family. Suzanne, BJ, Jennifer and Gabe sat together in one corner. Matt and Shane met their wives, Annie and Lily, as they rushed there as well. Vinny and Jobe stood near Tony, ready to offer support the minute they were needed.

Matt had reported that while Hernando was killed, Quentin escaped. The club and Hernando's businesses were raided and the number of children found in all areas was astounding.

"I can't believe that he got away," Jobe growled.

Lily placed her hand on his arm, and said, "But think of all the children we helped save tonight."

Just then a nurse came through the ER doors and looked around at the impressive group of men filling the room. A look of confusion crossed her face for a moment as she looked back at her file. "Mr. Alvarez?"

Tony stepped forward, but before he could say anything else, she said, "Ms. Mullins listed you as the fiancé." He nodded, unable to speak at the moment. She continued, "The doctor will see you in the consultation room."

He moved to follow the nurse, the sound of others behind him not surprising. As the nurse looked back, she pursed her lips and said, "This is for family only."

Tony glanced around, seeing Gabe, Vinny, and Jobe. "These are my brothers."

Jobe spoke clearly, "Where he goes, we go."

She nodded and left them in the small room. A few minutes later, a doctor walked into the room, startled at all of the men standing there. "Mr. Alvarez?" she asked, her gaze moving among them.

Tony nodded and stepped forward once again. The doctor smiled and said, "Ms. Mullins is doing very well, considering her ordeal. I am concerned about a concussion so we will keep her here for a while to make sure that she retains consciousness. We will of course have the hospital counselor see her and they will recommend a trauma therapist."

"So she's all right?" he asked, his voice breaking. He could feel his friends take a step closer, knowing they were closing ranks.

"Yes," the doctor replied. "I was concerned about the bruising on her abdomen, so we're doing an ultrasound to make sure there are no internal injuries. In fact, if you want to see her now she is just across the hall and you can be with her." With that, she turned and walked out of the room as Tony quickly entered the ER bay across the hall. Gabe, Jobe, and Vinny told him they would be right there until they knew for sure that Sherrie was all right.

The ultrasound technician was sitting next to Sherrie's bed, moving the wand across her abdomen from one side to the other. Tony walked to her side and leaned down to kiss her forehead as she weakly smiled up at him.

Her eyes red-rimmed and the dark bruising on the side of her face made Tony want to bring Hernando back from the dead just so that he could make him suffer again.

The technician's voice cut into Tony's anger and he quickly tamped it down so that Sherrie had his undivided attention.

"It appears that her kidneys and other internal organs are just fine. That was one of the things that the doctor wanted us to check. And of course, I know you are most anxious to hear that the baby's heartbeat is strong and it's very tightly settled in her uterus. This ordeal did not hurt the baby, just the baby's mama," he joked.

Tony stopped breathing. The sounds of the ER receded to the back of his consciousness as he replayed the technician's words. *Baby? Baby? Oh, Jesus, oh, Jesus.*

Looking at Sherrie, he saw the shock on her face before her expression broke out into the most amazing smile. Overwhelmed, he leaned down for a kiss, tasting her tears on her lips. A kiss of awe. Of amazement. Of celebration. Of family.

"Okay, daddy," the technician said. "If you can move out of the room for just a second, I need to get this equipment over to the other side so they can get the portable x-ray out of here since she won't need that."

Looking down at his beautiful woman, he choked out, "I'll be right back, babe. I'll just go across the hall and tell the men."

She smiled and nodded as she saw his chin quiver. Giving him another kiss, she whispered, "I love you."

"I love you too, babe."

Stepping out of the way of the equipment being moved in the small space, he went across the hall seeing the expectant faces of his men. His friends.

"She's going to be fine," he said, his voice breaking. "And...we're going to have a baby." A sob tore from his lips as his legs gave out from under him. Dropping to the floor, he knelt as more sobs continued to rack his body. The wall of men dropped with him, each kneeling around, placing one hand on their friend. Silent tears slid down the faces of the other three men as they supported the one in the middle.

Gabe, Vinny, and Jobe remembered the last time they knelt around Tony in such a way. That day, five years earlier, they supported their friend as he buried his wife and baby girl and then watched as he closed himself off to life. Until Sherrie came along. And they had watched as Tony slowly, painfully allowed life, and love to come back in.

Tony slowly became aware of his surroundings, but felt no shame. There was nothing hidden from these men. Nothing they had not shared. Standing, he wiped his eyes before looking at each of them in turn. They all smiled. Sucking in a huge breath, he let it out slowly. "Seems like we've got some celebrating to do, but if you don't mind, I think I'll go back to see the mother of my baby."

TWO WEEKS LATER, Sherrie Mullins became Mrs. Tony Alvarez. Tony had insisted that they marry as soon as possible and showed her the ring that he had bought, but had been waiting for just the right time to give her. She insisted that she did not want a large wedding—just Tony's father and friends. And Bernard to give her away.

Bernard had been shot in the side of his chest, the bullet just passing through muscle. Within two weeks he was ready to walk Sherrie down the aisle, although with the injuries to her feet, they made a slow pair moving toward Tony.

Standing in what was now their living room with the minister before them in front of the fireplace, they said their vows. Their friends sat in chairs moved in just for the occasion, with the dining room table loaded down with food for the reception.

Sherrie, overflowing with happiness, looked into the caramel eyes gazing back at her. Dressed in a flowing, ivory, knee-length dress, her blonde hair streaming down her back with Baby's Breath interwoven throughout, she looked like the princess he thought she was. The news they were having a baby had stunned her, but like Tony, she was ready to begin their lives together. No waiting. No second thoughts. Smiling, she pledged her life to him.

Tony, resplendent in a dark suit, kept his eyes locked on the beautiful woman at his side. He had a second chance at love and planned on making every moment count.

His father, standing next to him, glanced at the mantle noticing the small, framed picture of a smiling Tony with Marla and newborn baby Sofia. *Sherrie did that,* he knew. She had brought Tony out of the past while still celebrating all of life. Next to it was another framed snapshot, this one of Tony and Sherrie in the snow with the frozen lake behind them. And the two pictures looked perfect side by side. He knew that the mantle would soon be full of other pictures of them. Now, and later with children. *Life goes on,* he thought. *And thank God it does.*

Tony kissed his bride with all the love and passion he had for her, holding her tight as he handed her an envelope. Turning to the gathering, he proclaimed, "I have a gift for my new bride. One that holds a special meaning to us."

She looked up in confusion, her hand holding the plain envelope. "What is this?"

"Open it, baby," he said gently.

Licking her lips nervously, she opened the envelope and pulled out the sheaf of papers. *A deed?* "Oh my God!" she shouted, throwing her arms around his neck. Looking at the questioning gazes of their friends, he explained. "Mr. Marks sold the mountain cabin to us."

The laughter rang out in the room as his wife's tearful smile filled his vision. *Yeah, life goes on.*

CHAPTER 26

WAKING UP IN the cabin several months later, Tony looked over at his wife. Her cherubic face with the mass of blonde hair spilling on the pillow had him holding his breath for fear of disturbing her. She opened her eyes, blinking at the light. Focusing on him, she smiled.

"Hey, you," she said softly.

"Hey back," he answered.

Leaning in to kiss her, he then pulled back and lifted an eyebrow.

She huffed as she said, "Yes, of course," and moved to get out of bed. Returning a few minutes later, she climbed back under the covers. "It cuts down on the spontaneity when this baby is sitting on my bladder," she groused.

Chuckling, he kissed her again before turning her over and pulling her back to his front. Reaching down, he noticed her lack of panties. "Ummmm, you are ready," he murmured in her ear.

"Always for you," she whispered back.

Sliding into her, he curled one arm under her neck with one hand down cupping her swollen breasts while the other rested on her protruding belly. Slowly and deliberately he moved in and out, not willing to hurry the process.

It did not take long for the delicious friction to build and she began to pant as she climbed toward ecstasy. His cock was touching so deep within her, she could feel the tingles as her inner walls began to convulse, grabbing tighter to him as she flew over the edge. Screaming out his name, her orgasm rushed over her as she squeezed her eyes tightly, the electricity sending jolts to her whole body.

With only a few more strokes, his neck corded as the veins stood out, grimacing through his release. He felt his child kick and he could not help but chuckle.

"Mmmm, you woke the baby," she said, pretending to grumble. He nuzzled her neck as they panted their way down from shared breathlessness.

"I love you, Mrs. Alvarez."

She rolled over to face him, placing her hand on his jaw. "And I love you, Mr. Alvarez."

Later that day, they walked to the pier and sat on the edge, feet dangling in the water. "This will be such an amazing place to bring our kids for vacations," she said.

"We'll need to add a bit to it," Tony said, looking back at the small cabin.

"It was big enough for the Marks and they had two kids."

"Yes, but we need a bedroom off to ourselves. One

where when you scream out my name, the kids can't hear."

Giggling, she playfully slapped his arm. They sat in companionable silence for a few minutes. She turned toward him and looked into his warm eyes, handsome with the little laugh crinkles out from the sides. "Are you glad you followed me to this cabin in the storm?"

Taking her face in both of his hands, he gazed deeply into her eyes. Kissing her lightly, he pulled away, saying, "More than you can ever know. Baby, I may have come out here to save you, but that storm, this cabin, and you...saved me.

HAND IN HAND, Tony and Sherrie walked through the cemetery. Stopping first at Charisse's gravestone, Sherri smiled. Tony had purchased the beautiful marble stone engraved with her name and the title, *Beloved Sister.*

She knelt and brushed some grass from the base. Holding her large stomach, she said, "Oh Charisse, I wish you could have been here to be with me. But all I can wish for you is peace. I love you, sis."

Tony assisted her up and they made their way to the other graves. Stopping in front of Marla and Sofia's headstones, Tony also knelt to brush away some grass. This place used to represent all that he had lost. All that had been taken away from him. And now? He smiled, realizing how lucky he was that life had given him a second chance at love. At living. At being a husband and a father. "You two will always be in my heart," he said softly. Standing, he turned to see Sherrie smiling at him. "And you, baby," he said, moving closer to take her face into his hands, "have crept into my very soul." Leaning in he kissed her. A kiss of promise. Of life. Of love. Of forever.

TONY PUSHED SHERRIE'S damp hair from her face, waiting for the next contraction. They were coming fast and furious now and the doctor looked up from between his wife's legs and said, "Not much longer."

He was a wreck. In the past few months so many of their friends had had babies. Annie and Shane, as well as Jennifer and Gabe, had baby boys, Matt and Lily had a baby girl, and Suzanne and BJ had twins. With each one, he was reminded of having been in the delivery room years before, but this time was different. No other thought went through his mind other than Sherrie and this baby being healthy.

The contraction came once more and he assisted her forward so that she could bear down. "Only a few more like that and your baby will be here," the doctor called out. They had decided not to learn the sex of the baby, preferring it to be a surprise.

Helping her lay back down, he wiped her brow and stared into the eyes of the woman who had saved him.

Brought him back. Brought him forward. "You're doing great, babe," he encouraged, awed by her strength.

"This is it," the doctor said. "Push."

With one more push, Tony's son was born. A big, healthy, boy.

And life began again.

THE END

If you enjoyed Tony, please leave a review!
Next up is Vinny.

Keep up with the latest news and never miss another
release by Maryann Jordan.
Sign up for her newsletter here!
goo.gl/forms/ydMTe0iz8L

Other books by
Maryann Jordan
(all standalone books)

All of my books are stand-alone, each with their own
HEA!! You can read them in any order!

Saints Protection & Investigation
*(an elite group, assigned to the cases no one else wants...or
can solve)*

Serial Love

Healing Love

Revealing Love

Seeing Love

Alvarez Security Series
*(a group of former Special Forces brothers-in-arms now
working to provide security in the southern city
of Richland)*

Gabe

Vinny

Jobe

Love's Series

(detectives solving crimes while protecting the women they love)

Love's Taming
Love's Tempting
Love's Trusting

The Fairfield Series

(small town detectives and the women they love)

Carol's Image
Laurie's Time
Emma's Home
Fireworks Over Fairfield

I love to hear from readers, so please email me!

Email
authormaryannjordan@gmail.com

Website
www.maryannjordanauthor.com

Facebook
facebook.com/authormaryannjordan

Twitter
@authorMAJordan

More About Maryann Jordan

As an Amazon Best Selling Author, I have always been an avid reader. I joke that I "cut my romance teeth" on the historical romance books from the 1970's. In 2013 I started a blog to showcase wonderful writers. In 2014, I finally gave in to the characters in my head pleading for their story to be told. Thus, Emma's Home was created.

My first novel, Emma's Home became an Amazon Best Seller in 3 categories within the first month of publishing. Its success was followed by the rest of the Fairfield Series and then led into the Love's Series. From there I have continued with the romantic suspense Alvarez Security Series and now the Saints Protection & Investigation Series, all bestsellers.

My books are filled with sweet romance and hot sex; mystery, suspense, real life characters and situations. My heroes are alphas, take charge men who love the strong, independent women they fall in love with.

I worked as a counselor in a high school and have been involved in education for the past 30 years. I recently retired and now can spend more time devoted to my writing.

I have been married to a wonderfully patient man for 34 years and have 2 adult very supportive daughters and 1 grandson.

When writing, my dog or one of my cats will usually be found in my lap!

Made in the USA
Las Vegas, NV
07 May 2024

89654937R00225